SLEEP
LIKE
DEATH

BY KALYNN BAYRON

For older readers

Cinderella Is Dead

This Poison Heart
This Wicked Fate

You're Not Supposed to Die Tonight

For younger readers

The Vanquishers
The Vanquishers: Secret of the Reaping

SLEEP
LIKE
DEATH

KALYNN BAYRON

BLOOMSBURY

NEW YORK LONDON OXFORD NEW DELHI SYDNEY

BLOOMSBURY YA
Bloomsbury Publishing Inc., part of Bloomsbury Publishing Plc
1385 Broadway, New York, NY 10018

BLOOMSBURY and the Diana logo are trademarks of Bloomsbury Publishing Plc

First published in the United States of America in June 2024 by Bloomsbury YA

Text copyright © 2024 by Kalynn Bayron

Bloomsbury books may be purchased for business or promotional use.
For information on bulk purchases please contact Macmillan Corporate
and Premium Sales Department at specialmarkets@macmillan.com

Library of Congress Cataloging-in-Publication Data
available upon request
ISBN 978-1-5476-0976-5 (hardcover) • ISBN 978-1-5476-0978-9 (e-book)
ISBN: 978-1-5476-1710-4 (exclusive edition A)

Book design by Jeanette Levy
Typeset by Westchester Publishing Services
Printed and bound in the U.S.A.
2 4 6 8 10 9 7 5 3 1

To find out more about our authors and books visit
www.bloomsbury.com and sign up for our newsletters.

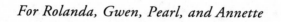

For Rolanda, Gwen, Pearl, and Annette

SLEEP
LIKE
DEATH

CHAPTER 1

It is easier to track an animal—or a person—if it is bleeding.

Drops of crimson in the snow are easy to follow. Blood on fallen autumn leaves or the earth tones of a harvest forest floor is harder to spot but still easier than relying on footprints alone. The method works for tracking people, too. An arrow through the thigh or the flank is sure to leave a trail I can follow.

Tracking is an art. Huntress can spot a leaf bent ever so slightly out of place from a distance. She can tell the weight and age of a bear, a wolf, or a wild boar by leaning close to its tracks and measuring the impression with her fingertips. Her tactics don't work as well on people, which is why I am mostly disinterested. The things I put my mind to must be in service to my true purpose. If the lesson is not shortening the path between myself and my enemy, what is the point? Huntress has assured me that I will eventually learn to savor the hunt. In my mind, the only way that happens is when I have *him* in my sights.

"Eve," says Huntress. "I need you to focus."

Focus.

Easier said than done when I'm lying under a darkening sky, across a scattering of jagged rocks and damp earth, trying to press myself flat so the gathering of deer in the clearing ahead of us can't see me or the arrow I have trained on them. I prefer the blade, but Huntress insists that I improve upon my skills with the bow. A part of me believes it is because she would prefer not to feel her blade scraping the bones beneath the wounded flesh. She likes the distance a bow provides. I have no such reservations.

Huntress is happy I've managed to track the deer to the clearing, but I haven't been honest with her. I've had help. I can still hear him, my gentle helper, as I lie still—the sound is less like a voice and more like a low hum that works its way up my back and settles at the nape of my neck. Each delicate intonation contains a meaning—fear, curiosity, happiness—I know them all. I've been listening to the sounds of the forest my entire life.

My helper is pacing on the other side of the meadow, just beyond the tree line. He has brought me here. We have always had an understanding, he and I.

"Draw back the bow and bag us a deer to take back to your mother," Huntress whispers. "I'm tired of lying in the dirt."

I notch my arrow and feel the muscles across my back

tense as I pull the bowstring toward my shoulder. I breathe in, listening to the beat of my own heart. My arrow will hit its target if I let it fly between breaths, between beats.

The deer's slender neck is fully exposed. It has wandered just away from the others, but that is enough.

One.

Two.

Three.

I let go and my arrow hits its mark with a soft, wet thud. The animal stumbles and then falls on its side. I stand, shaking off the dirt and damp, and walk into the clearing. The other deer scatter, leaving their fallen friend behind. I kneel at the animal's side and put her out of her misery with my freshly sharpened dagger.

"Good," says Huntress. "We cannot allow them to suffer, and we do not take more than we can use."

"There are some who should suffer," I say.

Huntress pushes a few errant strands of her graying hair away from her face. "That thinking will do you no good." She strides up to me and puts her finger in my shoulder. "Your head should be clear. Revenge, bitterness—arrogance. They'll rot you from the inside."

I sheath my knife and sling my bow across my back.

"You think I'm arrogant?" I ask.

She huffs and slaps me hard on the shoulder. "I *know* you are."

Huntress pulls a length of twine from her bag and ties the deer's legs together so we can transport it back to Castle Veil.

As she busies herself, I spot my helpful friend as he emerges from the underbrush.

His fur is shining and black as the evening sky, as are his wide curious eyes. His tail and each of his four paws are tipped with red. The hum in my head grows louder as he approaches. He is curious. I breathe deep, steadying the beat of my heart.

I mean you no harm.

The fox's ears lay flat as he angles his head down in a sort of bow. I tap the ground with the sole of my boot, and he scurries off.

Huntress watches him leave and then glances at me with a look of utter disappointment in her eyes.

"Please tell me you didn't," she sighs, rubbing her temple. "You used the fox to lead us here? Were you even trying to track the deer at all?"

"I tried," I say. "It's harder than it looks."

Huntress straightens up and faces me, her expression pinched. "You have to learn to do it on your own. You must be the one to do the work. You can't cheat every time, Eve."

I don't see why not. I can hear the unique signature of any animal. The hum from the fox is like a twinge behind my neck. Birds are like melodic whistling. Horses are low and resonant. Each animal has a voice that I can hear and understand, each and every one of them. I don't see it as cheating in the way Huntress does. If she had this ability, I know she would use it just as I do.

A rumble ripples through the cloud cover, and there is a loud crack in the distance. The air around me is suddenly alive, and the pitter-patter of rain sounds on the leaves and branches. Within moments, the sky opens up and we are stuck in a torrential downpour.

"We got the deer, didn't we?" I ask. "That's all that matters."

"It is not all that matters," Huntress says, her tone clipped. "I'm in awe of your gifts, Eve, you know that, but you can't just—"

A loud crack splits the overcast sky, and the forest is lit up like midday for a brief moment as lightning arcs over the canopy.

"Wonderful," Huntress grumbles.

She quickly slides her walking stick through the deer's legs and motions for me to grab the other end so that we can hoist it up and carry it home.

I reach for the stick when something—a distinct rumble—reverberates in my bones. It is not the thunder or the crack of lightning, but another animal's call. This is only the second time in my life I've heard it. A shudder of fear ripples through me, but I deny it and tightly grasp my dagger.

"Get behind me," I say.

"What is it?" Huntress asks, panic invading her voice. She glances around, then moves just behind my right shoulder without another word.

Only I can hear the animal's voice. It sounds in my head, getting louder as the seconds pass, and when I finally see it through the sheeting rain, it is too late to run or hide, though I would have done neither.

Huntress inhales sharply as the wolf steps into the clearing in front of us. Common wolves wander in and out of Queen's Bridge often enough that people know to avoid them or come prepared with a weapon when traveling through the woods. I know their call, but this is something different. It is not a common wolf at all. It is a dire wolf. A giant of its kind, lethal to nearly anyone or anything that has the unfortunate luck of crossing its path.

Its eyes are level with mine as it moves deeper into the clearing. If it were to stand on its hind legs it would be taller than me by an entire length of my own body. In the rain it is a hulking, monstrous shadow, with yellow eyes and long glinting teeth.

We came to the forest to hunt deer and pheasant. Huntress and I are both armed but not heavily enough to defend ourselves against a wolf this size. Huntress takes a step back and the animal crouches low, pinning its ears back, baring its wicked fangs.

"Do not move," I say in a tone so low it is barely a whisper.

The wolf growls and the sound overpowers even the rain. The wolf sniffs at our kill, and once it has the scent of blood in its nose it becomes protective of the carcass. Claiming it as its own, it now turns to me and settles back on its haunches, preparing to launch itself directly at me.

My heart beats like a bird in a cage as I let my gaze drift to the sky. Thunder rumbles in the distance, and I slowly extend my arm above my head. I open my fingers as the wolf snarls. The massive creature launches itself at me as an arc of white-hot lightning slices through the sky and finds its way to my outstretched hand. There is always pain when I harness lightning, but I've learned to welcome the shock of it. It reminds me that I am alive and possessed of something more powerful than almost anything or anyone in Queen's Bridge.

I grip the bolt, and as it disconnects itself from the sky it becomes a weapon made of heat and light. A nearly weightless sword, conjured from the storm itself. It is a weapon unlike any other in existence, and it will exist for only this moment. A shudder runs through my body as my skin is raised to gooseflesh.

I pull it through the air as the wolf lands just a few paces ahead of me and digs its paws into the muddy ground, skittering to a full stop. The hum of its unique voice falters inside my head. We stare into each other's eyes. It is a magnificent creature, but I need to get home to my mother. I am all she has left, and I will not be separated from her for any reason.

The wolf prepares to lunge again, but as its gaze drifts to the shining blade, it reconsiders. It sniffs at the deer one more time before skulking off into the underbrush. I don't move until its voice is gone from my head.

Huntress rests her hand on my shoulder, and I open my death grip on the sword. It dissolves into the air with a wispy puff of black smoke as the rain continues to sheet down around us.

"I thought we were in trouble," Huntress says.

"We were," I say as I try to catch my breath. "I haven't seen a wolf that big in years and certainly not anywhere near here."

"There has been one lurking near Rotterdam," Huntress says. "I've heard rumors it is hunting people."

"Gossip," I say. "Let's get the deer home."

Huntress nods, and we begin the long trek through the western forest of Queen's Bridge toward home.

———————————

Huntress and I carry the deer between us, having left our horses in the stables. It was only meant to be a brief hunt, a tracking exercise with a small prize for our efforts. I hadn't fully expected us to snare a deer this size, and by the time Castle Veil comes into view, we're both sweating, exhausted. The rain has stopped and the clouds are moving out, allowing a bit of sallow light to break through.

"Let's take it to the kitchen immediately," Huntress says. "I'm sure your mother would enjoy a bit of venison for dinner this evening."

We haul the animal through the labyrinth of passageways that snake through the castle and drop the spoils of our hunt at the feet of our head cook, Lady Anne. She looks on the kill with disgust.

"Well, what am I supposed to do with this?" Lady Anne asks, her round face slick with sweat, a light dusting of flour covering her apron front. "You didn't even field dress it?"

"I thought you'd want to do that yourself," I say. I've known Lady Anne my entire life, and I know full well that she can't stand the sight of blood and has never in all her long years skinned and harvested the edible bits off a freshly killed deer.

"Either you handle it, or I'll have to call on Mr. Finley to take care of it." There's a little ring to her voice when she says Mr. Finley's name. "In fact . . ." She trails off like she's lost in her own thoughts.

"I'll go get him," Huntress says. "I'm sure he'd be happy to do it."

"You're going to go get him right now?" Lady Anne asks, snapping herself out of whatever daydream she'd gotten lost in. She tucks a few stray pieces of her curly black hair under her head scarf and wipes her hands on her apron.

Huntress rolls her eyes. "Of all the people in Queen's Bridge, of all the people you could possibly choose, you've set your sights on Mr. Finley?"

Lady Anne looks to me. "You disapprove?"

"No," I say. "It's just, well . . . he's bald."

Lady Anne sighs as if she's picturing him in her head. "He's beautiful."

I try very hard not to laugh. I think it's sweet, but Huntress looks absolutely disgusted.

Lady Anne shoos Huntress out of the kitchen. "Oh, stop. Go get him."

Huntress goes off mumbling something about Mr. Finley under her breath as Lady Anne continues to primp and preen.

"Ignore her," I say as I help dust off Lady Anne's apron. "She's just upset no one is as happy to see her as you are to see Mr. Finley."

"Is there ever a time when she isn't upset?" Lady Anne asks. "That woman lives in a perpetual state of unhappiness."

It's a bit harsh. "It's just her way," I say. "You know that."

Lady Anne shakes her head and tries standing in several different positions as she glances toward the door. "Your mother was looking for you earlier," she says. "She was in her drawing room last time I checked."

I nod and put my hand on her arm. "I'm sure Mr. Finley will be happy to see you."

Lady Anne gently touches my cheek, then shoos me out of the kitchen. I make my way to the uppermost floor where my mother's private chambers are. Her drawing room is just off the landing, and as I approach, the door sits ajar. I catch a glimpse of my mother pacing in front of a long table.

I slip inside, and she gives me a tight smile. She's not alone. Captain Amaranth Mock, head of the royal guard, is here. Lady Harold in her constant state of worry is also present. She is my mother's second closest adviser—second, because I am her first.

They are leaning over the table, staring with concern at a map of Queen's Bridge. I move to the window where a gilded cage is situated and listen to the russet-colored nightingale fluttering on its perch, singing sweetly as my mother stews.

"Their land is overrun," Captain Mock says. "Their other crops are being choked out. It is an absolute disaster, and we cannot allow it to continue."

"Hasn't he been harvesting?" Lady Harold asks, a clear ring of annoyance in her tone.

"I believe he has," says Captain Mock. "But at a rate that cannot compete with what is being produced. The surveyor has informed me that if this continues, the overgrowth will reach the River Farris in less than a month."

"The entire Queen's Bridge water supply comes from the River Farris," I say, approaching the table.

My mother's discerning brown eyes are so dark they're almost black as she places a small weight on the outline of a farm near the river. Her hair is braided around the top of her head and her crown, a halo of golden maple leaves dotted with bright green emeralds sits nestled in among the errant coils. She palms a small emerald cut into the shape of a star that hangs from a silver chain around her neck. The smooth brown skin on the back of her right hand is flawless aside from a jagged scar running from her thumb to her wrist.

"The water supply will indeed be in danger if this continues," says Captain Mock. "What do we do, my Queen?"

My mother rests her long slender fingers on the map. "Sir Gregory has always been a good steward of these lands. He is watchful, and it is entirely unlike him to allow this." She sighs and pushes her hand down on the table. The dagger on her waist glints in the afternoon light, and she taps the heel of her riding boot against the stone floor. She suddenly turns to me and rests her hand on my shoulder. "Eve, I know you've just come from a hunt, but would you like to accompany me? I'd like to talk to Sir Gregory myself."

I nod. She knows she doesn't have to ask. There is nothing I wouldn't do for my mother.

"Let us make a little trip, then," she says.

"Is that necessary, my Queen?" Captain Mock asks. "It is concerning, yes, but surely it doesn't warrant a visit from her Majesty."

I turn to face him and roll my eyes. I want to make sure he sees how ridiculous I think he is. Captain Mock clenches his jaw and looks away from me. The captain is oppositional, always. My mother thinks it's wise to have someone on her council who isn't afraid to voice a differing opinion, but I have always thought the captain enjoys it just a little too much. He is enamored with royal life. So much so that he often makes disparaging comments about the residents of Queen's Bridge. My mother never fails to put him in his place, because it is her firm belief that she is meant to serve the people and that everyone under her eye is worthy of protection and concern. Captain Mock also never fails in ceding to her will.

My mother shoots him a glance that says even if the trip isn't necessary, it is happening and there will be no further conversation about it. Captain Mock bows his head and takes a step back.

I trail my mother to the stables where she mounts her horse, a midnight black mare with a silver-plated saddle and the Miller family crest embroidered on a flag draped over its side. The crest is a wheel set against an emerald backdrop, said to represent the unrelenting passage of time. Golden bands unfurl from either side of the wheel, forming a flourish in the shape of a crown at the bottom. It is the symbol of my family, a line of Millers stretching back generations, so far back that our history has taken on a life of its own in the folklore of this land. Nothing from the time before my great-grandmother's reign has survived except our crest, our name, and our responsibility to this place and its people. For my mother, that is all that is required. She is a queen by birth, by right, but more importantly in the hearts of the people, and she does not suffer anyone who would put them in danger.

As she climbs into her saddle, the horse whinnies and shakes its head. My mother glances at me. I can hear her horse's low hum in my head.

"How is she?" my mother asks.

There is always other information carried in the unique voices of the animals. I had sensed fear in the dire wolf, curiosity in the fox, and now I concentrate on my mother's horse.

"She's well," I say. "She was reshoed yesterday and I think she's eager to get out of the stable."

"Ah," my mother says, patting the side of the mare's neck. "She'll get what she wants today."

I prepare to mount my own horse, a smaller mare with a deep brown coat and the same crest draped across her back. She's older but reliable, and I can tell by her unique hum that she could also use a little time in the fresh air. I lean my face against her neck, and she gently presses her head against my shoulder. She smells of straw and the wind. I run my fingers through her mane and give her a good scratch between the ears. The hum in my head goes from low and resonant to a higher pitch, almost frenzied. It is excitement, anticipation.

"Let's go, then," I say as I pull myself into the saddle and take hold of the reins.

I follow my mother out of the stable as the sun cuts through the partially overcast sky. Queen's Bridge looks like a vision when the light is just so. Cobbled roads snake through sleepy stone buildings. Smoke billows from chimneys and curls upward, mingling with a layer of low-lying clouds. The greenspaces that dot the landscape are not so green as autumn leans toward winter, but they are still full of the town's residents. Harvest time is upon us and there is all manner of goods for sale at stands and open carts as Queen's Bridge prepares to settle in for the coming winter.

As we near the center of Queen's Bridge, a woman cradling a small child rushes out of her home. My mother brings her horse to a stop and dismounts. The other woman starts to lower herself into a low bow but my mother catches her by the elbow, bringing her back up.

"You and I have known each other too long for you to risk dropping this precious child in the leaves for the likes of me," my mother says, hugging her and taking the baby into her arms.

The woman is named Nina, and she has known my mother longer than I've been alive.

My mother coos into the baby's cheek, and Nina gives me a gentle smile. "Princess Eve," she says. "Looking fierce as ever."

I dismount and stand near my mother. Nina is a friend, but I don't let my guard down for anyone. My mother suddenly thrusts the baby toward me, and I step back.

"No," I say. "I don't want to hold it."

"It?" Mother asks, her brow knitting together.

Nina casts a concerned glance from me to the baby. It is no secret that there are many within our queendom who fear me but Nina should know that despite my aversion to her drooling child, I would not do him any harm.

"Princess, his name is Aldis," Nina says gently. "And he's not made of glass. Hold him. He might grow on you."

I might drop him directly on his head, but I don't say that out loud. My mother pushes the child closer to me and I take him up. I keep him at arm's length. I'm wearing all black and I don't want him throwing up on me as babies are known to do. Why are their insides always upset? Why do they feel the need to empty their stomachs or bowels at the most inopportune times?

Mother and Nina cluck like hens as they laugh, and while I hold tight to the boy called Aldis, more than once I consider just putting him down on the ground to fend for himself.

"I'm off to see about some business at the Gregory farm," my mother says. She takes the baby from me, and I've never felt more relieved. She kisses him and hands him back to his mother. "Be safe. You know where to find me if you should need anything."

My mother treats Nina the way she treats all residents of Queen's Bridge—with kindness and respect. Captain Mock has expressed how nervous this makes him. He says that blurring the line between royalty and common folk is dangerous. My mother disagrees and has set him so firmly in place that he rarely brings it up anymore. I stand with my mother—the people of Queen's Bridge are its lifeblood, and it is our duty to serve them, to protect them against all enemies, no matter how formidable they may be.

As we leave Nina behind, my mother glances at me. "He is just the cutest thing, isn't he? Baby Aldis?"

"Is he?" I ask. "I think I've seen cuter things. He has a quite a large head."

My mother laughs uproariously until little tears stand in the corners of her eyes.

"I hope you're not expecting that of me," I say, glancing back toward Nina's home.

My mother reaches across the space between our horses and pats my leg. "What I expect of you is whatever you deem appropriate. I want you happy." Something unreadable passes over her face, an expression drawn tight like a mask. I notice but say nothing.

Sir Gregory's farm is at the foot of the mountains, near the head of the River Farris, and as my mother and I push our horses in that direction, they gallop hard, their hearts beating, their muscles taut. They race along, their voices harmonizing in my head. When we arrive, they are nearly singing with content.

As we approach Sir Gregory's farm, I get a clear sense of what the issue is and why everyone had seemed so concerned. Sir Gregory grows flax, keeping nearly twenty acres of it. He is a regular at the market and is known for the impeccable quality of his crop. I am surprised to see that the fields of flax still retain their purple blooms but even more surprised to see that the plants have overflowed their acreage and are now spilling across the road into the neighboring field, creeping their way toward a wide swath of the River Farris. My mother dismounts, and I do the same. I tether our horses to a fence post.

"Stay put," I say to them. I listen for their response and they both seem agreeable.

I follow my mother up the overgrown path to Sir Gregory's front door. I stop and break off a sprig of the flax to examine its insides. The stalks are well formed and the green wick of the plant is wet. They are in perfect health, so I am at a loss. Why didn't he cut them and take them into town to sell? I toss the plant aside and, as it lands on the damp earth, one of the stalks sprouts a lavender purple bloom right before my eyes. I grab my mother's elbow and point to the newly sprouted stalks.

"Look!" I say. "They're—they're growing. Right in front of my face."

My mother examines the stalk. As she leans forward to get a better look, another one sprouts from the earth and blooms. She gently touches the petals and her expression changes from wonderment to quiet concern and then—to something else. Her mouth turns down at the corners and some of the color in her normally beautifully deep umber skin drains away from her.

"Mother," I say. "What magic is this?"

She straightens up and lets her gloved fingers rest on the dagger at her hip.

"Come," she says. "Let us see what Sir Gregory has to say."

CHAPTER 2

I knock on Sir Gregory's door, and a moment later he answers. Sir Gregory is a balding older man with kind eyes and an even kinder heart. He's gracious to a fault.

"Queen Regina," he says, bowing his head slightly and then turning to me. "Princess Eve."

"May we come in?" my mother asks.

Sir Gregory's eyes grow wide, and his lips part just slightly. He quickly reins himself in, looking flustered. My skin pricks up. It is unlike him to be so reticent. It stirs something in me. I have my dagger, as does my mother, though I will not give Sir Gregory or anyone else a chance to make her draw it. I breathe in. The moisture in the crisp autumn air is heavy. Good. It is yet another tool I have at my disposal should that become necessary.

"Of course, my Queen," Sir Gregory finally says. "Please come in."

He opens the door wide and Mother and I step over the threshold into a chaotic scene.

Sir Gregory's children, of which there are eight the last time I checked, are running in circles gathering up bundles of harvested flax plants and tying them with thread, then loading them into wicker baskets. The rear door to their cottage bounces open and a tall young man stumbles in with a sack full of freshly cut flax. Sir Gregory's wife rushes up to my mother, and they greet each other warmly.

"Oh, your Majesty," Lady Gregory sighs. "If I'd known you were coming, I would have cleaned up a little."

"Please," says my mother, brushing off Lady Gregory's concerns in the kindest way possible. "A messy home is usually a happy one."

"I'm sorry to say that's not entirely the case at the moment," Lady Gregory says.

"Latrice," Sir Gregory says. In his voice there is something like annoyance, and I cast him a dagger of a glance. He softens his tone immediately. "Her Majesty and the Princess don't want to hear about our problems." He comes over and stands between my mother and Lady Gregory. "Is there something I can help you with, my Queen?"

"Actually, I came to ask you the same question," Mother says. "Your crops are overflowing. They're making their way to the River Farris and, as I'm sure you're aware, that is the main supply of fresh water to the heart of Queen's Bridge. We cannot allow it to be impeded. It would be disastrous for everyone south of here."

"My crops aren't anywhere close to the river, my Queen," Sir Gregory says.

"Yes, they are," his oldest son chimes in as he drops a bushel of flax onto the table. "They're nearly to the bank."

"Gods, Mekhi! Don't tell me that!" Sir Gregory looks like he might faint. He grabs hold of the edge of the table. A thin film of sweat breaks across his sun-beaten brow.

Mekhi cradles his father's elbow to steady him. The boy's brow is deeply furrowed in what I can only assume is concern for his father. Sir Gregory puts his hand on the boy's shoulder. "How bad is it?"

Mekhi only shakes his head, his eyes downcast.

I study Sir Gregory carefully. His reaction seems genuine, but I could see his crops encroaching on the River Farris's banks from the road. If he hasn't seen it, if he doesn't understand how bad it is, it means he's choosing not to look, which presents the only question that really matters: Why?

Sir Gregory slumps into a chair at the table and holds his head in his hands. Mekhi keeps his hand firmly on his father's back as his gaze flits from me to my mother.

A thunderous rush of footsteps sounds and suddenly, from the back hall, a little girl with her hair in two little puffs on either side of her head rushes out. She makes a beeline straight for me and tugs on my trousers.

"Miri," Sir Gregory says. "Show some respect for the Princess."

The girl gives a wobbly little curtsy and then pulls from

her skirts a small wooden dagger and pretends to poke me in the leg with it.

"Miri, please," Sir Gregory says, shooing the girl away.

"It's fine," I say. I take out my dagger and angle it so that it catches just a little of the daylight streaming through the window. It glints in the sun and the girl's eyes grow wide.

"Can I hold it?" she asks.

I mask the amusement that courses through me.

"Miri," Mekhi says softly. "You can't hold it—"

"Why not?" I ask. I size Miri up. She's a stout girl with a round frame, absolutely perfect for wielding a dagger.

"She doesn't know how to use it," Mekhi says. "I'm teaching her, but she's not quite ready yet."

Miri pulls back her arm and jabs the end of her wooden dagger into my leg. I'm lucky the blade isn't made of metal because despite Mekhi's assessment of her skills, she would have put the blade straight through me if it had been real. She twists her wrist, a technique that would have ensured the wound—had she made one—would not have closed.

I feign a grievous injury, and her expression quickly turns to concern. She pats my leg as her eyes well with tears. I quickly right myself and smile at her. She exhales sharply and relief relaxes her brow. At least she's prepared to defend herself, unlike the slobbering baby Aldis.

"You know what to do, but you don't know what you will feel," I say quietly, slipping my very real dagger back into its sheath. "No tears for the wicked, sweet girl." I wipe her damp face with the sleeve of my shirt.

"Eve," Mother says sternly. "Let the girl have her fun."

"I'm sorry, Princess," Sir Gregory says as Lady Gregory ushers their children, including the girl with the little dagger, out the back door to allow us some privacy.

My mother moves aside some of the endless piles of flax and sits down, pulling her fur-lined cloak in close and folding her hands in front of her. I pull up a small stool and sit beside her.

"My surveyors have seen drought in some of the farmland west of Queen's Bridge," my mother says, her voice low and deadly serious. "Even in areas where the drought conditions are minimal there has been an influx of insects, vermin, and disease in the plants. People are struggling to maintain their crops." She glances around the room. "It seems you have no such issue."

"We've had some drought here, too," Sir Gregory says quickly. "Rot as well. In the roots."

"It doesn't affect the flax?" Mother asks, raising her brows and keeping her unflinching gaze on Sir Gregory. She leans forward and looks Sir Gregory directly in the face, the way she does when she asks a question to which she already knows the answer. It is then that I understand that my mother is holding back. She knows something about this situation and is giving Sir Gregory the opportunity to tell her the whole truth. I hope for his sake that he does. My mother did not get where she is by allowing people to lie to her.

Sir Gregory strums his fingers across the tabletop. "I'm getting older. Keeping up with the farm is a lot of work and only some of the children are old enough to help. I've had to take on some extra work." He gestures to a tall cabinet in the far corner of the room. It is filled with wood forms in the shapes of slender legs and arms. Painted faces stare out at us. "Marionettes," Sir Gregory says. "I've become quite good at crafting them."

"I can find you some help for working the land," I offer. "There are always people who are willing to help. We can cover their wages and meals."

My mother nods but remains silent.

"I don't want help," Sir Gregory says. His tone is clipped. He seems angry, but I still can't piece it together. "It's not necessary. I assure you."

My mother holds up her hand, and Sir Gregory looks down at the tabletop. His shoulders roll forward. He is trembling.

"You don't want help," Mother says, measuring her words precisely. "What *do* you want? Or should I say—what is it you *wish* for, Sir Gregory?"

For a moment, I don't register what she's just implied, but as the expression on Sir Gregory's face melts into a mask of abject terror, I finally understand.

"No," I say aloud, unable to disguise my disbelief. "Sir Gregory. Tell me you're not that reckless."

Sir Gregory's pitiful expression reveals everything. A bolt of anger ripples through me and the small fire in the hearth wavers. A slim flame, orange as the setting sun, leans ever so slightly in my direction.

"Eve," Mother says. "Not now."

I breathe deep and the fire returns to its steady state.

My mother gives her head a shake and runs her hand over her mouth before continuing. "You made a wish, didn't you?"

I stare at Sir Gregory as he tries and fails to hide the terrified look in his eyes. He is a kind man with a big heart, but I have never known him to be the type of person who would go seeking wishes.

Sir Gregory huffs as he builds up a façade of nonchalance. He shrugs stiffly. "It was simple. I swear. Nothing to be concerned with, Highness. Nothing at all."

"Nothing is ever simple with *him*," my mother says. "You know that. Everyone in Queen's Bridge knows that. Why would you risk it?" She glances to the back door on the other side of which is Sir Gregory's precious family, the thing he holds most dear. "Your family is now in proximity to him. How could you be so thoughtless?"

"Thoughtless?" Sir Gregory's mask slips. "I thought it through. Thoroughly."

"Clearly not," my mother says.

"I wanted double the crop in half the time so that I could make my harvest and settle in for the winter sooner." He runs his hands over the top of his head. "I'm getting older. I want to spend as much time with my children and my wife as I can and—"

My mother sighs, sitting back in her chair. "Was it for payment or terms?"

"Terms," says Sir Gregory quickly, as if that makes it

better somehow. "I didn't have anything he was particularly interested in as payment and so he offered terms—I make the wish and he will grant it exactly as I've asked. I know it wasn't smart but—"

"What were they? The terms?" my mother asks, abruptly cutting him off. "Tell me what you wished for."

I brace myself for what Sir Gregory might say. Every word will be important. Every potential double meaning will need to be known.

Sir Gregory's hands begin to tremble and he clasps them together in front of him, pressing his elbows into the table. "I told him that I wanted to double my yield of flax in half the time it normally takes me," Sir Gregory says. "I asked for an abundance of flax."

My mother presses her hands into the tabletop so hard the wood groans in protest. "No," she says firmly. "Tell me *exactly* what you said to him."

Sir Gregory is defeated. He slumps down. "I—I said, 'I wish for an overflowing abundance of flax for the remainder of the season. A crop so hardy that nothing, not disease or drought, can keep it from seeding.'"

My mother pushes her chair back and stands up. "When have you ever seen the terms of a deal with him work out as intended? You should know better."

"How did you even find him?" I ask.

My mother draws her mouth into a tight line, and I worry I've already given myself away.

"I was hunting elk in Hastwich Pass with Mekhi," Sir

Gregory says. "East of the River Farris. I saw his castle on its course through the mountains just by chance. I wasn't looking for him, but there he was." He shakes his head. "I sent my son home with our bounty and continued on alone."

"You had it in your mind to ask him for a wish and so he suddenly appears, allowing you to track him," my mother says. "That is no coincidence."

"No, I suppose it's not." Sir Gregory opens and closes his hands and sighs. "That drought you spoke of, it *did* affect me. I had sweetgrass and a good, sturdy grain, but it all went to rot in a month's time. We couldn't weave baskets. We could scarcely feed ourselves save for the wild game, so I turned to the flax. It's food, fiber, and fuel all in one. I thought I could make up for what we lost but the grow time is obscene. I couldn't wait a hundred and twenty days for them to mature. I was desperate." Sir Gregory slouches even further into his chair as if he's hoping it will swallow him.

"All who bargain with him are," I say.

Sir Gregory narrows his eyes at me, and I flick my wrist toward the fire. It jumps up, lapping at the bricks, funneling itself into a short column. I don't bring it to meet my hand; instead I allow the flame to retreat. Sir Gregory stiffens in his seat.

"You couldn't reach out to your neighbors?" my mother asks. "To me?"

"And have you know that I can't provide for my own children?" He shakes his head. "No. I couldn't do that." His eyes are glassy, like he's pulling something from the depths of his memory. Something he'd buried, never intending for it to surface again. "It wasn't at all like people say," he says quietly. "It's not a castle as much as it is a great hulking beast made of metal and rivets and steam and darkness—like a living, breathing, moving shadow."

A shudder runs through me.

"How many people have tracked down his abode and never made it home?" my mother asks. "You have a family. How will they cope without you? Did you stop to think of that?"

"I know," Sir Gregory says, hanging his head. "But I did it for them. I was just so desperate for rest and I wanted to have more time with them."

Something softens in my mother's face. She rests her hand on Sir Gregory's shoulder. "I'll send a few people around to help cut the crops back, keep them away from the river until the season ends." She draws her hand back and narrows her eyes at Sir Gregory. "I trust you will not make this mistake again. I understand you're a proud man but do not let your pride keep you from asking trustworthy people for help."

Sir Gregory paws at his dampened eyes as my mother gestures for me to follow her out the front door. The horses are grazing on the flax, and I swear, in just the time we had spent inside Sir Gregory's house, more of the errant crop had pulled its way across the dirt road.

"I can't believe he made a deal with him," I say as I untether my horse and pull myself into the saddle.

My mother mounts her horse and sighs, turning her face

to the sky. "I can. A wish granted is a very seductive thing, Eve. That is his power."

Of all the things we are granted under my mother's watchful eye, there are things that the people of Queen's Bridge desire that are out of her hands. What Sir Gregory wanted was beyond the reach of a queen's power—but the Knight is not a queen or any other sort of royalty. He is not even a man.

He is a myth made real.

A monster.

CHAPTER 3

My mother sits at the long table in her drawing room, her fingers tented under her chin, her face drawn tight with concern. Made from the trunk of a walnut tree, the table's grain is so dark it looks as if my mother is sitting at the head of a great black void. She stares at the map of Queen's Bridge in front of her, its corners pinned to the table by heavy brass candlesticks. I sit in silence, knowing that when she's ready to speak, she will. Until then, I have some concerns of my own.

"Why would Sir Gregory risk tracking down the Knight?" I ask. "His castle is almost impossible to find no matter where it's settled." The nature of the Knight's traveling castle is an enigma to the people of Queen's Bridge. Despite many sightings of it, no one is entirely sure what magic powers it. "Wherever the castle settled, the journey to it would have been a perilous one."

"Unless *he* wants you to find it," my mother says quietly, her gaze still fixed on the map. "If he wants you there, the path is wide open."

"You think the Knight lured Sir Gregory in?" I ask.

My mother tilts her head. "It doesn't matter. What's done is done. The wish was made. The Knight's terms are ironclad. Sir Gregory's wish was as simple as a wish could possibly be and still it has gone to rot because the Knight would have it no other way." She sighs and shakes her head before standing and sweeping over to the gilded cage by the window.

She opens the little door and puts her hand inside. The nightingale hops off its perch and stands on her outstretched fingers.

"Sanaa, my love," my mother coos. "We know better than most how the Knight's deals work, don't we?" Mother strokes the nightingale's soft plumage and it hops back to its perch. My mother leaves the cage open, blinking back tears. "I don't want her to feel like she can't be free if she wants to be."

I go to her side and put my arms around her. She buries her face in my shoulder.

"There is no such thing as a fair deal with him," she says, pulling back and looking me over. "He will continue to tempt those looking for something more. He knows how to play to their deepest desires."

"He must have known how desperate Sir Gregory was to spend more time with his family," I say.

My mother nods. "It has always been this way. We live in the shadow of the havoc he creates." She glances up at a large portrait of my other mother, Queen Sanaa, as she was before everything went wrong. A bottomless pit of grief threatens to swallow me whole if I step too near its edge, and so I look away from the portrait to the cage where Queen Sanaa now resides. It is the Knight's betrayal of her that fuels my mother's frustration with Sir Gregory.

Queen Sanaa's fate is as much a part of me as anything else. It directly links us to the Knight like a shackle. The story is burned into my mind, a cautionary tale I have heard since the incident itself occurred. It echoes in my mind, in my mother's voice, just as she told it to me those many years ago.

There had never been a wish that was spoken aloud with such clarity that it could not be twisted in some way. But hers was a simple wish. Nothing so vague as to be misunderstood or misconstrued in any way. He couldn't cheat her if she was concise. She had practiced in the mirror. She knew the words by heart.

She trekked into the mountains and found his castle by the light of the full moon, which, in her experience, was the best way to find such a place. It was nestled in a rocky outcropping near a steep cliff. The structure was never in the same spot for long. Had he meant for her to find him so easily? Perhaps, but that meant he knew she was coming and that, in turn, meant he was already a step ahead. Still, she braved the frigid cold and treacherous path to get to him.

The castle's doors opened under their own power, and a narrow corridor beckoned her in. She followed it and came upon him as he stoked a fire hot enough to dry her dampened skin in an instant.

"I must admit I did not expect to see you here," he said, his voice like the echo in a cave.

"I want to make a wish," she said.

He turned and stared at her, though she could not make out his eyes through the narrow slit in the black helm. None now live who had ever seen him without it.

"Terms or payment?"

"Terms," she said.

His head tilted to the side. "So be it."

She knew what to say, all that was left was to say it aloud.

"I am ill," she said.

"And you wish to be cured of what ails you?" the Knight asked.

"No," Queen Sanaa said. "The sickness has stolen something very dear to me and I want it back." Queen Sanaa took a breath and touched the delicate skin of her neck. Her illness had stolen her ability to sing, a talent she had curated since the time she was small. She stilled herself and spoke her wish aloud. "I wish that my singing voice was the loveliest in all the land."

Simple. Direct. No room for error.

The Knight didn't move or speak for so long, she began to wonder if he had forgotten she was there.

"Three days' time," he said finally.

She turned and left. As soon as she was clear of his castle, she heard a great rumble. Behind her, the castle, a mass of blackened bricks and twisted metal, rose up and lumbered away from her like some beast from a nightmare.

She felt she had done it. She had recited the words just as she'd planned. Her wife would be pleased. She would use her *renewed talent to serenade her love the way she had when they were courting, and she would lull their tiny girl to sleep.*

By the third day, nothing remained save for a pair of wild, terrified eyes situated over a black beak and mottled brown feathers. The nightingale frantically beat its wings as the little girl cried and Queen Regina wept. In her last moments before the change was complete, she'd revealed to her love her terrible circumstance and how it had come to be.

"Fight him with everything you've got," she said.

"I will," said Queen Regina. "I swear it."

The Queen became despondent but was pulled out of her grief by the hand and smile of her little girl. Her laughter took the place of the unending sobs.

The girl was all that mattered.

I stand looking at the nightingale in the gilded cage. Queen Sanaa wished to have the loveliest voice in the land, all in a bid to serenade my mother, to be able to sing me to sleep. The Knight turned her into a nightingale, granting her wish in the most literal sense. She now has the lovely voice she wished for but is cursed to live the rest of her days as a bird. Her song is high and melodic, but her calls are fearful. They ring with despair.

Where the Knight obtained this terrible power and how he continues to wield it without consequence are the questions that keep my mother up at night, pacing the floor in her chambers. The Knight roamed these lands long before my mother's reign and had terrorized generations of Miller Queens. If he has his way, he'll be here when all the rest of us are dead. He has always been a figure to be feared and still people think his treacherous deals will work in their favor—they think they are special. They are wrong.

"My hope is that one day, we will end him once and for all," my mother says as Queen Sanaa flutters to her shoulder. She says the words like it is her sincerest hope, but there is desperation in every syllable. "I will not rest until he is held accountable. The people of this land deserve some justice, some peace."

"As do you," I say.

I often think of what my mother's life would be like had she not been burdened with this constant threat, if she had not had the love of her life ripped away from her so cruelly. She and I exchange glances. I have spent my entire life training for a confrontation with the Knight. My abilities are formidable. My skills, both learned and granted by virtue of my birth, have been honed. I am a weapon at the ready, and still my mother speaks as if she is unsure of what to do.

"I will end him," I say. "One way or another."

My mother stares at me and cups my face in her hands. There is sadness in her eyes. "I hope it will not come to the two of you at the end of the world."

"You're afraid to let me face him," I say.

"Yes," my mother says. "I am."

"Why?" I ask. "Do you think it is a coincidence that I have these abilities?" I stretch my hand toward one of the candles on the table and the flame elongates and arches toward my open palm.

Mother gently pushes my arm down. "You know that

magic is a part of this land the same way the trees and rivers and animals are. There have been people born with all manner of abilities that defy explanation."

I huff. "I've never heard a whisper of anyone who can do the things I can."

"No, but there are witches, conjurers of all sorts," my mother says, avoiding my eyes. "What I mean to say is that while you are unique, there is no reason to assume that you've been granted this magic to use against the Knight." Mother grips my shoulders a little too tight. "You are not bound to him if you don't want to be."

"If I am bound to him then it should be because I will be the one to kill him," I say. "He should be worried if our fates are intertwined." I sigh and try not to let my mother's saddened expression seep into me. I have been ready to tear down the world for her for much, much less. "Let me deal with him. There is no one better suited."

She shakes her head. "I plan on stopping him long before it comes to that."

"Before it comes to what?" Huntress stands in the doorway, her hand on her hip, her eyes questioning.

"Nothing you need be concerned with," Mother says, dropping a mask of calm over her face.

Huntress steps into the room. "Are you certain?" She strides up and puts her hand on my mother's shoulder. "You looked upset."

My mother shrugs away from her and closes the birdcage as Queen Sanaa hops back onto her perch.

"Take Eve for another lesson," my mother says.

"She needs no more lessons aside from tracking," Huntress says.

"Still," my mother says. "I'd rather be overprepared than underprepared. Agreed?"

Huntress bows her head. "Yes, my Queen."

My mother nudges me toward the door, leaning close to my ear. "Do not be easy with Huntress."

I best Huntress four out of four times with the dagger. A small cut on her cheek drips crimson as evidence.

"I'm sorry," I say. "I didn't mean to actually cut you."

"You didn't?" she asks, wiping the blood away with the sleeve of her shirt. "You swung your dagger in front of my face. What did you expect would happen?"

"I thought you would duck."

She and I look at each other in silence, and then she begins to laugh. She doesn't know that I was holding back. I always am. I could kill her easily.

Huntress chuckles to herself as she dabs at her cheek. "It's like I said to your mother the other night, you have excelled at everything I have to teach. We've brought in outside people to work with—sparring, swordplay—and you've bested them all. Even if you cheat, you still win."

I look her over, trying to discern if she's joking. She's not.

"You keep accusing me of cheating in some way," I say.

"It isn't your fault," Huntress says. "You have those

36

powers by birth. You can conjure a weapon out of anything in nature. You're not better than anyone else because you can do that, and you shouldn't rely on those things all of the time."

Her words are harsh, but I am not prone to having my feelings hurt.

"Maybe you're mad that I had you on the ground so quickly today," I say. "No conjured weapons needed. I think I set a personal best."

Huntress huffs. "There's that arrogance again. It will be the death of you, Princess." She hesitates on the verge of saying something more. She readjusts her grip on her dagger and shakes her head. "Your mother and I would have you prepared for anything," she says. "And we have done just that, but I fear it may not be enough to contend with your ego."

Magic like mine is rarely seen in Queen's Bridge, but it manifests in me and I don't see anything wrong with being proud of that.

"I can beat him," I say. "That's all that matters."

Huntress is quiet for a long time before speaking again. "I think we're done here. You should wash up and check in with your mother. I'll see you in the morning."

"Right," I say.

Huntress shrugs out of her fitted breastplate and tosses it to the ground. She turns on her heel and heads for the door without another word.

"Huntress," I call after her.

She stops. "I don't want to talk about the Knight. Speak to

me about something else or I'll take my leave and see you in the morning."

"Fine," I say. "Will you help me talk to Mother about my birthday plans?" I ask, changing the subject to something different but equally taboo.

Huntress pauses. "I thought she asked you not to speak of it."

My seventeenth birthday is in less than a month, and as it approaches my mother becomes less and less interested in my ideas for a celebration.

"Doesn't seem fair that I can't plan my own birthday," I say.

"I'm sure she has her reasons," Huntress says. "When I told you to talk to me about something else, I didn't mean that."

I let a smirk pull itself across my lips. "You didn't specify."

"And you are too smart for your own good." She stretches her hands over her head and sighs, walking back over to me. I have known Huntress my entire life, and our relationship grows more complicated the older I get. She prefers to think of me as a little girl, as someone who should lean into my role as my mother's right hand, helping her with planning and supporting the people of this queendom when I would much rather be her sword—her vengeance.

As Huntress stares at me, I see in her eyes a mother's worry and concern, though she does not hold that title.

"Do you even know how to dance?" Huntress asks.

"What?" I ask.

A smile breaks across Huntress's lips. "A celebration usually involves dancing, and I don't think we've covered waltzing in any of our previous lessons."

I have always pictured myself dancing at a celebration but have never had the opportunity to do it. "It can't be that hard."

Huntress chuckles. "Right. Come here. Stand up straight and take my hand."

"Why?" I ask, horrified as Huntress holds out her hand to me.

"We'll have a lesson right now," she says. "If your mother changes her mind, you should be prepared."

"You can teach me?" I ask. "Do you know how?"

"I dance with your mother all the time."

I'm shocked. My mother doesn't dance. Neither does Huntress. And they have been dancing together? I have more questions, but Huntress roughly takes my hand.

"One, two, three. One, two, three," Huntress chants in a rhythmic way as she slowly moves her feet to the count.

I try to mirror her steps, but she's pulling on my hand and trying to steer me alongside her. I grip her hand back and try to make her slow down.

"Stop," Huntress says. "You can't always lead."

"Well, I don't want to do it, then," I say.

Huntress laughs. "You can't be this stubborn. Gods, Eve."

I loosen my grip. Huntress sighs and leads me in a sweeping circle as I try to keep up with her. By the time we've gone around a half dozen times I've tripped over my own feet a hundred times and almost elbowed Huntress in the neck as she tried to turn me. I break her grip and sit down on the ground. Huntress dabs at her brow with a cloth and shakes her head.

"Maybe we've found the one thing that is absolutely impossible for you to do," she says.

"How did you learn to dance so well?" I ask, trying to catch my breath.

Huntress grins. "Practice with a good partner." She pushes her hand down on her hip. "I don't think we should have a band at all during this celebration. We can't risk it. If you can't kill the Knight with a sword, maybe you should invite him to the celebration and make him die of sheer embarrassment."

"It's that bad?"

"Yes," Huntress says with absolute sincerity.

I pluck a handful of dried grass from the ground and toss it at her. "Leave me alone!"

She and I laugh together until we can hardly breathe. It's nice to feel so carefree for once.

"Let's not press our Queen about it right now, though," Huntress continues. "Especially after this latest business with the Knight. You know how she loathes him and her frustration is renewed every time one of the people of Queen's Bridge thinks they can outsmart him. She's left to clean up the messes he makes, and it wears on her."

"As a birthday present, she should let me relieve him of his head," I say. "It's what she's been preparing me for my entire life."

Huntress narrows her gaze at me. "We'll see. Let us discuss it tomorrow because right now you smell awful, and my feet are bruised from you stepping all over them. After I make my rounds in the stable, I need to rest. Getting beaten up by you all afternoon is tiring."

She takes her leave, and I make my way to the upper floor of the castle.

In my quarters, I wash up in the basin and practice the steps Huntress had taught me with an invisible partner. I can't imagine who might dare to dance with me, but surely someone will ask. I find that, alone, I'm not so bad at it. A rustle draws my attention to the washbasin. I stop to listen but whatever it is has moved on. Most likely a mouse seeking shelter from the cold. I stomp around and give the washbasin stand a swift kick to scare away any rodents that might be lurking, and then lie across my bed, letting the knots in my back and shoulders unwind. I am beyond tired in my body and my mind. I think about my mother's long history with the Knight, how he betrayed Queen Sanaa the same year I turned eight, and how none of us have been the same since. His presence in Queen's Bridge and in our lives is like a dark, heavy shadow. My hatred of the Knight has blossomed from the time I was first made aware of him. It has grown like a ragged weed, now living in every part of me. I've been taught that revenge is not noble, not befitting of a princess. My mother urges me toward justice. I cannot tell her that when the time comes for me to exact the punishment the Knight so rightly deserves, it will be vengeance that guides my sword.

I get up and make sure my door is tightly closed. Locking it is never an option but I do slide a short wooden stool in front of it to act as a warning should someone try to enter. I then retrieve a large wooden box from under my bed and sit down next to it. I pull up the lid and move aside the folded woolen quilt I'd placed on top of the things that really matter. I shuffle through hand-drawn maps of Queen's Bridge and the surrounding lands—Queen's Bridge at the northeastern corner, Hamelin to the west, Rotterdam to the north, the Forbidden Lands and Mersailles to the southwest. The different territories are marked off by thick black lines signifying my presence in each place. I'd traveled to each of them, trying to feel out the edges of the Knight's influence, collecting his stories from places near and far. The tales became stranger the farther I went from Queen's Bridge. There had been sightings of him as far north as Dead Man's Peak and even on the border of Hamelin. But Queen's Bridge is his home, and so it is here that he inflicts the most damage.

The box is a vault of secrets, unspeakable tales, accounts from people who had seen the Knight or his sentient castle. I pull out a small collection of notes in my own hand. They are wrapped in a cloth and bound with twine. These are some of my most precious possessions. They are the actual wishes made by the people of Queen's Bridge to the Knight, accounts of the actual words used and the often catastrophic outcomes of even the simplest of wishes.

The first account is that of a woman whose husband was named Midian. He went to the Knight and wished for gold and riches to be heaped upon him. He was crushed by a priceless emerald as he worked in the South Steps mine.

A woman named Hazel wished for her eldest daughter to

be the belle of the annual winter solstice gathering; the girl was transfigured into a brass bell as soon as she arrived at the festivities.

A jealous man asked the Knight to make his neighbor's wife think of him and only him. She became so obsessed with him that she thought of nothing else, not food or drink, not sleep, nothing. She died, and he was killed by the woman's husband.

There was the story of the Kingfisher and his seven sons, though how the Knight was involved with this man and seven of his children was never made clear to me. This story was not a firsthand account but rather a tale that came to me in fragments—a man cursed by the Knight and each of his sons cursed in turn because of something the man wished for. The details are vague and the story is always secondhand, but the outcome is clearly the same as all the other accounts of the Knight.

There are dozens of accounts, each of them more terrible than the one before.

Ruin. Rot. That is all the Knight is capable of granting.

I envision the Knight falling under my sword. I can almost feel the weight of a weapon in my hand. I can imagine the look in his eyes when he realizes that my face will be the last thing he ever sees. There is suddenly movement to my left. I'm on my feet in an instant, my fingers curled around my dagger, my heart pounding wildly. The flash of black had come from the small round mirror over my washbasin.

I glance around my quarters. I am alone, of course, and all

is still aside from the fire burning hot in the hearth. The stool remains propped securely against the door. My skin is raised to gooseflesh, and the sense that I am not alone overwhelms me. I approach the mirror and peer into it. I see only myself. The long black curtains that cover my window sway slightly in the draft that is pushing its way through the bricks around the window. I set my dagger on the small table next to the wash-basin and sigh.

I change into my nightclothes and twist my hair into a knot on the top of my head. I light a small lamp and make my way to my mother's private chambers just down the hall from my own. Her door is closed, as it always is in the late evening when she breaks from solving the problems of Queen's Bridge and steals a few moments for herself. I raise my hand to knock but stop short. My mother's voice drifts out from under the door. Her words are low and almost frantic. She is saying something I cannot quite make out. I lean closer to the door.

"Please," she says, her voice tight. "Tell me what I can do."

Someone answers her.

I glance out the small stained-glass window at the end of the hall. It is well after dark and I cannot imagine who she would be receiving company from at this hour.

"You already know," the answering voice says. It is a low, husky declaration—and it is unnatural. It sends a shiver straight through me, setting me on edge. Both close and faraway in the same breath. "Stop this pleading, my Queen. It is folly."

"It isn't!" my mother snaps. Her words are all fire and anger. "It doesn't have to be this way."

My instinct is to kick the door in and defend her. Instead, I knock.

"Mother?" I call. "Are you all right?"

There is a long pause, and I put my hand on the door, preparing to open it regardless if I am granted an invitation.

"I'm fine," Mother says finally. A shadow moves under the door as if someone is standing just on the other side, but when my mother speaks again her voice echoes from somewhere deep inside her chambers. "Good night, Eve. I love you very much."

"I love you, too." I know my mother, and I know that as she tells me this, she is crying.

I stand there like a shadow. How long, I do not know. After some time, I make my way back to my room. Flames lap at the blackened bricks in the hearth. I tie a scarf over my hair and crawl into bed, pulling the covers up to my neck.

I hate that my mother is upset, but something else sticks in my mind. A memory claws its way up from wherever long-ago thoughts go to sleep. It's something about my mother—and that voice from behind her locked door.

I have heard it before.

CHAPTER 4

I wake as soon as the sun slants through my window. I slip out of bed, dress, and go into the hall. From somewhere below, the clang of pans and the scent of bread wafts up. The castle is just now waking, but my mother is already up, dressed, and pacing in her drawing room.

"Good morning," I say as I slip into the room and sit down. "You were up with the sun."

"I think I beat the sun," she says. "I haven't slept."

"What's wrong?" I ask. "I heard you in your room last night. You sounded upset."

She avoids my gaze and instead stares out the window. A layer of frost has laid itself across the land like a glittering blanket. "I have to send some workers out to help Sir Gregory manage his disastrous mistake. Would you be willing to help?"

"Of course," I say.

She smiles and her shoulders roll forward a little.

"I spoke to Huntress about my birthday," I say.

This time, she turns and looks me dead in the eye. "We have been through this."

"Yes," I say quietly. "But I was hoping you would reconsider."

Even as I say it, I know it sounds ridiculous. The Knight is wreaking havoc in our lands, and I want a celebration. But it's for that very reason that I'm hoping my mother will change her mind. I want a moment, even if it is just a few small hours, to be free of the constant worry. There is a growing part of me that wants to wear a pretty dress and dance the night away and pretend that life could always be like that.

"Seventeen is no different than sixteen and you managed that without much fanfare," Mother says.

Without any fanfare, if we're being honest. I haven't celebrated a birthday properly since I turned thirteen. Every year since then has been a game of wait and see, and it appears this year will be no different. Huntress comes in and takes a seat by the window.

"I don't want to talk about this anymore," my mother says. "The Knight's influence is ever present. Do you not feel it? How can we celebrate at a time like this?"

"But if we could just do something small?" I ask. "I spend so much of my time fighting, I'd like a moment to let my guard down."

"Let your guard down?" My mother repeats the words as if she cannot understand, and I know I have said too much.

"I've never heard anything so reckless in my life." I am struck silent. She is not the kind of parent or ruler who has led with anger. She is kind and gentle, understanding but fair. Firm but willing to listen. But in this moment, as she heaves, her hand pressing into the table, I feel a twinge of fear.

"My Queen," Huntress says in a plea for calm. "She's distracted. She has been for weeks."

It feels like Huntress is digging at me, and I straighten up.

"Was I distracted when I bested you yesterday?" I ask. "Was I distracted when I bagged the deer or when I saved your life in the woods?"

Huntress laughs. "My life was never in danger."

"The wolf would have disagreed," I say.

"Wolf?" My mother's brows push up as she narrows her gaze at me. "You said nothing of a wolf."

"It was nothing," I say. "I frightened it away."

"It was a dire wolf," Huntress says.

Mother's mouth opens into a little O and her eyes widen. "In Queen's Bridge? There hasn't been one here in years."

"Maybe it's a sign," Huntress says.

I cannot help but roll my eyes, and Huntress immediately takes umbrage.

"Don't look at me that way," she says, leaning forward.

"I'll do as I please," I say, staring at her unblinking.

Huntress's expression goes slack as she leans back in her chair. She roughly taps the side of Queen Sanaa's cage. "Look at your girl. Just as headstrong and arrogant as you were."

I'm about to say something that will absolutely earn me a reprimand from my mother, but she beats me to it.

"You will remember your place," Mother says. "Do not ever speak disparagingly about Sanaa in my presence."

Huntress stands and bows her head. "I meant no disrespect, my Queen. Only that Sanaa—"

"*Queen* Sanaa," my mother interjects. "She is still here and you will address her with respect befitting of a Queen." My mother's chest heaves and those last words barely make it past her quivering bottom lip.

Huntress nods and presses her hand to her chest. "Yes, Highness. Queen Sanaa was undoubtedly headstrong. I should not have used the word arrogance to describe her. My sincerest apologies."

My mother holds her steely gaze for another moment and then looks away, letting her arms fall heavily at her sides before turning back to me. "Do not bring up this business of a celebration again. Too much is at risk and with the Knight interfering more and more every year . . ." She sighs. "We will focus on the task at hand—the matter of Sir Gregory's farm and keeping Queen's Bridge safe—and nothing else. Is that in any way unclear?"

I search her face for some kind of sign that she regrets having to make this decision but find nothing but fear and anger in her eyes. I let my gaze wander to the floor.

"Yes, my Queen," I say. I get up and move toward the door.

"Where are you going?" my mother asks.

"I need to clear my head," I say. "I'm going for a ride. I'll be back this afternoon."

"No." My mother comes around the table and stands in front of me. "Huntress will accompany you to Sir Gregory's and you will help organize the effort to keep his flax from choking off our water supply. You are not to step one foot past Sir Gregory's land."

I spin around and look at her. She meets me with narrow, steely eyes.

"You've never put restrictions on how far I can ride out," I say. "I know how to take care of myself."

"You do," she says. "And still, you will go no farther. End of discussion."

She turns and busies herself with her maps as Captain Mock comes in. Following close behind him is Lady Anne, balancing a tray of sliced bread and a kettle spewing steam from its spout. She sets the tray on the side table and sweeps over to me.

"Only three more weeks," she says in a whisper. "Seventeen. I can hardly believe it. You know, I've been here for every step. Your first words. Your—"

"Stop." My mother's voice snuffs out Lady Anne's enthusiasm like a candle. She doesn't look up from the map. Her body is rigid and her fingers press hard into the tabletop. "Have I not made it clear that there is to be no talk of this particular subject?"

Lady Anne turns to face my mother. "I have children of my own, my Queen. You know them well. I understand that seeing them grow up and become their own people is a terrifying thing." She laughs lightly. My mother does not. Lady Anne approaches her and gently puts her hand on my mother's shoulder. "My Queen, please. The girl deserves a celebration. It can't be training and fighting all the time."

My mother raises her head and stares Lady Anne directly

in the eye. "You have children. You love them and you'd do anything to keep them safe, isn't that right?"

"Of course," Lady Anne says. "Anything."

"As would I," my mother says. She straightens up and clears her throat. "I will say this one more time just to be sure that I am crystal clear—do not bring up Eve's birth, a celebration, nothing that has to do with any of that in my presence or in the privacy of your own quarters. If I so much as hear another whisper about it, I will make you regret it." She turns to Captain Mock. "Set a decree and let it be known to everyone in Queen's Bridge."

Captain Mock simply nods and hurries out of the room. Huntress keeps her gaze fixed on the floor.

"A decree?" I ask. "Is that really necessary?"

"Seems it is," my mother says as she stares accusingly at Lady Anne.

Lady Anne unflinchingly meets her gaze. "In all my years I have never seen you act this way. What is troubling you?"

"Troubling me?" My mother huffs. "I am carrying burdens heavy enough to crush us all and you ask what troubles me?" She shakes her head. "That will be all, Lady Anne," my mother says curtly and slumps into her chair, her face in her hands.

Lady Anne pauses, then gives a little bow and leaves the room.

I approach Mother and stand opposite her as she breathes deep, like she can't catch her breath, like she's panicked. Because her hands are covering her face, it takes me a moment to realize she is desperately fighting back tears.

51

"Mother," I say gently.

She holds up her hand. "Go see about Sir Gregory."

There is no getting through to her in this moment. I leave the room and rush out of the castle to the stables. The low hum emanating from my horse has a distinct singsong melody to it and it offers some comfort. Huntress saunters into the barn and leans against a post, her arms crossed over her chest.

"Why is she acting like that?" I ask through gritted teeth. I am so angry I could scream. "The way she spoke to Lady Anne—that woman nursed her when she herself was a baby."

Huntress shakes her head. "I know, and I don't fully understand it either. She has been on edge for days. She's been trying very hard not to let it show."

"I guess she gave up on pretending."

Huntress nods. "I guess she has. She instructed the staff early this morning to not mention your upcoming birthday at all. Anyone who does is subject to termination. But you know how Lady Anne is."

"I do," I say. "And I know how you are, too. Why are you digging at me? Those comments about my arrogance—why say that?"

"Am I wrong?" Huntress asks.

"That's not the point," I say angrily.

"Yes, it is," Huntress says, stepping toward me. "Your arrogance, your anger, is fueled by your hatred of the Knight. I understand that, but you cannot let it rule you or you will put all of us, especially your mother, in danger."

I turn my back to her. "I don't want to talk about putting

my anger away anymore." I sigh and lean my forehead against the side of my horse. "I would rather wield it as a weapon."

"Of course you would," Huntress says. "And here you are, once again, proving my point."

I hate that she is right. "Why order people to ignore my birthday? What is so wrong with allowing me even one moment to leave everything else behind? Doesn't she understand that I am burdened by the Knight's presence in all our lives, too?"

Again, Huntress seems at a loss. "She's working through something. Maybe it's exactly like Lady Anne said. Watching your children grow up is a gift but it's also a reminder of your own mortality. I remember when you were little, now look at you." She smiles. "All grown up and trying to take on the world."

"Not the world," I say. "Just the Knight."

"You don't need a celebration," Huntress says. "It's time to grow up."

I glance at her. Her jaw is set and her gaze is fixed on me. Anger colors her expression, but as soon as she realizes I'm watching her she masks it with a smile and raises her brows.

"We should head out and see about Sir Gregory," she says.

I mount my horse and, with Huntress following close behind, ride away from the castle, away from my mother, hoping the wind in my face will clear my head some.

———————

Sir Gregory's flax crop has pushed so far beyond the borders of his farmland that from a distance the pale purple blooms look as if they've overtaken the entire land of Queen's Bridge. A small group of residents is busy cutting back the overgrowth when Huntress and I arrive. Sir Gregory's children are pitching in where they can but most of them are too small to do much more than run water and food to the others. Sir Gregory comes to meet us, and we walk toward the river to survey the crop up close.

"I think we've finally got it under control," Sir Gregory says.

It doesn't look like he has it under control at all. New stalks of flax are sprouting from the ground under my boots. "Are you trying to convince me or yourself?" I ask.

"The Queen is angry, then?" he asks in the way a child might ask.

Huntress rolls her eyes. "Your deal with the Knight has endangered everyone in Queen's Bridge. So yes. She's angry."

Sir Gregory keeps quiet as we move closer to the river's edge. A tall woman in a gray woolen dress and apron swings a scythe and cuts a dozen stalks of flax off just above the ground. She stands back, one hand on her hip, the other clutching the handle of the scythe so hard her knuckles pale.

"Wait for it," she says breathlessly.

The cleanly cut stalks sprout new offshoots and within a few moments they are fully regrown.

"You wished for an abundant crop," I say to Sir Gregory. "It looks like you got exactly what you wished for."

Huntress grabs a long, curved blade from a man napping on a bale of hay and gets to work hacking away stalks of flax.

I tilt my head up to gauge the fullness of the gray clouds

high over my head. They're dark and wispy, but that is all that is needed. I extend my hand toward the sky and breathe deep. The clouds swirl into a long snakelike tangle that coalesces in my palm. I will the clouds to pack themselves tightly, to form a handle and then a blade longer than I am tall.

"Stand back," I say to the others who have gathered to help cut back the flax. They look upon me with a strange mix of fear and wonderment.

I swing the blade across the stalks of flax, cutting it off just below the ground in a wide swath. Dirt and stalks fly through the air. I bring the blade cleanly across the stalks again and gouge out more of Sir Gregory's land. As I step back, letting the weapon dissipate in a puff, the new stalks slowly begin to push their way up from their severed ends. I sigh. It was worth a try, but it is of no use.

The others fall back into the rhythm of swinging their scythes in an unending battle to keep the flax from overtaking the river. Sir Gregory shakes his head and meanders toward the riverbank. I follow him.

He stands quietly as the water rushes by, fed by the snow-capped mountains to the north. Mixed in the rapid rush of water are thousands of purple blooms. It might be beautiful if I didn't know that the Knight was behind it.

"I didn't know it would be like this," Sir Gregory says.

I dig my heels into the muddy bank. "The Knight's deals never work out the way they're meant to. Everyone in Queen's Bridge knows that."

He sighs and shakes his head. "I was desperate."

I glance at him. I do pity him in some small way. He has a big family and I'm sure his responsibilities are many, but now we are all in danger of losing our water supply because of him. "My mother makes sure the people of Queen's Bridge are taken care of. If there was a problem, you could have gone to her."

"I didn't want to," Sir Gregory says. "I wanted to handle this on my own."

"And look where that got you."

He raises an eyebrow and presses his mouth into a hard line. I'm sure he's holding back a few choice words.

"We'll rotate volunteers to keep the flax away from the river and make sure no one is being overworked," I say. "You're certain you only asked for this to last through the end of the growing season?"

Sir Gregory nods. "I'm thankful I didn't leave it open to interpretation. The Knight would have taken full advantage of that."

I focus on the river. "You never should have made the wish at all. We will have to wait for the end of the growing season to see if you have been as concise as you think you have."

The sound of the rushing river fills the silence between us. The sky is clear and the air is crisp. I can see for miles, and in the distance I catch a glimpse of something that shouldn't be there—a puff of black smoke. It breaks from the mountainside like steam from a kettle and billows high into the air.

"Look," I say.

The dark smoke trails across the snowy peak and though I cannot see where it is coming from, I don't need to. I can tell from the way it puffs up every few seconds in a new location that it is coming from a moving structure, and that can only mean one thing . . .

"It's him," Sir Gregory says. "His cursed castle is making its way through the mountains. Probably on his way to Rotterdam, maybe Mersailles. Who knows what dreadful business he'll conduct there."

I track the black smoke as it moves into the distance, and a sinking feeling settles in my gut.

"What magic is it that allows him to do that? To move his infernal dwelling from place to place like that?" Sir Gregory asks with a tone of wonderment. "You know, when I was a boy, my mother told me the Knight's castle had the legs of a wolf and it would carry him to wherever he wanted to go because he has dominion over the beasts."

I've never seen the Knight's castle up close though I've collected many firsthand accounts of it. None of them have ever described it that way but Sir Gregory's stories tell me that rumors and gossip permeate all talk of the Knight in Queen's Bridge. Some say he's ten feet tall or that his sword is unbreakable or that he can control the animals of the forest. I don't know which nightmarish stories are fact and which are the fears of the people made manifest, so I have prepared for them all.

Sir Gregory sighs. "The snow makes the castle easier to track. The castle leaves a distinct footprint in its wake."

I say nothing but keep this little piece of information in my mind, repeating it so that I don't forget.

Sir Gregory runs his hand through his graying beard and looks at me from the corner of his eye. "You are very curious, Princess. You speak of him with such contempt." Sir Gregory lowers his voice as he says this, like the Knight can hear him. "Do you not fear the Knight as your mother does?"

"She does not fear him," I say firmly, knowing that it is, at least in part, a lie. "And neither do I."

I take a last glance at the mountainside. The little plume of black smoke is gone.

Sir Gregory huffs. "You should."

He walks away, leaving me at the river's edge.

CHAPTER 5

Evening falls over Queen's Bridge. The night air is crisp, and the tendrils of winter are working their way under the skin of autumn. Snow has already come to the mountains and soon it will pull itself over the entire land like a shroud, as we bury ourselves in the darkness of winter.

I have yet to speak to my mother since returning from Sir Gregory's farm. I go to her door a half dozen times but find myself unable to knock. Things cannot be left as they are, though I have no idea what to say. Something is eating away at her. I can see it in her eyes every time we speak. I suppose it has always been there, an air of melancholy that clings to her like a wet blanket, but it has become so much more prevalent of late. It worries me.

I pad down the hall toward my mother's chambers once more. The castle is sleepy. Everyone has retired for the night, and the only sounds are the echoes of my own footsteps in the hall. I stand in front of her door and, as I raise my hand to knock, I again hear her voice coming from inside. I think she's crying, but I cannot be certain.

"Mother?" I call through her closed door. "I wanted to talk to you before it gets too late."

"Tomorrow, Eve."

There is something in her voice that leaves me unsettled. A slight tremble in her tone, a wavering in the timbre of her words. I back away from her door and stand still and quiet. Her voice echoes from inside and, while now I am sure she is crying, she is also speaking in a frenzied, hushed way. I can't pick it apart, but I do hear my own name spoken over and over, like a prayer.

I quickly return to my room and change out of my sleeping gown and into something more fit for climbing.

Outside, the night is full dark. Twinkling specks of starlight dance high above me, magnified by the frigid nighttime air. The rush of cold makes me rethink my plan. I could return to the warmth of my hearth and bury myself in blankets, but my mother's sobs echo in my head.

I move to the rear grounds, checking to see if anyone is close by. When I am sure I am alone, I raise my hands high over my head. I do not close my eyes but instead keep my gaze focused on the sky. I have made weapons of thunder, of lightning, of ice and snow, but the night sky is not for making tools of destruction. It is for nurturing and comfort, for protection.

In my mind's eye I see the nighttime sky fold over on itself like a flag in the wind. I imagine what it would feel like to touch it and, as I do, my fingers brush against something billowy and soft as goose down.

I close my fingers and grasp, then I wrap it around myself. Cloaked within the night itself, I feel safe.

More importantly, I feel invisible. The folds of the cloak meld so perfectly with the darkness around me, anyone looking would only have seen a hazy outline. They may even mistake me for a shadow. Of all the things I can do, this trick unsettles my mother and Huntress most. Mother discourages me from using it and Huntress outright forbids it during our hunts and exercises.

I scale the rear wall of the castle, using the rough, uneven faces of stones to hoist myself up. I climb slowly, finally reaching my mother's balcony. The doorway is flanked by two floor-length windows, one of which is standing open. I crouch low and peer inside. My mother is standing in her nightgown with her hair loose around her shoulders, her face wet with tears.

"I cannot do this," she says. "I grow weary of your constant torment."

Leaning in as far as I dare, I try to get a better look at whom she is talking to. Mother takes a step to her right, and I am struck silent.

Standing before her is a large mirror, higher than she is tall. Its rough outline juts up sharply on one side but the reflective surface is black as the night sky. I can see her silhouette reflected in it as she talks . . . to herself.

"Leave me alone!" she shouts. "I cannot do this! I will not!" She collapses into a chair, and her body trembles as she sobs into her hands. "I have done what I could but I will not do this! You cannot ask this of me!"

My mother is a fierce protector of Queen's Bridge, of her people, but she has clearly neglected to protect herself from the strain her position puts on her. I understand the pressure she is under as Queen to provide for the people of Queen's Bridge. I feel terrible for bringing up my birthday after she'd told me she didn't want to discuss it. Now she is talking to herself in the mirror?

I stare at the mirror. I have never seen this particular looking glass before. Her quarters are modest, home to only a four-poster bed, a small table with two chairs where she and I have spent countless hours talking and laughing, a washbasin, and a rug made of the soft hide of a brown bear.

I straighten up and put my hand on the balcony's rail when my foot slips and knocks a clay planter on its side. It rolls to the edge of the balcony and, before I can catch it, tumbles to the ground below and shatters. The sound splits the air like a thunderbolt, shattering the silence.

I vault over the rail and cling to the underside of the overhang. If anyone were to look up at that exact moment, they would see only a patch of starry black sky stuck to the Queen's balcony.

My mother suddenly appears and rests her hands on the rail. My shoulders ache as I struggle to hold on. I try not to breathe or move or make a sound. My mother looks over the edge and then returns to her chambers, closing the door and drawing the curtains over the two windows flanking the entryway.

I exhale and my grip slips. I tumble down, my fingers scraping at the bricks as if I can stop myself from falling. I land on my back in the frozen grass. The air punches out of me and for a moment my vision goes completely black. There is a brief moment of silence and confusion before the pain rushes in. My back, my leg, my shoulder. Everything hurts, but I can't suck in enough air to produce the agonized groan caught in my chest. I roll onto my side, my mouth open, eyes watering, gasping. Standing up is nearly impossible, but I manage it. I discard my cloak of stars and it disintegrates, as all my tools do when I'm done with them.

I hobble to my room and lie across my bed as I try to ignore the pain blooming at the back of my head.

The morning sun brings with it a new wave of pain that leaves no part of my body untouched. I decide to tell anyone who asks that I fell from my horse. It feels like that's exactly what happened, so I won't feel too terrible about lying.

My mother does not join me for breakfast. She is not in her drawing room when I check for her there.

"She's still in her bedchamber," Huntress says from the doorway. She leans against the frame like she's holding it up. "She took her breakfast in there this morning. She isn't admitting anyone. I would be lying if I said I wasn't worried."

"I was hoping to speak with her," I say. "She didn't want to talk last night. At least not to me." I still cannot fully understand what I saw. She was talking to herself last night, but I *had* heard the voice of another behind that same locked door. I'm sure of it.

Huntress shakes her head, and I go to the golden cage where Queen Sanaa sings a chipper melody. The hum of it echoes in my ears and inside my head.

"Do you think she knows me?" I ask as I gently press my fingers against the side of the cage. Queen Sanaa beats her wings as she flutters around inside the cage. Her unique voice sounds like bells, but it is hard for me to separate what I'm actually hearing from what I wish to hear. "Sometimes I wonder how much of her is still in there," I say. A knot crawls its way up my throat. "I don't know what is worse—thinking that any part of her that remembers me is gone forever or that she's still in there and completely aware and unable to do anything about it."

Huntress shrugs. "I don't know," she says. "I cannot fathom the type of magic the Knight has at his disposal. It is unlike anything—" She stops short, staring at me. "Well . . . almost anything."

"I am not a wish-granting monster," I say.

"No," Huntress says. "But you were born with a power that rivals his. You are both a product of the magic that Queen's Bridge is steeped in."

"I don't care what kind of magic it is or where it comes from," I say. "All I care about is finding a way to make him leave us and the people of Queen's Bridge alone forever."

"He'd have to die," Huntress says bluntly. "He would have to be in the ground."

I glance at her. "I'm fine with that."

Huntress gives a short, forceful laugh. "So am I." She sweeps in and stands next to me, staring into the birdcage. "We have another issue. I don't mean to sound heartless, but we need your mother to put her best face forward. I'm afraid the stress of this latest business with the Knight has been taking its toll on her. The people look to her for comfort."

I sigh and let my gaze drift to the window. "I don't know what to do."

"You're already doing it," my mother says.

I spin around to see her standing as still as a statue in the doorway. The whites of her eyes are red, the skin around the sockets puffy, like she's been crying. Huntress gives her a quick bow and takes up a position by the door.

Mother sweeps over to me and takes my face in her hands. "You're already doing everything I need you to do. You're learning the limits of your power, learning to wield it. That's where your attention should be focused."

"That's hard to do when I'm so worried about you," I say. "You look like you haven't slept. Ever since we found out what Sir Gregory did, you've been . . . different."

She sighs and moves to the table where she sits down and stares at her map. "I am running out of patience. I feel like I cannot escape him—the Knight—no matter how I try." She glances at the birdcage and her mouth flattens into a tight line. There is pain in every shadow on her face, and it breaks my heart into a million pieces. "I cannot avoid what I see when I look in the mirror." She inhales sharply, like she's trying to draw the words back into her mouth. "What I mean to say is that what I see there is the reality that I have very few choices left when it comes to handling the Knight."

"Very few choices?" I ask. "It seems like you only have one option—kill him."

My mother lets her gaze wander to the window where the midmorning light is just beginning to warm the sill. "Easier said than done," she says in a voice that is a ghost of her normal tone.

"I'm with you no matter what," I say. "To whatever end. Isn't that what you've been training me for?"

She sighs. "It is, but I have never wanted it to come to that. I still hope it can be avoided."

"Why?" I ask. "If that's what needs to be done, why not allow me to end him?"

She takes a deep breath and shakes her head. "Would you give me and Huntress a moment?"

She's not going to give me an answer, so I let the conversation fall away. "Of course," I say.

I gently touch her hand, then turn and leave her and Huntress alone. They close the door and, as bits of their conversation waft from under the door, I make my way to my mother's bedchamber as fast as my legs can carry me.

Outside her room I make sure the hall is clear before gently pushing the door open and slipping inside. The bed is made and her basin is half empty on the stand in front of a large oval mirror. This one I'm familiar with. It hangs in a gilded frame and has been in the same spot on her wall my entire life. I don't see the larger looking glass she was staring into the night before.

I tiptoe through her room to the windows near the balcony. Standing with my back to them, I try to recreate the angle I'd seen her at. Had she dragged the mirror in from somewhere and then taken it out again before the sun rose? It didn't seem practical. The mirror was taller than her, wider too. It must have weighed a considerable amount. I can't imagine why she would have needed to keep it a secret. Maybe she had help moving it. Still, it doesn't feel like that is the right answer.

I consider giving up my search when something catches my eye—a triangle of black fabric protruding from between the large flat stones that make up the floor near the hearth. I kneel and try to pick it up, but it won't budge. It is attached to something under the floor.

I run my hand along the seam in the stones and up the adjoining wall next to the hearth. At eye level there is a brick that is smaller than the others and well-worn in the center, as if someone has run their finger over it hundreds, maybe thousands, of times. I gently press on the spot and a soft click sounds under my feet. I stumble back as the stone floor in front of the fireplace slides open. A solid object draped in a thick black cloth silently rises out of the floor.

My heart tumbles in my chest as I cling to my mother's bedpost. When I'm finally able to gather myself, I move closer to the object that had been secreted under the floor. I gently tug on the cloth, and it falls to the ground in a heap. I had thought the object was a mirror. I'd seen my mother reflected in it so clearly, but, as I examine it, I realize it is something else entirely.

The frame is made of intricately carved wood in a rich brown hue. The glass has not been cut to fit the frame; instead the frame was constructed around its oddly shaped edge. I examine it and to my amazement, realize the reflective surface isn't glass at all—it is an onyx-colored stone polished to such a high shine that it reflects everything in front of it. I see myself in it—my hair is pulled into a bun at the nape of my neck, although a few errant coils have freed themselves around my ears. I can see the creases in my shirt and trousers.

I have never seen a stone like this. When I run my fingers over its surface it is smooth as ice and just as cold to the touch. I lean in, putting my face so close to it my breath fogs the shiny surface. It doesn't make sense. It is completely flat—flawless. There are no tool marks, no cracks, no imperfections. It's like looking into a flat calm sea in the dead of night. There is a depth to the stone that seems impossible. As I lean closer, I feel suddenly as if I am on the edge of a cliff and that moving any closer will pitch me over the edge. I lean away from it, from my own reflection—no. Not my own reflection. In a dizzying haze of confusion, I realize that I am not seeing my own face in its reflective surface anymore. Instead, a pair of wide, gray eyes stare out at me.

I step away from the mirror, my hand moving to my hip

where my dagger should be but isn't because it's early and I haven't armed myself yet. The gray eyes are set within an angular face that commands all my attention, even as a body solidifies within the mirror itself. I whip my head around, certain I'll find that someone has entered the room without my noticing and is standing near me, but I am alone.

Tap. Tap. Tap.

The figure has raised its hand and is using its fingers to tap on the stone's surface . . . from the inside.

I am frozen. Stuck to the floor. I can't breathe or move, and all I feel is the terrible unease of knowing this is not something I should be seeing. There is a young man in the polished stone. He angles his body and gives a little bow. When his gaze returns to mine, his full lips part and, as his eyes move over me, the corner of his mouth pulls up just slightly.

In the glassy surface another figure appears, and this time I know it is not some figment of my own imagination—it is the reflection of my mother who is standing behind me. I hadn't even heard her come in as I stood transfixed before the person in the mirror.

"What do you think you are doing?" she asks, her voice whispering and cold. She doesn't look at the mirror at all. She keeps her gaze locked on me, her face a mix of utter disbelief and anger.

"I—I saw you last night," I say, my gaze darting from her to the mirror where the figure is still staring out at me. "You— you were upset. You were talking to the mirror."

My mother snatches the black cloth from the floor and

drapes it over the stone. The figure of the young man disappears behind the shroud, and I swear, for just a moment, I hear a faraway laugh.

"What is this?" I ask, the terrible weight of overwhelming dread settling upon me. "What is going on here?"

"Get out," Mother says. She doesn't yell. Her words are heavy with grief and disappointment. I've overstepped some boundary, and whatever this is, she will not be explaining it to me at this moment. Maybe not ever. I walk to the door, and, as soon as I'm over the threshold, she closes it, bolting it from the inside. Her weeping echoes down the hall.

CHAPTER 6

By morning the next day, there is a heavy wooden crossbeam on the inside of my mother's chamber door. I catch a glimpse of it while three hulking laborers grunt and sweat as they heave the massive beam into place. My mother watches the workers while I watch her from the hall.

"How will you secure the door yourself?" I ask her.

She doesn't answer me. She doesn't even acknowledge the question. When the workers finish, she again retreats to her room and does not emerge for the rest of the day.

It goes like this for two days and two nights, and in the castle a rumor begins to seed itself. Behind cupped hands and closed doors there are whispers—our beloved Queen has gone mad.

It only makes sense on the surface. No one has seen the way she fought and clawed through her grief to give me a life after Queen Sanaa was remanded to her gilded cage. She didn't let the sorrow of it make her heart cold. We have cried together and spoken of our shared anger and grief and then finally of our fond memories and hopes for the future. There are still moments of melancholy, of abysmal sadness, but what is happening now is something different.

I sit outside Mother's door on the third night. I speak to her because I know she can hear me.

"I spent the morning training with Huntress," I say as I press my forehead against the door. "Another lesson in tracking. I'm still terrible at it, in case you were wondering. It's the one thing I can't seem to get a handle on without using my other skills, which Huntress tells me is cheating." I sigh. "It's not and I think she knows that."

There's a murmur from inside her bedchamber, but nothing distinct.

"We're planning on having another lesson," I continue. "Huntress says I'm still not allowed off castle grounds without supervision. If she goes with me, it's not breaking your rules, right?"

A soft sigh against the inside of the door. She must be standing right on the other side, and still she won't open it.

"Mother," I say, my throat tight, my eyes wet with tears. "Please. You should hear what people are saying about you."

"I don't care," she says from the other side of the door.

Hearing her voice is like feeling the warmth of the sun on my face after a cold dark winter. "I know," I say. "I don't think it's born out of any kind of malice. I think the people are worried about you. So am I."

There is a rustling from inside the room but no response.

The torches lining the hall cast deep shadows all around as night pulls itself across Queen's Bridge. The stained-glass windows at either end of the hall go from green to black as the light fades outside. I close my eyes.

I'm suddenly shaking myself awake. I've dozed off in far less forgiving places than this. I prepare to gather myself up and go to my room when the low notes of a voice reach me. At first, I think it has come from somewhere below me, the kitchen or the great hall, but after a moment I realize it is coming from my mother's room.

I press my ear to the door and hold my breath. It's my mother's voice. Her tone is again frantic and pleading.

"More time . . . please . . . I need to—she's just a girl."

My heart kicks up and I press closer to the door. I'd fallen asleep, but I surely would have awoken if someone had entered the room. The crossbeam would have been moved and the near-impossible task would have made enough noise to rouse me from even the deepest sleep. A hand suddenly clamps down on my shoulder.

I whip around, knocking into the door and scrambling to my feet. My mother's muffled voice goes silent.

Huntress stares at me, her eyes narrow. "What are you doing?"

I straighten up and try my best not to look suspicious. "Trying to talk to my mother."

"And?" Huntress stares blankly at me.

"And it is pointless."

Huntress slings her arm around my shoulder and pulls me

down the hall. We duck into my mother's drawing room, and Huntress closes the door.

She sinks into a chair and rubs her temple. "The door is barred because you were being nosey."

"That's true," I admit. "But is it really necessary? She could have just told me to stay out."

"Would you have listened?" Huntress asks.

I pause.

"See?" she says. "She knows you better than you know yourself." She leans back in her chair and rubs her neck, sighing. "That crossbeam must weigh a few hundred pounds. And you're correct when you say that it feels excessive, even if it is to keep you from sticking your nose in business that isn't yours."

I huff and cross my arms over my chest.

"Don't be such a child," Huntress says. "It doesn't suit you." She leans forward and clasps her hands together in front of her. "What did you see while you were in there that upset her?"

I look at her quizzically. I assumed my mother would have told her something about all this, but she seems just as confused by these events as I am. "She has a mirror in there. One I've never seen before in her bedchamber or anywhere else."

Huntress's entire frame stiffens, and she lets her hands drop into her lap.

"What is it?" I ask. "You know about it?"

She shakes her head. "I cannot understand it."

I walk over and kneel beside her, keeping my voice low. "Everyone in the castle thinks she is going mad."

Huntress rolls her eyes and shakes her head. "Vicious gossip."

"See?" I say. "You don't believe that and neither do I, but look at her behavior over the last few days. *Something* is happening to her."

"She is not mad," Huntress says. "She is in trouble."

My heart jumps into my throat. My hand instinctively goes to my dagger, which is now affixed firmly to my hip. It doesn't feel adequate. I glance out the window at the cloudy nighttime sky. I could forge a blade from those wispy strands of windswept clouds sharp enough to split a human hair down the middle.

"I don't know if this is something your magic or anyone else's can help with," Huntress says as if she'd plucked the thought from my head.

"What is happening?" I ask. "Please be honest with me."

Huntress leans close to me in the shadows of the drawing room. There are no candles here, no torches, but even in the blackness I can make out the pained expression on her face.

"What I tell you will stay between us. This is not a request. It is an oath. Swear to me."

"I swear it," I say without hesitation.

"Was the mirror you saw black and is it surrounded by a polished wooden frame?"

"You've seen it?" I ask.

Huntress nods. "Only once. I was here when it was brought into the castle."

"Recently?"

"Fifteen years ago. Just before your second birthday. It came into the castle under cover of night and was taken to her chambers in secret. Not even Lady Anne or Captain Mock knew about its arrival. I wasn't meant to know either, but I happened to be on watch that night and strayed a little too far from my post." She sighs and leans even closer to me. "And it is not a mirror."

"What?" I ask.

"No," Huntress says. "It is a seeing stone. The largest one I've ever seen."

"A seeing stone?" I try to remember where I've heard that term before.

Huntress narrows her gaze. "It's a tool used by witches to glimpse the future, the past, even the present."

I am having a hard time gathering my thoughts as I turn this revelation over in my mind. "My mother—she's not a witch."

"I am not saying she is," Huntress says. "What I am saying is that she has a witch's tool. Why and to what end, I still don't know. I wasn't even certain she still had the seeing stone in her possession until you spoke of it."

"It's hidden under a slab in the floor." I lower my voice until it is barely a whisper. "I saw her speaking to it—to the stone. And then when I went into her room, I saw someone reflected in it but I was alone."

Huntress's head snaps up and she gazes at me for a long time before she speaks again. "I have always believed that the seeing stone is cursed."

"Why would you say that?" I ask.

Huntress glances around, making sure no one is within earshot. She leans close to me. "Because after the stone arrived, your mother was different. She and Sanaa argued constantly. Queen Sanaa wanted your mother to destroy the stone, but she refused. Whatever it is, whatever its purpose, it cast a shadow over this place. I could feel it."

"Magic exists," I say. "We see it all the time in the Knight's misdeeds, in me, in others who have less prominent gifts." I open and close my hand. "Just because she has a magical object doesn't mean it's cursed."

"You were born with magic in your blood," Huntress says. "And you use it in defense of your mother and the people of Queen's Bridge. The Knight uses his magic to cause chaos and torment. There are any number of magic wielders in this land and those beyond our borders. Magic is not good or bad or black or white. It is whatever the practitioner of it wants it to be. Who's to say the person who created the seeing stone didn't have some ill intent."

"You're saying she didn't create the seeing stone herself?" I ask.

"No," Huntress says, her tone deadly serious. "Like I said, it was brought here from somewhere else." She sighs and shakes her head like she's exhausted. "Your mother is harboring a tool, a witch's seeing stone, though she is not a witch herself."

"Let us say she didn't create it," I say. "Fine. But she is clearly using it. She's talking to it while she's locked up in there alone." All I can think of are the sounds of her weeping and her panic-filled pleas. "Why?"

Huntress shakes her head. "I don't know, but you will speak of this to no one. Give your mother some time, and we will approach her together."

I nod, and Huntress leaves me in the drawing room alone. I won't breathe a word of what we shared with each other, but I also won't sit and do nothing. Huntress feels the seeing stone is cursed and, while I'm hesitant to agree with her, if there is any possibility that it is, there is no telling what torment my mother has suffered because of it.

No.

I won't sit by and allow this to continue. The seeing stone should be destroyed, and I will be the one to do it.

———————

Lady Anne leaves a tray of food outside my mother's door. Mother retrieves it and slides the tray back out when she's done. On the fourth day of her self-imposed exile, I position myself at the far end of the hall, pressing my back into the wall inside the dusty alcove behind a statue of my grandmother in the hallway. The shadows are deepest there and, while it's not as easy to hide myself as it was when I was little, it will have to do for now. Lady Anne soon approaches and leaves the tray of food for my mother, pleads at the door for her to emerge, and, when she doesn't, disappears down the hall in tears. My heart breaks for her.

As soon as Lady Anne is out of sight, I grab the tray and secrete it in my room before returning to my post.

I wait and soon a loud scraping sound cuts through the silence. The door yawns open and my mother appears. Her hair is loose, the hollows under her eyes are dark, and she's draped in a black sleeping gown that brushes against the floor as she steps into the hallway. She looks up and down the vacant hall. I hold my breath and try my best to sink into the shadows when what I really want to do is run to her and put my arms around her.

She huffs and mumbles something to herself as she pulls the door closed behind her and pads down the hall. When I hear her soft footsteps at the bottom of the stairs, I break from my hiding place and slip into her room as quickly and quietly as possible.

This is a terrible plan, but whatever hold the seeing stone has on my mother probably can't work if the cursed thing is broken. I touch the hidden notch and, as the mirror rises out of the floor, I grab a heavy poker from beside the hearth. Taking hold of the black cloth draped over the mirror, I raise the poker high over my head.

"Wait," says a gravelly voice.

I spin around, expecting to see someone in the room with me, but I am still alone. The heavy black cloth falls to the floor, and as I turn back to the seeing stone, the strange figure of the young man I'd seen before appears in the glassy surface.

"You don't want to do that," he says.

His voice is coming from inside the seeing stone. I blink the confusion away.

"How—how are you speaking to me?" I stammer.

"The same way you are," he says, his tone flippant. "I open my mouth and words come out. Imagine that."

I grip the poker, trying to stem the trembling in my hands. "My mother has been talking to you?"

The corner of the young man's mouth pulls up, as if he's trying not to smile. His gray eyes glint like stars in the night sky. He moves closer to the inner surface of the seeing stone. His gaze sweeps over me from head to foot. The look in his eyes is full of wonderment and something I think might be sadness. He sighs, and my skin pricks up.

"Answer me. Who are you?" I demand. "I saw you in the seeing stone before. How are you doing that?"

"I owe you no explanation," he says. His voice is deep and each syllable sends a tremor through the room.

"You do," I say. "And I will have it . . . or your head. The choice is yours."

He puts his hand on the seeing stone's surface. It is as if I am viewing him through a pane of glass. Strumming his fingers on the invisible surface, he lets his gaze move to my face as the hard angles of his jaw soften and his lips part.

Despite the twist in the pit of my stomach, I raise the poker and prepare to swing it directly into the stone's surface when—to my horror—the young man grips the frame and pulls himself out of the seeing stone.

CHAPTER 7

I stumble back until I'm pressed against the post of my mother's bed. I keep the poker raised, ready to strike, as the young man takes a step toward me.

"Don't come any closer," I say. I have reined in my fear, and now I let it simmer under my skin as it fuels my focus.

"Are you going to hit me with that?" the young man asks in a low, husky voice.

"Yes," I say. "And if you doubt it, please, take another step."

He stops, and I have a moment to take in the sight of him more clearly. His dark hair is pulled into a small bun at the back of his head. Several wavy strands have broken free and brush gently against his face. He is draped in a flowing black cloak that looks as if it is made of shadow and smoke, like something I might conjure. It curls around him as he narrows his gaze.

I square my shoulders and step toward him. "Who are you?"

"My name is Nova." He stares directly into my face, but I cannot read his expression. He betrays nothing. "And you're Eve, aren't you?"

My heart kicks in my chest. "How do you know my name?"

He tilts his head back, exposing the smooth skin of his neck, and laughs. "A little birdie told me."

I lower the poker, not because I'm not prepared to swing it but because I can fashion a better weapon from the fire in the hearth if need be. I toss it aside, and it clatters across the stone floor. "You mock me?"

Nova's mouth turns downward. "I didn't mean anything by it."

His words sting in a way he cannot possibly understand.

"Who are you?" I ask again.

"I've already given you my name."

Although not mocking me, he is being evasive and vague, which is stirring an anger in me. "What business do you have here in my mother's chambers?"

"I am a liaison to the Knight."

He says it in a way that is so offhanded that I repeat the words in my head to make sure I heard them correctly. It is no minor confession, and I am struck by how casually he says it.

"You admit you are in league with him?" I ask.

"I am his messenger. His enforcer. I am his servant." Firelight glints in his eyes as he speaks these words, not with a boastful air but plainly, as if the words hold no real meaning for him.

"But what are you doing *here*?" I demand. I feel the warmth gathering in my palm as the fire in the hearth laps at the blackened bricks.

He blinks repeatedly as if my question doesn't make sense to him. "Did you not hear what I just said? I am a liaison for the Knight. A go-between for those who have entered into deals with him."

"I heard you, but—" It falls on me like a wave breaking against the shore, or maybe a wave thrashing me against the jagged rocks in some darkened cove. Nova is the go-between for the Knight and those he has made his crooked deals with, and he is here—in my mother's chambers. "My mother made a deal with the Knight?"

Nova pulls his bottom lip between his teeth and runs his long slender fingers over the side of his face, letting them trace the angle of his chin. "I cannot speak to the dealings of others. If you're not privy to the deal, I cannot reveal it to you. Maybe you should be asking these questions of someone else."

No. I cannot fathom it. A white-hot anger ignites inside me. My mother spends every day of her life trying to keep the people of Queen's Bridge safe from the Knight. She takes care of them so that they never have a need to seek the Knight's help. And for those who do, like Sir Gregory, she is constantly cleaning up their messes. She hates the Knight for what he has done to our people. She would never willingly enter into a deal with him. Never. So now I understand that Nova is a liar and vow to treat him as such from this point forward.

Nova clicks his tongue behind his teeth and shakes his

head. "So much confusion. What is it? You think there are no secrets between the two of you?" He laughs lightly. "The secrets she keeps could fill an ocean."

"She doesn't keep things from me." Even as I say it, I know it is a lie. The mirror is proof of that, but I don't want to believe it.

"Aww, Princess," Nova says. Now he is indeed mocking me. "You are in so far over your head you cannot see that you are drowning. You cannot even begin to understand it. You should leave all of this alone before you are overcome. You're not equipped to handle what might be revealed."

As a surge of anger courses through me, I conjure a sword of fire and ember. Its hilt forms in my hand, and I grip against the sting of it. I bring it down in a flaming arc, aiming for Nova's head, but he quickly steps back into the seeing stone. The fiery blade makes contact with the glassy surface and a loud crack splits the air. A fracture blooms on the surface of the stone, creating a spider's web of jagged lines, but it does not shatter. Nova laughs, the sound muffled now that he's retaken his place in the mirror. I slam my hand against the stone's surface. Nova's frame fades away like mist dissipating with the rising of the sun.

A sharp intake of breath over my shoulder draws my attention to the doorway. My mother stands there motionless, her hands balled at her sides, her gaze locked on the seeing stone as the hazy remnants of Nova's shape fade into the dark.

I allow the weapon I'd conjured to disintegrate, and the ashes fall to the ground as I brush past my mother without a word. I hear her door close and lock as I go down the hall and into my room.

The next morning, I sit at one end of the table and my mother sits at the other as the morning light slants through the high stained-glass windows in her drawing room. Huntress had been here, but my mother dismissed her almost immediately. A million unsaid things hang in the air between us.

Finally, my mother sighs, places her hands flat on the table, and levels her gaze at me. "You will not speak of what you saw in the seeing stone to me or to anyone else. Ever. Do you understand?"

I stare down the table at her. She has never been cold or dismissive of me in any way, but now there is both fear and cold, collected anger in her voice.

"You said there were to be no secrets between us," I say softly. As angry as I am, I cannot disguise the hurt. "And now I see that you're the one who has been keeping secrets from me."

"This is different," she says.

"Who is Nova and how is he able to show up in the mirror like that?"

My mother's eyes widen, but she says nothing.

"I've heard you talking to someone in your room," I say, avoiding her eyes. "And not just in these past days either. I heard a voice in there with you a long time ago. Was it him?" Nova didn't look much older than me so maybe it wasn't him I'd heard years ago, but it had been someone. "How does he come out of the seeing stone like that? What magic is it? I don't understand."

Mother sits bolt upright. "Out . . . out of the seeing stone?" Her brows knit together. She brings a trembling hand to her lips. "He showed himself to you? Fully formed? Not just a reflection?"

"I nearly killed him," I say, thinking of how my palm had burned with the heat of the blade conjured from the fire.

When I meet Mother's gaze her normally glowing brown skin is ashen, her eyes are wide and horrified. Her mouth is open, and I expect a scream to claw its way from her throat at any moment, but she stays silent.

"Mother, who is he?"

"Do not ask me this," she says, her voice trembling.

"Why?" I ask. "I share everything with you! We have no secrets!"

"We don't?" she asks. "Have you shared with me everything you have in that box under your bed?"

I'm struck silent. "You opened it?"

She shakes her head. "I would never. But I know it's there and I know that whatever is inside it consumes your thoughts more and more with each passing day. I know you've taken journeys that I know nothing about to places that are known to be cursed."

"They are accounts of the Knight's wishes." I offer her this without hesitation. Maybe if I am open with her, she will be the same way with me. "That is what is in the box. I wanted to study his deals. I've collected the accounts of people who knew the details of his treacherous wish granting."

A panicked look spreads across my mother's face.

"I've been honest with you," I say, even though it is not the entire truth. My plans for tracking and killing the Knight are in that box, too, but I can't tell her that. Not now. "You should tell me the truth about the seeing stone and about Nova."

She slams her fist down on the table and the candlesticks rattle. She stands up and heaves as she leans on the table. Without another word she pushes her chair back, knocking it over, and storms away, pausing in the doorway. She glances back at me, her eyes wet with tears, her bottom lip trembling. She grips the doorframe so hard I think it might break. She opens her mouth to speak but then turns abruptly and disappears down the hall.

I stare into my lap as a knot grows in my throat. Tears sting my eyes, and I let them fall in little rivulets down my cheeks. My mother has made a deal with the Knight and I cannot fathom why. After everything she has seen, after all the chaos he has created, she should know better than anyone that it cannot end well.

One thing is absolutely certain: my mother will not reveal the terms of the deal to me or to anyone else. She might lock herself away again, and the thought of it makes me so angry I have to stand up and walk it off.

I make my way to the stables and sit in the back of one of the stalls until I calm down enough to think clearly. Mother will not reveal the details of her deal with the Knight, but that doesn't mean they are impossible to uncover. The young man in the mirror—Nova—knows the terms, too, but if I don't have access to the mirror I won't get a chance to press him about it again. There is only one other person who would know the specifics of the deal, and I've trained my entire life for a possible confrontation with him.

I saddle my horse and ride away from Castle Veil as fast as I can. I arrive at Sir Gregory's farm in the early afternoon. He is sitting on the porch whittling away at a piece of wood that looks like it will become an arm for one of his marionette creations.

"You can tell the Queen we've got everything under control," he says when he sees me. "We're working in shifts cutting back the flax. I think the growth is slowing."

I gaze out over the fields where the flax does indeed look like it is blanketing less of the Gregory farm than it had been only days before.

"That's good," I say, "but that's not why I'm here. Is Mekhi available?"

Sir Gregory pauses, then gestures toward the river. "It's his shift. He's out there cutting back the crop. What do you need him for?"

"He's a tracker," I say. "I gathered that from our conversation before. That's why you had him with you at Hastwich Pass, isn't it?"

Sir Gregory nods. "Doing a little hunting?"

"Tracking isn't one of my strong suits," I say. "But there is a wolf menacing some residents in the northernmost territories." The lie is a plausible one. "I was hoping he could help me find it."

"I'm sure he'd be honored to assist you, Princess," he says

as he roughs out the fingers on the marionette's arm. "Just make sure you bring him back safe and sound."

"You have my word," I say.

I turn and make my way to the riverbank where Mekhi and three others are hacking away wide swaths of flax. The stalks grow back but not quite as aggressively as they had before. The season is coming to an end and so the terms of the Knight's deal are reaching their conclusion. They are lucky that this will be all that is wrought. Mekhi spots me and gives a little bow, removing his cap and pressing it to his chest.

"Princess Eve," he says. "My father is at the house—"

"I've seen him already," I say. "I'm not here to talk to him. I need your help."

"Me?" he asks, confused.

"Can you come with me for a moment?"

He replaces his cap and tosses his scythe to the ground, hurrying toward me. "Any excuse to get out of this. My shoulders are aching. I might ask my father to carve me a new set of arms after all of this is over."

"He was working on an arm just now," I say. "I'm sure he'd make you the best wooden arms and legs in Queen's Bridge. He's masterful at that hobby of his."

"He's taken to it more gleefully than he ever took to farming this land," Mekhi says. "I admire his passion." Mekhi falls a few steps behind, and I turn to look at him. "He's a good man," he says, keeping his gaze on the ground at my feet. "He worships my mother. He loves me and my siblings with his entire heart. There is nothing he wouldn't do for us, which is why he—"

"I know," I interrupt. "That has never been in doubt. My mother knows it, too. If that's what is on your mind at this moment, defending your father, set it aside. I don't really care about any of that right now. What I need to speak to you about has nothing to do with what your father did."

Mekhi tilts his head quizzically. "All right?"

"Not here," I say. "Privately. Let's go for a little ride."

Mekhi hesitates.

"What's wrong?" I ask.

He shakes his head and kicks at the cold, hard ground with the toe of his boot. "I mean no disrespect, Highness, but—you're not going to kill me, are you?"

I laugh, but Mekhi's face is a mask of seriousness.

"Oh, you're not joking," I say. "Why would you ask me something like that?"

"Your reputation precedes you, Highness." Mekhi avoids my gaze as he speaks, measuring his words carefully. "They call you the Queen's fury."

"Who is *they*?" I ask.

Mekhi runs his hands over the top of his head, then clasps them together in front of him like he's praying. "People all over Queen's Bridge. They say your presence is why soldiers from Hamelin and Rotterdam don't dare tread on our territory without an invite."

I clench my jaw to keep from grinning. Perhaps this is the arrogance Huntress speaks of because the thought of armies of well-equipped soldiers being fearful of me makes me giddy.

"Rumors," I say.

"That start with something true," Mekhi adds. "People see your training exercises. Especially when it's stormy, and they are terrified of you."

I cannot help myself. I smile wide. I train in all conditions, in many different areas across Queen's Bridge, but my favorite place is a small glade in the lowlands west of Trapper's Ridge. When the sky is a swirling mass of gray and it breaks itself apart with every clap of thunder, every bolt of jagged lightning, I use each thing—the rain, the heat from the lightning, the damp earth—to conjure weapons. It had never occurred to me that people might be watching me that far out, but apparently they have.

I mount my horse. "Come," I say. "No harm will come to you under my watch."

Mekhi nods and runs to fetch his horse from the stable. He returns a few moments later on a black stallion with a shiny copper mane, a gorgeous creature with a low resonant hum emanating from him, distinct from my horse or my mother's. The horse is agitated and huffs loudly as Mekhi scratches between its ears.

I home in on the sound. Agitation again, and just the slightest ring of pain.

"Check your saddle straps," I say. "Your horse is irritated."

Mekhi reaches down and loosens the strap. The horse whinnies and shakes itself. The call is low and calm as it echoes in my head.

"That's better," I say.

I nudge my horse on and ride past Sir Gregory's farm until

the trees become thick and the air is sharp with cold. We're at the base of the vast mountain range that dominates the landscape running up to the northernmost edge of Queen's Bridge. A dusting of snow blankets the ground. I dismount, tethering my horse to a nearby tree.

"Are you going to tell me what this is about?" Mekhi asks as he, too, hops down from his horse and stands beside me. He keeps nervously looking over his shoulder, and I try my best to calm him.

"You're a gifted tracker," I say. "That's what your father says."

Mekhi's eyebrows arch up. "I—thank you?"

"I need to know if you can track someone for me."

"A person?" Mekhi asks. "I don't really do that—track people, I mean."

"It's not a person," I say as I step closer to him. "It is the Knight."

Confusion colors Mekhi's face for a moment before the realization of what I'm asking sets in. He huffs out a nervous laugh, and his warm breath turns to steam in the frigid air.

"Is something funny?" I ask.

"Yes," he says. "Can I be honest with you, Highness?"

"I would have it no other way," I say.

Mekhi takes a deep breath, the air puffing out of him in billowing clouds. "I watched you when you came to the house, when you spoke of the Knight. I don't know if you're aware, but your hatred of him is palpable. I could feel it running off you."

"I don't deny it," I say.

"Have you ever met someone who hates him as much as you do?" Mekhi asks.

It is an odd question but I answer him as best I can. "My mother, perhaps. Most people fear him. Their hatred is tempered by how much they worry he might take advantage of them or someone they love."

Mekhi nods. "I didn't think there was anyone in Queen's Bridge that could hate him as much as I do—until I met you."

I angle my head and look at Mekhi. His face has changed somehow. Where once there had been a happy, almost vacant expression were now a pair of steely brown eyes and a hard-set jaw. The face I'd seen before was only a mask—this is his true self.

"What did he do to you?" I ask. It is the only adequate question. "It cannot be this business with your father's crops."

"It isn't," Mekhi says. Even his voice is lower in tone. "There was a girl . . ." He trails off, and I see him putting the mask of innocence back up.

I rest my hand on his arm. "No. Don't do that," I say. "Tell me. And don't spare the details." This story, whatever it will be, is going in the box under my bed, and I can tell from Mekhi's entire visage that it will be among those whose details will haunt even my waking hours.

Mekhi stares out over the snowcapped mountains where I last saw the distinctive plume of black smoke that emanates from the Knight's dwelling.

"Two years ago, I met a young woman from Hastwich

Pass," he begins. "Her name was Fairouz and we fell in love as soon as we laid eyes on each other. Her hair was so black it was almost blue, her eyes were the deepest brown. She was beautiful and smart and I would have done anything for her. I brought her home to meet my family. Everyone loved her. *I* loved her." Mekhi's breaths come in long drawls, and he balls his fists at his side. "My mother adored her, but she reminded Fairouz of her own mother who had died when she was little."

My heart ticks up.

"Fairouz mourned her mother every single day of her life and then one day she asked me to meet her in secret along the bank of the River Farris where it spills from the foot of the mountains." Mekhi takes a step away from me. "She told me she had done something—something terrible. When I pressed her, she told me that she had sought out the Knight and asked him to bring back her mother from the dead."

I inhale sharply. "Just like that? Was that the exact wording of the wish?"

Mekhi nods.

"Terms or payment?" I ask.

"Payment," Mekhi says. "She gave him seven silver rings that her father had given to her."

"He never cares for such things," I say. So few of the Knight's deals involve payment. Most people think they can satisfy him by simply paying him some unimaginable price, but they are almost always wrong.

"I think it was a formality," Mekhi says. "He seems bound by rules that are difficult to understand. Fairouz chose

94

payment, and he only told her what that payment would be after she made her wish. He didn't care about the value of the rings, only that it soundly fulfilled the deal. In return he brought her mother back from the grave."

A chill runs straight up my back.

"As I stood listening to her tell me this, her mother emerged from the woods like something out of a nightmare." Mekhi's voice is trembling as he continues. "She was a shambling, rotted corpse. Her bones were visible through her torn flesh. The white of her skull looked like a polished stone. And the noises she was making, it wasn't human. Her eyes were empty—dead . . ." He trails off, and his own eyes become glassy and unfocused.

"You don't have to continue," I say.

He refocuses, his gaze locked on mine. "I was afraid," he says. "I drew my father's sword and Fairouz stepped between us. She begged me not to do it, but I did. I cut her mother's corpse down."

I instinctively grasp the hilt of my dagger at the thought of a reanimated corpse stumbling its way toward me. I can't imagine what Mekhi must have been thinking.

"She hated me for it," Mekhi says. "Fairouz. She screamed and cried and struck me with her closed fists. All I could do was stand there. She wanted her mother back and she got what she wanted but I took it from her."

"No," I say. "You did the right thing."

Mekhi stares ahead, unblinking. "She picked up what was left of her mother and put the pieces in the river and then she, too, went into the water. I tried to stop her and she told me she hated me, that she never loved me, that she wished me dead." Mekhi breathes deep. "She let the current carry her away."

We stand together in silence for a long time before I work up the nerve to say something.

"I want to end the Knight once and for all," I say. "I have been preparing for this, but I need help tracking him."

Mekhi moves closer to me. "Do you really think you can do it? After everything we know him to be capable of, look me in my face and tell me you truly believe you can end him."

I stretch my hand toward the snow-covered ground. In my mind's eye, I see the weapon form. The white powder stirs itself into an undulating orb. It folds in on itself over and over again. I put my hands on the frigid surface and press the orb into a flat disk until its edge is razor sharp. Grasping it firmly, I curl my arm toward my chest. With a flick of my wrist, the disk flies out of my hand, whizzes by Mekhi's terrified face, and embeds itself in the trunk of a towering pine tree. A little shower of snow and browning pine needles, knocked loose from the branches, rains down on us. I breathe deep, letting the frigid air fill me up. The newly formed weapon feels like it is an extension of myself, a vessel for all my rage, all my mourning.

"I will kill him and free us and the people of Queen's Bridge," I say. "You have my word."

Mekhi looks over at my weapon and gives me a nod, then returns his gaze to the mountains.

"Your father said the castle leaves a distinct mark in its

wake," I say. "I know you've seen it. I need you to help me track it down. I can pay you if that makes a difference."

"And if neither of us live long enough to pay or be paid?" Mekhi huffs.

"Then we will be dead, and we will have nothing left to worry about," I say.

"How do you imagine it will go?" Mekhi asks as he shoves his hands in his pockets, bracing himself against a gust of cold air. "We track him down and—what?"

"I'll do what must be done, but I also need to find out about the terms of the deal he made with someone else."

Mekhi pulls at the back of his neck. "Do you really think he's going to just give up that kind of information?"

"He won't have a choice," I say. "The other details aren't important. Get me there and I'll handle the rest. Are you in or not?"

Mekhi hesitates. "I am but I cannot lie to you; it feels impossible."

"I understand the seriousness of what I'm asking," I offer. "You said that your father would do anything for your family, that he was willing to go so far as to seek out the Knight himself. This is no different. I need to do this. I'll pay you twenty silver pieces."

Mekhi's eyes grow wide. "A half year's wages?"

I nod.

"Will you give it to my father instead?" he asks. "Give it to him so that he can focus on his new hobby for a time without distraction."

I stick out my hand, and he grasps it. We shake, signaling that we've come to our own deal. When he tries to pull away, I grip his hand tight. "Let's be clear on the details. I will pay you half now and half when we get back. You don't say a word about this to anyone. Ever. Tell your father we're going to hunt a wolf. Understand?"

Mekhi nods, and I put a small coin purse in his hand containing the silver I'd promised.

"Meet me at Highmoore Bridge tomorrow at sunset," I say. "Come alone. Bring whatever you need to track him."

He nods again, and I mount my horse and ride away before either of us can change our minds.

CHAPTER 8

Of all the stories I have heard of the Knight, none of them include anything personal or insightful about him. His cruelty and disregard for anyone's safety is on full display every time he engages in his insidious game of trickery, but I've never heard anyone give even the slightest hint of what kind of creature lies under his monstrous façade.

No one knows exactly who or what the Knight actually is.

There is a rumor that he used to be a mortal man who crossed paths with a witch and was cursed to wander the land for all eternity. If I pick up a rock anywhere in Queen's Bridge and throw it, it is guaranteed to hit someone who claims to have had dealings with a witch. It's not impossible. Queen's Bridge has magic in its midst. The Knight is evidence of that, and so am I. But witches are mostly healers who deal in the care and concerns of other women and are known to keep to the woods, away from the prying eyes of the public. There had been rumblings far north of Queen's Bridge that a witch had once brought a man back from the dead. But I believe those were scary stories told to children to make them take heed of strangers and to stay out of the woods. If the Knight was cursed, it wasn't a witch's doing.

I am almost certain the Knight is not now, nor has he ever been, a mortal man. I am convinced he has honed his magical abilities over an unnaturally long life and in that time has come to enjoy watching people suffer. Huntress often says that no one is evil without a reason, but I don't believe her. For the Knight, his cruelty is the point.

As the evening descends, I layer my clothing to stem the damp cold that comes with trekking through snow. I pull on my sturdiest pair of boots, secure my hair in at the nape of my neck, and tuck my dagger into the sheath on my hip.

Over the washbasin, a small oval mirror in a silver frame hangs on the wall. I catch a glimpse of myself and the sternness in my own expression stops me. I look down into the basin.

"So serious," a familiar voice says.

I snap my head up and look into the mirror. Nova is standing over my right shoulder. I instinctively spin around, my hands raised in clenched fists, but he isn't there. Turning back to the mirror, I find him staring at me. Smiling.

"I would very much like to remove that smirk from your face with the tip of my dagger," I say.

Nova's eyes widen. "Are you always so morose?"

"What does it matter to you?" I snap.

"It doesn't," Nova says. "But it makes you exceptionally boring to be around."

I lean closer to the mirror, letting a fake grin twist up my mouth. "The good news is that no one asked you to be here. No one wants you here. You won't be missed when you're gone so you should probably just . . . go."

Nova blinks twice as if he's trying to absorb what I've just said.

"You're preparing for a journey," he says, the smile now gone from his lips. "Would you like some company?"

I almost laugh aloud. "Whose? Yours? No."

Nova puts his hand over his heart. "That hurts my feelings."

I glare at him through the glass. "Ask me if I care."

Nova tilts his head, and I am again struck by the glint in his eyes. He hasn't taken anything I've said to heart even though I was trying to cut him as deeply as any words could.

"Your mother leads me to believe you are an exceptionally caring person." He lets his eyes drift over me from head to toe. "I think she may be wrong."

My mother has been telling him things about me? I don't even attempt to hide how angry that makes me. "I care about the people of Queen's Bridge. I care about my family and I love my mother, but I don't care about you, or your feelings. Whatever you've been talking to my mother about is upsetting her. She hasn't been out of her room for longer than a few minutes in the past several days."

"That is your fault," Nova says.

I'm taken aback for a moment before a seething hatred seeps in. "Excuse me? How is any of this my fault?"

Nova raises his shoulders, and the corner of his mouth lifts. "Asking too many questions. Nosing around her private chambers without permission." He clicks his tongue behind his teeth. "I can see why she locked herself away. Seems she needs some privacy."

I grab my dagger and slam the handle into the glass. As it fractures into a lacework of broken fragments, Nova's laugh echoes through the room. I can still see him in the fractured glass, his face a patchwork of broken pieces. I wish his face was broken in real life and not just in the mirror.

I hoist my bag over my shoulder, secure my dagger, and ease into the hall. I stand still—listening. The floor is quiet as is most of the castle. A few hushed voices float up from somewhere below. Halfway to the stairs I stop. The beam on the inside of my mother's chamber door groans as someone slides it away. I duck into the shadow of a statue and hold my breath. I expect my mother to emerge, but instead Nova sweeps from the room, his flowing black cloak draped around his tall frame. I leave my hiding spot and rush up to him just as he pulls the door shut behind him. I hear the lock slide back into place from the inside.

Nova stands, hands clasped, as if this is exactly where he belongs. He sees me, and as his gaze drifts over me, his cloak transforms into a pair of black fitted slacks, dark brown riding boots, and a billowing black shirt open at the neck. His dark hair is pulled away from his face.

I narrow my gaze at him. "What are you doing here?"

"I could ask you the same thing," he says.

I scowl. "No. You couldn't. This is my home."

Nova laughs. "Whatever you need to tell yourself, Princess."

It is my title, but from his lips it has a terrible ring. I put my hand on my dagger and Nova grins.

"What will you do?" he asks. "Stab me?"

"Yes," I say, without even the slightest hesitation.

Nova takes a step back and looks me over. Almost as if he's seeing me for the first time or maybe reassessing whatever conclusions he had come to about me. Good. I straighten up, push my shoulders back, and lift my chin.

"So serious," he says again. "If it means anything to you, I won't hurt you."

I draw my dagger and stick the point in his chest. "I wouldn't give you the chance to hurt me." As I press the blade, there is almost no resistance. I feel as if I could slice straight through him. "What are you?"

Nova looks down at the blade, then back to me. "I am a messenger. Nothing more."

I put away my dagger. "Do you have something to tell me? Isn't that what messengers do?"

Nova lets his gaze drift to the hall behind me. "Not yet, but will you tell me where you're going? You look like you're headed into battle."

"Maybe I am," I mumble, pushing past him. He's a liaison to the Knight, which means he will almost certainly give him a heads-up if he finds out I'm on my way to try to end him. "I wouldn't tell you if I was," I say. "Because you're prepared to run back and tell *him*."

Nova rears back, like he's offended. "No, I—I don't think that's necessary."

I stare at him, confused. I don't understand why he's here if he has no message to convey and if he doesn't plan on reporting back to the Knight.

"I'll come with you," Nova says. The grin hasn't faded from his lips, and it's starting to wear on me.

I glance at my mother's bedroom door. "Get away from me."

Nova's mouth turns down in an exaggerated scowl. "Again, you're hurting my feelings."

"You keep saying that," I say. "And somehow you don't seem to understand that I could not care less about your *feelings*." I sidestep him and go down the hall to my mother's drawing room. I need a map and had decided not to take my own copy because I didn't want to remove the pins and notes I'd attached to it.

I light a small torch on the wall, which washes the room in a warm amber glow. Queen Sanaa coos quietly on her perch inside her gilded cage. I swipe a rolled-up map from my mother's table and shove it in my bag. As I turn to leave, I find Nova has silently entered the room and is standing next to the golden cage.

"Stay away from her," I say angrily.

"She's lovely," Nova says. "But I find it barbaric that you would keep such a beautiful creature in a cage."

My hand instinctively moves to my dagger and the light from the lamp flickers. I rein in my anger. "You have no idea what you're talking about."

"I see a bird," Nova says. "She belongs in the wild, don't you think?"

I march straight up to him. He is taller than I am by a few inches, broad shouldered. I keep one hand on my dagger and with the other, I lift the little cage door and the nightingale flutters out and lands on my shoulder. "She isn't a prisoner. And she's not a bird . . . at least, she hasn't always been."

Nova stares at the nightingale and then shifts his gaze to me. "Explain."

"Why should I? You act like you already have all the answers so why don't you know that this nightingale is my mother, Queen Sanaa, transformed by the hand of the Knight?"

Nova's face goes blank. The nightingale that was once my mother circles my head, her tiny wings beating, then returns to her perch. I slide the cage door closed and step closer to Nova, who remains silent.

"You don't know as much as you claim to," I say. I take an almost unfathomable amount of satisfaction in that.

"Perhaps," Nova says quietly. "There were . . . rumors."

"Rumors? You don't know a single thing about me and I'd like it to stay that way, so keep your distance." I turn and leave the room.

In the stable I load my pack onto my horse and lead her away from the castle, toward Sir Gregory's farm. The land is sleepy and still. Columns of smoke billow from chimneys and mingle with the gray cloud cover high above my head. As I traverse the narrow road that leads away from Castle Veil, I realize with a sudden start that I am not alone in the encroaching mist.

The galloping of hooves on the road sounds from somewhere behind me. I pull up the reins and bring my horse to a slow trot, hoping the person behind will continue on their way, but their horse's footfall slows as well. My heart ticks up. I feel the weight of my dagger at my side, but I want more cover. I hold out my hand, and a warm tingle spreads from the center of my chest into my arm. The fog pulls in close to me. My horse whinnies, and I gently scratch between her ears to calm her. With a gentle tug on the reins, I bring her to a complete stop.

We wait, draped in fog, weapon at the ready. The rider approaches but doesn't pass me by. They stop alongside me. The dense fog separates us, and I hold my breath—waiting.

"I can't see you but I know you're there," says a familiar voice.

My hesitation swirls into a white-hot anger. I send the fog rolling back with a flick of my wrist and Nova, mounted on a midnight black stallion, appears in front of me like a ghost.

"I wasn't at all subtle when I told you I didn't want your company," I say, letting my fingers glance over my dagger. "But just in case you need a reminder—I don't want you here."

"Ah, so you see, I have the opposite problem," Nova says in a tone that is too happy, too gleeful to do anything but make me more irritated. "I was *too* subtle. So let me remedy that right now." He shifts around in his saddle and pulls his billowing black cape in close to him. "I know you don't want me along, and I don't care. I go where I please, much like you."

I have never wanted to cut someone down so badly, save the Knight, in all my life. "Go away," I say through gritted teeth.

"I won't hinder you," Nova says, shrugging his shoulders. "I'm just curious as to where you're going on a night as black as this one. You could just tell me and save us both the hassle."

"Or I could tell you to mind your own business and leave me alone before I wrap this fog around your throat." In my head I picture the swirling tendrils of gray fog encircling his neck, and right before my eyes the fog begins to do just that. It coalesces in a thick band and swirls around him, but I take a deep, wavering breath and it dissipates. I'm not here to destroy him. It is the Knight I want and killing Nova right now means I'd need to hide his body. I simply don't have time.

Nova gazes down the road and then back to me. "You're headed out of the castle district—why?"

I spur my horse and leave Nova behind, pushing my horse to her limit. We ride like a hawk on a tailwind, and when I reach Highmoore Bridge, Nova and his horse trot up behind me as if they'd simply appeared there and not raced at a full sprint. Nova's horse has no voice, no internal hum that I can discern, and I begin to wonder about its nature. Mekhi is sitting atop his own stallion at the bridge. His eyes widen when he sees Nova approach.

"I didn't know you were bringing a friend," Mekhi says, his gaze darting back and forth between us.

"I didn't invite him," I say. "And he is no friend of mine."

Nova bristles, and I hope the insult stung. "Don't worry," Nova says. "You won't know I'm here."

"Who are you?" Mekhi asks.

Nova looks over Mekhi with the disinterest of someone watching a leaf tumble across the road in a stiff wind. "My name is Nova," he says.

"Don't talk to him," I say. It takes everything in me not to conjure a weapon and chase Nova away, maybe right into the icy river flowing beneath the bridge. His presence is putting all my plans in danger. I take out the map, hand it to Mekhi, and position myself so that Nova can't see it. "Can you show me the best place to start?"

Mekhi stares down at the map, then brings it close to his face. "I can barely see anything. Are you sure you don't want to do this in the daytime?"

I take a small piece of flint from my pocket and strike it against my horse's bridle. It sparks and from that little ember I produce a short but steady flame that I hold in the palm of my hand.

Mekhi's mouth falls open as the flame casts a hazy orange glow through the fog. "Doesn't that hurt your hand?"

"A little," I say truthfully as I nudge my horse a little closer to his. "It's cold out here, Mekhi. And I am irritated beyond belief." I cast a dagger of a glance at Nova. "So if we could get on with this—"

"Right," Mekhi says, flustered.

He flips the map around and, as he studies it, I glance at Nova again. He is staring at the flame in my palm as if he's never seen fire. His brow is furrowed, his mouth turned down. In the firelight, he almost looks pitiful.

"Here," Mekhi says. "I saw the smoke from his castle just beyond Trapper's Ridge in the late afternoon. He might not be far from there now. He never seems to go anywhere with any urgency."

I quickly take the map back and press my finger to my lips. I don't want Mekhi to say anything about what we're doing in Nova's presence. "Once it's in sight, you don't have to stay," I say to Mekhi. "I'm not asking you to get too close."

"Good, because I was planning on leaving you the moment the Knight's castle comes into view anyway."

"You're tracking the Knight," Nova says. It's not a question as much as a realization, and concern stretches tightly across his face.

I cast an angry glance in Mekhi's direction.

"I'm sorry," he says.

When I turn to Nova, the glinting reflection of the flame makes his eyes look as if they're glowing from within— shining stars against a backlit canopy of swirling fog. I crush the flame in my hand but the glow still simmers in his gaze.

"I told you none of this is your business," I say.

"Do you have a death wish or are you just reckless?" Nova asks.

I slide off my horse, as does Nova, and we approach each other in the dark. I don't care what magical abilities he possesses. I possess some of my own.

"I don't know how to make it any clearer," I say through gritted teeth, my hands trembling in balled fists at my sides. "This doesn't have anything to do with you."

"Oh, but it does," Nova says in a hush. His breath is icy in my face. As I stare up at him, his gaze fixes on me. "If you find him, what will you do?"

"I want to know what the details of his deal with my mother are."

Nova shakes his head. "He will not tell you."

I set my hand on my dagger. "Then I will extract the information from him."

Nova says nothing, and I'm glad. His presence irritates me. I am not usually affected by such things. Not even Captain Mock and his dismissive attitude have managed to get under my skin the way Nova has, and I've only been aware of his presence for a few days.

I turn to Mekhi. "If we're headed to Trapper's Ridge, we should go now."

"You don't want to wait for the light?" Mekhi asks again.

"No," I say firmly. "In fact, I think we should avoid it if possible. The dark will provide some cover."

Mekhi looks up at the darkened sky and holds his breath for a moment before sighing, resigning himself to the task.

"This is folly," Nova says. Something lingers in his voice, an edge that sounds very much like fear. "You have no idea what you're stepping into."

"Enough!" I scream at him, unable to keep my frustration at bay any longer. "You don't think we can or should go after him. Fine! Leave! Go away and leave me to it!"

"You will not convince him to tell you the terms of his deal with your mother," Nova says flatly.

I turn away from him, trembling with anger. "Because he's so secretive about his deals? Again, ask me if I care."

"That's not why," Nova says.

"Well, then what is it?" I ask.

"He will think you're trying to trick him," says Nova. "He will assume you already know something about his deal because it involves you."

CHAPTER 9

I spin around and find Nova blankly staring at me. Mekhi glances back and forth between us, then puts his head down.

"What did you say?" I ask.

"I was clear," Nova says. "His dealings with your mother involve you, and if you think you can—how did you put it? Extract it from him?" Nova shakes his head and approaches me.

I stand firm, digging my heels into the hard ground. I don't conjure a weapon because I feel as if I could tear him apart with my bare hands.

His eyes are darker now, the gray absorbing some of the blackness around us. I stare into his face and, of everything I should be thinking, I can only wonder at how young he appears. His smooth skin is slightly ruddy at the cheeks and forehead. It looks like he's warmly flushed and not freezing in the cold night air. His hair is tied back but in a messy, haphazard way. He pushes a few of the jet-black strands away from his face. He's my age, but that doesn't make sense. The way he spoke, it is as if he has been at the Knight's side for much longer than my nearly seventeen years.

"Even I am not privy to the details of his deal with your mother," he says softly against my ear as he leans closer to me. "I may not know everything, but neither do you, apparently."

I put my hands in the center of his chest and shove him. "Get back," I snap. There is heat running through every part of me. I can feel it pooling deep in my gut. "I mean to find out the terms of the Knight's deal, and I need to know right now if you're going to warn him of our approach." I extend my hand and pull a sword from the snow cover—a blade of ice and magic, deadly.

Nova lets his eyes move over me again, and his façade of calm collectedness falters. "No—I—I wouldn't." He stops himself, straightening up and putting his hand over his heart. "Your mother has kept you safe; why undo her work now?"

I raise the weapon and point it directly at him. "Don't speak of my mother."

Nova sets his jaw in a way that tells me he has nothing left to say, and I'm glad. It takes everything in me not to run him through. I mount my horse and allow Mekhi to lead the way toward Trapper's Ridge.

Nova follows along behind us, keeping enough of a distance that I can't reach him with the tip of my dagger but close enough for me to hear him huffing as Mekhi and I discuss the whereabouts of the Knight's castle. I have decided that if Nova is going to alert the Knight, then so be it. When I glance back at him, his eyes are fixed on some point in the distance, but he turns and meets my gaze. I quickly put my attention back on Mekhi.

As we cut a path through the dusting of snow that blankets the lower hillside, I cannot keep my mind focused. The terms of the Knight's deal with my mother involve me? A deep and uncomfortable sense of betrayal seeds itself in the pit of my stomach. My mother and I have always been close. She is my best friend and I am her biggest champion, her staunchest defender, and still she kept this from me. I cannot fathom what it could be, but I know it is nothing good.

The River Farris is fed by the perpetually snowcapped mountains that lie to the north. Along the banks of the river, against the current, the air turns biting and our pace slows. We stop several times, and Mekhi dismounts, checking the ground and the bent limbs of trees for a sign that someone or something has been this way.

"Here," Mekhi says finally, after hours of finding nothing. He gets off his horse and adopts the measured pace of someone who knows exactly what they're looking for, while all I can see is the endless blanket of white snow.

I join him, being careful not to distract him. He directs my gaze to an impression in the ground.

"What is it?" I ask. I don't see anything besides a short gouge in the snow. It could have come from anything—a fallen tree limb, another person on horseback, a wild animal.

"Look there." He points at an identical impression in the

114

snow farther away. "It is the same track. Made in one step by the castle itself."

"One step? How is that possible?" I ask. The scale is hard for me to grasp. If the track was made in a single step, its stride is as long as four or five lengths of my own body.

Nova, still seated atop his horse, grunts. I ignore him.

"I need to get a better look at things," Mekhi says, as he marches to the peak of a rise a short way off and immediately drops to his stomach in the snow.

I rush over and crawl up beside him. The peak overlooks a steep valley and there, nestled in the deepest crevasse, is the thing we are searching for.

It breathes like a living creature. It seems to expand and contract, and steam billows out of its many chimneys upon each exhalation. Its frame is made from sheets of shining black metal, the rivets that close the seams glinting in the moonlight that peeks through the gloom. The windows are shuttered, and the doors are giant slabs of splintered wood with black metal hinges.

It is the nightmare that is the Knight's castle.

"What now?" Mekhi asks, his voice trembling.

"He is inside," I say as I stare at the Knight's fabled abode. I have only ever seen hints of it—a trailing line of smoke across the sky or the shadow of its strange shape through the trees. Up close, it is the strangest thing I have ever seen. I wonder how it came to be and what kind of magic powers it possesses, but after a moment I realize it doesn't matter. I nudge Mekhi, bidding him to follow me back down the rise. I shimmy down

the slope and tie my horse to a tree. "I'll go on alone." I shoot
Nova an angry glance as he slides off his horse and stands like
a shadow in the mist. "You don't need to risk your safety for
me. I can handle it."

"Handle it?" Nova asks, his brow furrowed. He steps
closer. "How will you do that? What makes you think you
even could? *Handle it.*" He huffs and shakes his head.
"Ridiculous."

"What did you think I came all the way up here for?" I
ask. "To look at his castle from a safe distance?"

"No," says Nova. "But I thought when you got up here
and saw it in person, you would change your mind."

His bluntness catches me off guard. He so plainly thinks
I am a coward. It's insulting.

Mekhi exhales sharply. "Highness, maybe—"

"Maybe what?" I snap.

"Maybe he's right," Mekhi says.

"Or maybe you're both wrong and scared," I say. "I am
neither."

Mekhi looks wounded, and I immediately regret being so
short with him.

"I—I'm sorry," I say, making sure I look only at Mekhi.
"Of course you're scared. Look at this place." I shake my head.
"I'm not asking you to stay. I will go on alone, and I will not
fault you for it. I'll still pay you."

"It's not about that," Mekhi says quietly.

I pull my cloak around me and start down a steep, crooked
path into the void of the valley below. I don't expect them to

follow me but when I glance back Mekhi and Nova are making their way behind me.

The path is narrow and the trees are close. Too close. I suddenly feel crowded, and I pull at my collar. My cloak catches on low-hanging branches several times as I struggle to keep my footing on the slick surface. I stop halfway down and scuff the flat surface of my boot with my dagger to try to gain some traction.

What I notice most in the dark of the woods is the silence. When I was little, Huntress taught me to listen for the sounds in the wood, to know that dead silence means the animals have taken heed of something dangerous nearby. I learned that in the presence of something menacing, the animals would even quiet their calls, the ones only I can hear. And that is how it is now. Silent. Mekhi seems to come to this realization at the same time because he stays so close to me I can almost feel his breath on my neck.

"Something isn't right," he whispers.

The forest animals may be silent, but another noise sounds in the murky dark. A low rumble, like a growl deep in a wolf's chest. Low and ominous, it emanates from the Knight's castle in pulsing waves.

Is it alive? It cannot be. I can see the metal and wood that make up its structure as we come to a stop at the base of one of its four massive legs. My heart crashes in my chest as I take in the sheer scale of the monstrous place. I meant what I said when I told Mekhi I wasn't afraid—I am not. What I feel as I look up at the belly of the mechanical beast, the dwelling of the bane of Queen's Bridge, is something akin to dread. A certain knowing that all is lost. It is much worse than fear.

"You can still turn back," Nova says, as if he could hear my thoughts aloud. "You don't have to be this foolish."

I ignore him and search for a way inside. There are doors, but they are high above my head and are closed, with no visible handles or knobs. I reach out and run my hand along the side of one leg.

Mekhi recoils. "We should go. I was wrong. We can't best him. Look at this place." He gazes up at the structure. "We should get as far away from here as—"

A noise cuts through the air and steals the breath from Mekhi's chest. We all hear it—the unmistakable moan of pain and a shrill terrified scream.

"What was that?" Mekhi asks.

Nova hangs his head. "It seems the Knight is busy at the moment."

I quickly cast aside my cloak and find a foothold in the gaps between the leg's joints. Hoisting myself up toward a riveted panel on the underside of the castle, I draw my dagger and try to pry the rivets off with no luck. I think for a moment and then take out a piece of flint I keep in my boot pocket. I strike it hard against the leg, and it sparks just long enough for me to harness the fire and let it grow into a white-hot ember in my palm. Willing it into a blade hot as a blacksmith's forge, I draw it along the belly of the castle, right alongside the rivets, which burn orange as the heat warps their rounded shape. With the metal weakened, I'm able to pry off several of the rivets. As they fall to the ground, puffs of steam erupt where the damp snow snuffs out their red-hot glow. The hatch yawns open, and I peer into the blackness above. I grab hold of the edge of the hatch and prepare to hoist myself inside.

"Stop," Nova says. He glares up at me. "You shouldn't go any farther."

"Good thing I'm not inclined to listen to you," I say.

Nova tilts his chin up. "Your arrogance is going to get you killed."

"Arrogance?" I shimmy back down the leg and stand in front of him, my fists curled at my sides. "You think I'm here because I'm arrogant?"

Nova nods. "There can be no other reason."

I step toward him. "You saw what he did to Queen Sanaa. You see what he's doing to the people of Queen's Bridge, and you think *me* arrogant?" Rage floods in and clouds every rational thought.

"You haven't thought this through," Nova says. "You think you'll survive a confrontation with him?"

I huff. "I am prepared to die if it means defeating him."

Nova draws his mouth into a tight line, and the shine in his eyes seems to dull.

"That bothers you?" I ask.

"Yes," he says quietly, his face etched in steep shadows. "You cannot understand how much."

"Why?" I ask. "Why does it matter? You don't know me. Why should you care if I live or die?"

"I do not think your mother should be left without her only child," Nova says.

I turn away from him and glance up at the black void waiting for me.

"I'm going inside," I say. "If you stand in my way, I will kill you."

Nova hesitates, the muscle over his temple flexing like he's grinding his teeth. As I brush past him, I shove my shoulder into his, knocking him back a step.

"Are you coming?" I ask Mekhi. "You don't have to. You've brought me far enough."

He hesitates. I feel a pang of guilt for dragging him into this, but it is drowned out by the furious beating of my heart. Mekhi gazes upward. He has his own scores to settle with the Knight.

"I'm coming with you," he says.

I climb back up the leg and squeeze through the narrow hatch, hoisting Mekhi up behind me.

The heat inside is almost as stifling as the dark. The hatch leads to a cramped, narrow hall. Steam hisses from seams in the metal ceiling. A viscous black liquid drips down the wall and pools near my feet. A single flickering torch is set on the wall, washing the entire hall in a dim yellow light. The heat carries the smell of fetid air into my face, and I have to swallow the urge to gag. Mekhi cups his hand over his mouth and nose.

Nova appears beside him and another surge of annoyance ripples through me. He will not allow me to leave him behind, no matter how hard I try. But if he is here with us, that means he is not ahead of us, warning the Knight of our approach.

"Which way do we go?" Mekhi asks.

A shrill bellow cloaked in agony echoes through the cramped interior.

"Follow the screams," I say.

Pushing down the hall, with Mekhi and Nova on my heel, I make a left, a right, then ascend a short flight of uneven stairs slicked with the same black grime that had been dripping from the ceiling. The inside of the Knight's castle is a labyrinth. Some of the rooms don't have doors at all and are filled with various clutter. One small room is closed by an iron gate behind which lies a heaping pile of rotted straw and the remnants of some kind of loom now broken and near collapse. Another room contains only a long table on top of which is a large spool of black thread.

"We've been this way before," Mekhi says.

I glance back at him. "Have we?"

He nods, dragging his fingers over a deep gouge in the wall where it looks as if the metal has been ripped open by some clawed beast. I hadn't noticed the marking in the dark.

"We should turn here and then make another right," he says, gesturing to the forked hallway ahead of us. "Or we could leave. That's always an option."

I shake my head. "No. It's not."

Mekhi sighs. His lanky frame seems to collapse in on itself. His motives for helping me can't contend with his fear.

"You can go," I say, giving him an out if he wants to take it.

"Honestly, I don't think you'd be able to find your way out

without me," he says, avoiding my eyes. "You weren't lying when you said tracking isn't your strong suit."

Nova makes a sound. Like a stifled laugh. I ignore him and take the path Mekhi suggests.

We cross a threshold at the end of a twisted hallway and find ourselves in a room bigger than any we've come across. It is strewn with wooden tables of different sizes, and chains hang from the ceiling. A fire, stoked to blazing, burns bright in an alcove set against the back wall. Sweat beads on my brow and rolls down my neck, soaking my collar. A thick haze chokes the air around. Wrought iron implements—mostly fire pokers in various sizes, all thick with filth—hang on the wall. A putrid smell lingers in the air—excrement and sweat mixed with the metallic twinge of blood.

Footsteps sound in the hall behind us. My heart leaps into my throat. I grab Mekhi's arm and yank him against the wall closest to the door, pulling him down behind a large wooden table. I put one hand over his mouth, the other on the hilt of my dagger. I look back for Nova but find he has vanished.

Coward.

From our hiding place I try to keep my own panic from overwhelming me as a figure lumbers into the room. That I have never seen him with my own eyes makes no difference. This is the monster, the treacherous fiend who has wrought so much pain and suffering on the people of Queen's Bridge.

This is the Knight.

Clad in armor black as the midnight sky, every inch of his body is hidden behind the metal plates. He has a man slung over his shoulder who groans as the Knight sits him roughly on one of the tables. The man is naked and covered in filth and open wounds.

"Please," the man pleads. "I'll do anything you ask! Please! No more!"

"Anything I ask . . . ," repeats the Knight.

I have to bite my tongue to keep from gasping at the sound of his voice. It is every bit as horrible as the accounts I'd collected say it is. It drips with malice. He has spoken only three words, but they are enough to lay bare the makeup of his soul—he is wicked, through and through.

The Knight shackles the man's ankles and wrists to the table so that he is splayed out like a deer ready to be field dressed. The Knight runs his long, metal covered fingers over the iron pokers, tapping each one of them before plucking the largest one from its hook. He thrusts it into the fire, and, as he stands before the flames, the firelight lights up his frame. He is a massive figure. As broad across at the shoulders as an ox, taller than any person I've ever seen. He makes the room feel crowded and small. His chest rises and falls in a slow, steady motion. I cannot see his face though there is a narrow slit in his helm where his eyes should be. Behind it is only darkness.

"I had no choice!" the shackled man screams.

"There are always choices," says the Knight. He tilts his head up as he speaks. "They may not be choices you like, but they are choices, nonetheless."

Mekhi trembles so violently beside me I have to grip his

123

arm, digging my fingers in. I hope he understands what that means—do not move. Do not even breathe.

"My daughter—" the man begins.

"Our deal was clear," says the Knight. "Have you forgotten? You chose payment and I chose a fee befitting of the prize." He flicks the fire poker as it rests in the hearth and a flurry of sparks ascend the soot-covered chimney. "Tell me your wish. Speak the words to me as you spoke them to me on the day we made our pact."

The prisoner sobs. His tears trace down his cheeks, clearing away the dirt and blood that obscures almost every feature of his face. "I—I wished for enough silver to fill my coffers for twenty years."

The Knight turns his masked head toward the man. "And what was my fee? What was the payment I asked for in return?"

The shackled man presses the back of his head into the table beneath him. "My firstborn."

It takes everything in me not to gasp aloud, but the Knight shows no such restraint. He laughs, the sound splitting the air like a clap of thunder.

"I gave her to you!" the man shouts. "She drew a breath before her heart stopped. How was I to know? But it fulfilled the terms of our deal! I swear it did!"

The Knight draws the poker out of the flames and stalks toward the man, who tries desperately to free himself from his shackles. The Knight clamps his hand down on the man's leg, and the man screams. Mekhi jerks under my own grip, but I hold him tight.

"The girl was a twin," the Knight says.

The prisoner's mouth turns down. He tries to hide his shocked expression.

"You thought you could give me the lifeless shell of child and pretend the living one doesn't exist. You cannot keep her from me forever," the Knight says. "I *will* find her, and the terms of our deal *will* be fulfilled because that is how this works. That is how this has always worked. You will not outsmart me. You can't." He draws the poker across the man's bare belly, and the man yelps in agony as the smell of seared flesh fills the room. "Do you know how long I have roamed these lands?" The shackled man cannot speak to answer him. "You are not the first to think you are smarter than me," the Knight continues. "And you will not be the last, but it cannot be done. And until your terms are fulfilled, I will make this pain last and last."

"Please," the man says, defeated. "Please, Knight."

The Knight laughs. "Knight? That is what your wretched people have taken to calling me, but how can you plead with me and not know my name? The disrespect is almost too much to bear." He drags the tip of the red-hot poker across the bottom of the man's foot, and the man screams, then promptly loses consciousness, his head rolling to the side, his eyes half closed.

Mekhi retches. For a moment, I think the sound is lost in the roar of the fire and the clanging of the Knight's armor shifting as he moves to the head of the table. But to my horror, he slowly turns his head toward our hiding spot. He takes a step in our direction. Mekhi wipes the sweat from his lip and squeezes his eyes shut. His body betrays him, and he retches again. This time, there is no hiding it. I scramble to my feet, letting the Knight see me and hopefully not Mekhi, who stays crouched behind the table.

I can tell nothing from the position of his body. I cannot see his face, but I sense that the Knight is taking me in piece by piece.

"You," he says, his voice like an echo in a cave.

My heart almost stops. "You—you know me?"

His helm tilts just slightly to the right.

I stretch my hand toward the orange flames lapping the blackened bricks surrounding the hearth. The fire arches toward me and fashions itself into a blazing sword. The Knight's head moves from one side to the other as if he is tracking the flame.

Clutching the burning sword with both hands, I step toward the Knight. This is not what I had intended—to leap from a hiding place and catch him so unaware that he hasn't reached for his weapon yet. I always envisioned us dueling in some secluded spot, somewhere that I could burn his body after he fell and never tell anyone where his remains lie.

The Knight squares his shoulders. I still cannot see his eyes through the slit in his helm, but I can hear his breathing, which is measured, undisturbed by my sudden appearance.

Mekhi scrambles out from behind the table and runs toward the open door. The Knight turns his head toward him. I lift my sword, casting an orange glow all around. I plant my back foot and prepare to bring the blade down on his head. In this moment, I realize that all my training has come to this. I'm here. I've done it, and in this moment I feel as if I could move mountains.

I swing my sword down, and the Knight swiftly dodges the blade, ducking away to his left. The fiery blade glances off his arm plate, sending a shower of sparks cascading to the ground. I bring the sword up as a cry breaks from my chest. The Knight extends his hand and catches the blade mid-swing. The sudden stop jolts me to the side. As I scramble to regain my footing, the Knight rips the sword from my grasp, and it disintegrates in a puff of black smoke and swirling embers. He draws up his armored hand and brings the back of it across my face in one quick motion. The world dims, and for a moment there is no sound. And then pain comes rushing in like the tide, upending me. I'm sprawled on the floor, gasping for air, reaching for my dagger, which I know is pointless. It is woefully inadequate.

I stretch my hand toward the hearth again and as the flames reach for me, the Knight steps in front of them. He grasps the flame with his own armored hands, and the fire compresses itself into an undulating ball. Closing his hand, he quickly extinguishes the flame, black smoke curling from between his fingers.

The magic I possess is no match for whatever magic courses through the Knight. He doesn't have to draw his sword for me to know that—I can feel it in every part of me. This will be my end.

Suddenly, a shadowy figure is standing between me and the Knight.

Nova.

"If you kill her now," Nova says. "Your deal with her mother will be unfulfilled."

I scramble to my feet and step backward toward the door. My head is ringing, and my vision is still blurred. I can taste blood in my mouth.

"You have never allowed that to happen," Nova says. "Why should this be the girl who unravels all you have done? Is she really worth that?"

The annoyance I'd felt for Nova blossoms into a darkening rage. I want him in the ground and the Knight beside him. I reach for the fire again, but as the flame arcs up toward my hand, the Knight lifts his foot and brings it crashing back to the ground. It splits the floor in a jagged line that rips toward the hearth where it separates the bricks. Half the fireplace collapses in on itself. The flames sputter and go out, plunging us into a darkness broken only by one faltering torch on the wall.

"Eve!" Mekhi yells from somewhere down the hall. "Run!"

Nova's back is to me, and he turns his head just slightly so that I can see the shadowy outline of his profile. In his glinting gray eye there is the distinct look of fear.

I break for the door on unsteady legs as a clang of metal erupts from behind me like the rumble of a storm. Mekhi has pressed himself against the wall in the hallway and I grab him by the front of his coat, pulling him along behind me as I race down the hall. Fear floods my mind and my body. I glance back to see the Knight's hulking frame in the doorway, his sword drawn, the blade gleaming like an ember in the dark.

Mekhi gets his legs under him, and we race through the twisting maze of passages. Every hall looks the same to me. I have already lost my way after a few turns, and I can feel panic bearing down on me just like the Knight.

"Where do we go?" I scream.

Mekhi looks around frantically. "Left!"

I follow his instructions only to find that we're back in the hall leading to the Knight's torture chamber. The Knight has disappeared from the doorway, but his thunderous footsteps and the scraping of metal echoes somewhere down the hall. Suddenly, the entire structure seems to lurch to the side and I fall hard against the wall. Metal groans underfoot, and I get the distinct impression that we are listing to the side as if we were in the belly of a sailing ship.

"What is this?" Mekhi asks, his breaths quick and chest heaving. "What is happening?"

"We're moving," I say. "We need to get out of here right now!"

"I—I don't know which way to go," Mekhi stammers.

I push forward, looking for some sign of the hall that leads back to the open hatch. Just when I think we'll be trapped in the labyrinth for eternity, or at least until the Knight finds us and tortures us to death, I spot the gouge in the wall.

"Here! We're almost out!" I finally catch a glimpse of the hatch we'd entered through and race toward it.

The castle lurches, rocking to the side. Mekhi crashes to the floor in a heap. My legs go out from under me and I also crash to the floor. Pulling myself along, I grasp the frame of the hatch, preparing to throw myself down onto the ground, but that ground is much farther down than it had been before. The castle shifts again and the legs beneath it unfold, raising the belly of the structure higher above the treetops. A fall from this height will kill me.

"Gods," Mekhi gasps as he peers through the open hatch.

I brace myself in the hatch opening and cling to the upper strut of the castle's leg. The biting cold whips my face. A torrent of ice and snow twists around me. The numbing chill makes my bones ache, and I struggle to hold on to the freezing metal as feeling fades from my fingertips.

"Come on!" I shout to Mekhi as I shimmy down the castle's leg. "Follow me! Now!"

Above me, Mekhi's legs protrude from the hatch as he struggles to get his arms around the strut. I work my way down, willing my hands to move, though my joints are numb and stiff. I glance back up to see if Mekhi is making progress, only to find him gone and in his place, peering out from the opening in the castle's belly, is the Knight.

A startled gasp escapes my lips as I peer into the Knight's masked face. The slit in his armor where his eyes should be is a blackened abyss, and still I can feel the malice, the hatred, dripping from that blackened void. He moves away from the opening and then comes a sound, the likes of which I have heard before—in the throes of battle. There have been so few in these past years that I have almost forgotten what a man sounds like as he is dying. There is a guttural rasp and then a sort of wet gurgling. Mekhi's body falls from the hatch, and as it brushes past me, I catch a glimpse of his wide eyes and the nothingness behind them.

He is dead before he hits the ground.

The Knight's castle suddenly heaves, and I lose my already tenuous grip on the metal leg. I tumble back, and as I careen to the ground the tree branches claw at me like talons, tearing the flesh on my neck and hands. I land hard on my back, and, as the hulking shape of the Knight's castle moves over me like a beast leaving its ruined prey to rot, darkness consumes me.

CHAPTER 10

"Eve."

The faraway voice that calls me is familiar, but it brings me no comfort. In fact, it makes me want to burrow deeper into the empty pit where my mind has taken refuge.

"Eve. Get up. We have to go."

I stare up at the trees as my senses return to me. Pain comes rushing in like a gale-force wind, stealing my breath and making me cry out. Agony traces a path through my back and down my arm all the way to my fingertips. I turn my head to the side and see Nova's feet. I shut my eyes.

"Get away from me." Even speaking hurts. I groan as I roll up to a sitting position. It feels as if I am perched on a bed of broken glass.

"We need to get out of here right now," Nova says, looping his arm under mine and pulling me to standing.

I shove him hard in the chest, nearly knocking myself off balance in the process. "Get back! Don't ever touch me!"

I frantically look around. I have to get to Mekhi. Maybe there is still a chance. That is the lie my mind keeps repeating. "Where is he? Where?" I try to find the place where Mekhi had fallen, but I can see almost nothing in the dark. I flex my fingers and look up, pinpointing the brightest star I can find among the tangled canopy of barren branches high above my head. The light in the sky pulses, and as I turn my open palm to it, the starlight descends and gathers in my palm—a perfect orb of dappled starlight that brightens the surrounding wood. I stagger toward a depression in the ground several paces away.

Nova steps into my path but avoids my eyes as he speaks. "Please don't."

I glare at him. "Don't what?"

"You don't want to see him," he says.

"Don't tell me what I should want!" I scream. "Move aside or I will move you myself!"

"The Knight's castle walked over him after he fell," Nova says in a voice that is so much like a whisper, it takes a moment to reach me and for me to understand.

I can scarcely comprehend what he is saying. I push past him and peer into the deep gouge that had been made in the snow and damp earth by the feet of the Knight's castle.

Mekhi—or what is left of him—lies face down, his body pressed into the cold earth and snow. The edge of his coat shifts as the wind whips up, revealing that his torso is no longer connected to his lower body. I stagger back as the sour taste of vomit rises in the back of my throat. Nova steadies me with his hand, but I jerk out of his grasp.

"I tried to warn you," he says, glancing into the hole that now serves as Mekhi's grave. "All I could do was give you time to escape and still you tried to reach for a weapon."

"Do not speak to me," I say, my voice choked with rage. "Do not speak to me as if you were trying to help me!"

"What can any of us do against his power?" Nova asks quietly. "I am at his mercy as much as anyone else."

He is right, and I hate it. I had been so confident in my skill, my natural power, but they are nothing compared to him. I sit in the snow and hang my head. I have been training my entire life for a confrontation with the Knight. My mother and Huntress led me to believe that if I trained hard enough, if I used the power I'd been granted, that maybe I could end him once and for all.

Nova's words echo in my head like a nail pounded straight through my temple, shattering all thoughts of ending the Knight. He's roamed these lands for a very long time. He isn't just some monster I need to slay; he is a curse I need to break and nothing I have learned or trained for has prepared me for that. I am wholly inept. My weapons . . . useless.

Setting the starlight orb in the snow and stumbling to my feet as pain courses through my body, I can only look upon Mekhi's broken body. Guilt overwhelms me. It should be me in that hole. I am the one that should be lying dead, but it is instead Mekhi—a boy who loved his family, who had his own reasons for hating the Knight. A boy whose father will be destroyed by his loss and all because I'd been led to believe that I could somehow be a match for the Knight. Anger tries to crowd out the guilt, but I don't let it. I deserve to feel this agony, this regret. Leaning down, I gently close Mekhi's eyelids and touch the side of his broken and bloodied face. I stretch out my hands, beckoning the snow to gather itself and lay over Mekhi like a burial shroud.

When he is properly buried, I mount my horse and ride back to Queen's Bridge with Nova trailing me like a cursed shadow. I leave my horse at the castle gate and go to my mother's chambers, where I find the crossbar gone and her door sitting ajar. I enter without knocking and find her standing in front of the fire blazing in the hearth. Huntress sits in a chair in the corner, her legs crossed, her hands folded.

"Where have you been?" my mother asks. "I've been—"

She stops short as she looks me over. I glance at myself in her washbasin mirror. I am bloodied and bruised. My entire body is racked with pain.

My mother rushes to me and cups my face in her hands. "What has happened?"

There is no sense in putting up any pretense. "I was chasing the Knight."

Huntress leans forward in her chair, shaking her head. "Eve—"

"Spare me your hand-wringing," I snap.

"You will watch your tone," Huntress says.

"And you will remember that I am the Queen's daughter, *not* yours," I shout at Huntress.

She is wounded and immediately sits back, her eyes downcast.

"Eve," my mother says softly.

"No!" I shout. "No! All this time you've both been lying to me! The endless training, the constant work of learning to swing a sword and an axe and fight with my bare fists—for what?!" I rip off my dagger and throw it on the ground, then turn to face my mother. "You must have known that I could never best him. How could I? My power is nothing compared to his. Why would you spend all this time making me think I could defeat him?"

"We let you bury yourself in your duties," Mother says. "We allowed it, encouraged it. I—I didn't know what else to do." Tears glint in my mother's eyes as she speaks but she doesn't allow them to spill over.

"You didn't know what to do?" I repeat her words because I can't understand. "You let me think it was my fate to defeat him?"

"There is purpose in that duty, Princess," Huntress says without looking up.

"Mekhi Gregory is dead," I say. The words come from my gut because that is where my anger lies. "I was nearly killed myself."

A noise draws my attention to the doorway. Nova has appeared, looking mournfully upon the scene. I expect my mother to be frightened, pleading, as she had been when I overheard her speaking to Nova, but she is neither of those things. Her face is all fury and spite. She detests Nova and isn't bothering to hide it. My mother grips her sword, which even as she stands in her sleeping robes, hangs from her hip. She lunges toward Nova, and Nova effortlessly sidesteps her.

"You allowed her to seek him out?" my mother screams as she nearly upends her washbasin.

"As if I could stop her," Nova says. "She is your daughter, and I'm certain she gets her bullheadedness from you and you alone."

My mother huffs angrily. "You could have stopped her, but you didn't." She holsters her sword and approaches Nova more calmly this time, but that doesn't mean she will be kind. She narrows her eyes and her gaze is enough to send a chill straight through me. "You want him dead as much as I do. You hoped Eve would end him. Admit it."

I expect Nova to lash out at her accusation, but instead he blinks, staring blankly at her.

"I will do no such thing," he says. "I would not wish his wrath on anyone."

My mother looks him over from head to foot. "Keep lying to yourself."

"I don't know if you're in a position to talk about liars," I say.

The entire room falls quiet, but the silence is heavy. It presses down on me and I step back, as if I'm trying to distance myself from the words. I've never been so angry with my mother in all my life. There has never been a need. She always encouraged me to speak my mind, to say exactly how I felt, and I had. But this is different. There is an anger in me that I cannot stifle for the sake of decorum.

"I will not allow you to speak to her this way," Huntress says.

I look at Huntress like she is small, and she bristles.

"No," Mother interjects. "No, I deserve that." She turns to me. "You're right, and there is no sense in keeping up this ruse any longer. I have not been truthful, and I fear my dishonesty has put you in even more danger than you already were."

The anger that had felt like a frigid block of ice around my heart begins to thaw. "You'll be honest with me now?" I walk to the fireplace and press on the small indentation and the looking glass ascends from its hiding place under the floor.

My mother is quiet for a moment and then nods. "I don't think I have any other choice." She slumps into her chair and massages her temple for a moment before gently resting her fingertips on her pursed lips. "Bar the door."

Huntress does as she is told, but as she secures the door, her hands are trembling. Nova moves to the rear of the room and stands like a statue, hands folded in front of him, his eyes downcast as my mother gathers herself. When the door is closed to anyone but us, my mother takes a shaky, uneven breath.

"What I will tell you now is something that is known only to myself, Nova, and the Knight. My beloved Sanaa knew, of course."

Huntress makes a sound, and I turn my back to her. Does she really think she is privy to every thought in my mother's head? Now is not the time for her petty grievances.

Mother inhales and lets the air hiss out between her teeth. "I made a deal with the Knight many, many years ago."

Hearing her say it out loud is jarring but not unexpected. I had deduced as much, but it stings nonetheless. I shift from one foot to the other, resisting the urge to ask her how she could do such a thing. How could she be so reckless when she handles the running of Queen's Bridge like a craftsman handles a delicate glass?

"As you well know, I came to the throne upon my mother's death. I married Sanaa and we were blissfully happy. I had never known such contentment in all my life."

Hearing her speak of Queen Sanaa this way puts an ache in my chest.

"We could not have been happier in those early days," my mother continues. "But soon after we married, we began to feel as if something was missing from our lives."

"What could you have been missing?" I ask. "You were Queen. You were in love. You had the wealth of Queen's Bridge—"

"A family," my mother says. "Not just a family. A child."

My heart sputters in my chest.

"There are ways of doing this," my mother says, avoiding my gaze. "But none of them seemed . . . right. So, for a long time, we accepted that it was not meant for us." She sighs and rests her hand over her heart. "We were never very good at lying to each other. Sanaa said she was fine, and I said the same but it wasn't true. We wanted a family more than anything, and so I—I broached the subject of the Knight. She refused to even consider it."

"For good reason," Nova says, his voice like the moaning of the wind—cold and hollow.

I still cannot speak. Some dreadful knowing pools in my gut.

My mother ignores Nova and continues. "In time, Sanaa warmed to the idea, but there was still a dreadful hesitation.

We both knew full well what might happen if we made even a single misstep. One evening, I was sitting alone at the window in my chambers as winter pushed in around us. I was distraught. I tried to busy my mind with mending one of Sanaa's favorite gowns and pricked my finger on a sewing needle."

My mother pauses and her body goes rigid. Her eyes glass over. She looks like she might rise from her chair and bolt from the room at any moment. I hold my breath as my heart gallops in my chest. "A single drop of blood fell into the snow," she continues. "And then suddenly, I was not alone in my chambers." She glances up at Nova, who turns away from her. "Nova appeared, reflected in the stained glass of the window. In his capacity as liaison to the Knight, he offered me a deal. He told me I could have my wish, that the Knight would make it so. I could have my child and my wife and all would be as I wanted but . . ."

"But what?" I ask in a whisper, my mind reeling. "Are you saying I am here because of the Knight? That I exist because of him?"

"No," my mother says. "You exist because of me and because of Sanaa."

Huntress makes a noise like she's trying and failing to keep a torrent of words sealed behind her lips.

"You made a deal with him for me to come into existence?" I ask in abject horror. A terrible thought occurs to me, something far beyond the circumstances of my making. "What were the terms?"

My mother doesn't look at me. "It was not a deal made of simple terms. It was for payment."

"What did he want for his fee?" I ask. My heart trips into a furious rhythm. My mouth is suddenly dry, and a clammy sweat slicks my palms.

"He would not tell me," my mother says. "He said I had to agree to the deal before he would reveal its cost. Of course, I could not agree to that and I refused." My mother sighs as if her chest is suddenly closed in a vise. "But then Nova appeared to me as I walked along the River Farris. A stone the size of a door lay buried in the ice and snow on the river's bank. The images he showed to me in it lifted the cloud of despair that had descended on me. I had the stone cleaned and brought to my chambers under cover of night. Once it was in place, I saw the image of a dark-haired, golden-skinned cherub of a baby. In the stone I saw us together, smiling, laughing. I saw Sanaa cradling the infant. Nuzzling her neck and gently squeezing her perfect little arms and legs." My mother suddenly has a faraway look in her eye. "I could hear the laughter. I could feel the warmth, the unbridled happiness." My mother's eyes mist over and her chin wavers. "Every day I saw the images. And after a time, I simply could not bear it any longer. I called to Nova, and he appeared in the mirror. I told him I wanted to make a deal with the Knight. I was willing to give whatever he wanted as payment, thinking that maybe—"

"Maybe what?" I ask. "That he wouldn't ask something only a fiend would ask? That he wouldn't make you pay for the thing you wanted most?" I cannot fathom it and so I ask the question that matters more than anything else right at this moment. "What was his payment?"

Tears spill down my mother's face as her gaze finds mine. There is nothing but despair behind her eyes. "I wished for you, and his payment would be your life. I am to kill you by midnight on your seventeenth birthday. By my hand or another's, your death must come at my orders."

I am struck silent. I feel as if I am falling. As if the room is spinning. I stagger back. Nova's hand is suddenly on my back, steadying me, but I twist away from him.

Mother dabs at her eyes. "I thought—I don't know. I thought maybe I could find a way to—"

"A way to what?" Nova interrupts. "To outsmart him? To get out of your deal?" He shakes his head. "I thought you were smarter than that."

"You dare chastise me?" my mother asks heatedly. "After your part in all of this?"

My anger is with her but fault also lies with Nova. I turn to face him, and he presses his mouth into a hard line. He avoids my eyes.

"You tormented my mother with images of something she could never have," I say. "You tricked her into a deal with the Knight."

"No," says Nova. "I did what she asked. I helped her enter into her deal with the Knight. She knew full well what might happen."

"That's true," my mother says to Nova, her tone clipped. "But you're also not telling the whole truth."

Nova's brows push up. "That makes two of us, doesn't it?"

I turn to my mother. "What happened then? After you agreed to a deal?"

My mother dabs at her eyes with her fingers and sighs. "The Knight came to me, and I watched as he created you from the golden winter sunset and the shining stars. He pulled them down and breathed life into you, and there you were. I held you in my arms as you drew your first breath, and I knew that there was nothing I would not do for you. If the Knight required a life as payment, I would give up mine instead. If not, I would find another way."

I look down at my hands, my bare forearms. He'd made me from the things my mother loved most—the sky as the setting sun warms the horizon, the brilliant stars, the cold chill of winter. My power, which once seemed magical, now seems much more like a curse.

"And have you found it?" I ask. "Have you found a way to best him?"

My mother stands. "I have tried to think of a way to change the terms. I have requested an audience with him, and he has refused. The only thing I knew to do was prepare you to face him, maybe end him before he could collect his payment."

"The terms will not be changed," Huntress says. Her voice startles me. She'd been nearly silent as my mother let this story flow out of her. "How could you ever think he would change his mind? The more important question is what does he gain from it?"

"I don't know!" my mother snaps as tears cascade down her face. "I wanted Eve. My Eve! And I would give my life to keep her safe, but what I didn't want to admit then was that cruelty is the point of every deal with the Knight. He revels in the suffering, *my* suffering! And he will try to ensure that I will kill my own child." She looks at me. "I will put myself in the ground before I would harm you."

"No," I say in a desperate gasp. Angry as I am, I cannot listen to her speak of dying for me. She and I have both made terrible mistakes and miscalculations. Mekhi is dead because of me. We will find a way through them together, because if she goes into the ground I will follow.

"We are out of time and we are out of choices," Huntress says. "The Knight *will* collect what he is owed." She looks at my mother, pain stretched across her face. "If he cannot, he will exact a terrible revenge. You know this. Your life cannot be forfeit. I and every single member of your guard and the people of Queen's Bridge would lay down our lives to protect you because you are our Queen and that is our duty." She presses her mouth into a tight line as if she is bottling up the rest of what she has to say.

There is a heavy silence before Nova approaches us. It takes everything in me not to grab the flames from the hearth and fashion them into a dagger sharp enough to pierce his heart.

"There may be something that can be done," Nova says quietly. He folds his slender hands together in front of him and then stares at my mother. "A plan you concocted in a drunken stupor when you'd had your fill of the wine—when was it? Five years ago now?"

Mother avoids Nova's gaze.

Nova shakes his head. "A part of me believes you've been working toward it all along. Knowingly or not."

Mother closes her eyes tight. "It will require another kind

of sacrifice," she says, letting her eyes lazily flutter open again. "One that I am unsure any of us is willing to make." She suddenly steps in front of Nova. "You knew I had this plan and you said nothing to the Knight?"

"What plan?" Huntress asks.

"I can't trust you, Nova," my mother says. "You have always been the Knight's pawn. You do his bidding unquestioningly."

"We have known each other a long time, my Queen, but you don't know nearly as much about me as you think you do." Nova bristles. "I tried to stop Eve from confronting him. I distracted the Knight so that she could escape. And here I stand, ready to betray him yet again."

"Why?" my mother asks. "Why risk anything for us?"

Nova glances at me and there is something in his eyes that unsettles me—a genuine softness. He readjusts himself.

"It doesn't matter," he says.

A wave of frustration rolls over me, and I march toward Nova, gripping my dagger. I want to feel the pressure in my palm as I slip the blade between his ribs.

"You cannot best me," Nova says.

"You have no idea what I am capable of."

Nova backs away, his hands up. "You can't best me because I won't fight you."

I conjure a sword of fire and embers from the hearth. The flames light up the room and settle in my hand as I move toward him. "You are a coward."

Nova lets his hands fall to his sides. "Do it," he says. "End me."

I stop. He seems utterly defeated.

"What should I have done?" Nova asks.

"Not help the Knight torment my mother!" I shout. "Not help him at all! Why do you do it?"

"You stand at your mother's side," Nova says. "You are her right hand. I serve the exact same purpose for my father."

Huntress inhales so sharply she sputters and coughs. I let the flames of my weapon die out in a puff of black smoke.

My mother steps toward Nova. "Your father?"

Nova stares at the ground, his hands folded in front of him. "Cover the mirror."

My mother depresses the little notch, and the mirror sinks silently into the floor.

Nova's shoulders roll forward, and he holds himself around the waist as if he might fall apart. "He is my father and even he and I have made a deal, the terms of which I will never repeat."

"You're his child, and he makes you adhere to the terms of his treacherous deals?" I ask in utter disbelief.

Nova looks at me. "I thought you were aware of how cruel he can be, but clearly you have not been paying attention." He shifts from one foot to the other. "I have been at his side for a very long time and I know full well how terrible the consequences of not strictly adhering to his rules can be. You think watching a man being tortured is the worst thing you've ever seen?"

Something in his eyes tells me he has beheld horrors too gruesome to recount, and I shudder as my mind wanders to what that could possibly mean.

"You were at his side even as a child?" I ask.

"I have always been this," Nova says. "No older, no younger. Just . . . this."

I don't press him further.

Nova moves closer to me. "If your mother tries to get out of her deal, he will bring his wrath down on all the people of Queen's Bridge. No person, young or old, will be spared. And no one will face harsher consequences than the Queen. Except maybe you, Eve." He breathes my name like something that is half a curse, half a secret.

I turn away from him.

Mother steps away from Nova. "After all this time, why are you suddenly concerned?"

I can feel Nova's gaze on the back of my head, and I glance behind me. He is indeed staring directly at me.

"I can't say," Nova says. "I don't think anything I do will allow me to be redeemed."

"Redeemed by who?" I ask. "For what reason?"

"By anyone who might see me for who and what I truly am and not what has been made of me," Nova says.

"We are what we are," I say.

"Are you the Queen's fury?" Nova asks. "Or the girl who buried an innocent boy in the woods with such a heavy heart that I doubt you will ever fully recover from the loss?"

Nova holds my gaze until I look away, frustrated by how deeply those words cut.

"I don't know about redemption," my mother says softly. "I have much to account for in my own life, but if that's what you're looking for, if you think you can find it here with us, you start by swearing to me that you will not betray us."

Nova looks down at the floor. "I swear it."

His word means nothing to me, but Mother seems satisfied, at least for now.

Huntress stands and looks pleadingly at Nova and then at my mother. "What is this plan you speak of? I need to know." There is desperation in her voice, and I wonder, if she feels so strongly about me, why is she always so harsh?

"We must make him think that I have fulfilled the terms of our deal," my mother says quietly.

"And then you must live your lives as if you actually had," says Nova. "It is a ruse that you will have to keep up all the rest of your days."

"What ruse?" I ask.

"We must deceive him," my mother says. "We must plan and execute Eve's death by my hand and pray the Knight never finds out."

The Huntress throws her hands up in disgust and defeat. "You cannot be serious. Please, my Queen, tell me you are joking."

I turn to my mother, expecting her to be angry at Huntress's outburst, but she looks upon me with wild eyes. A spark I haven't seen in a very long time is ignited in her gaze.

"It may be the only way," she says softly.

Huntress's gaze darts between my mother and Nova. "Ridiculous. It will never work."

"It will," Mother says. "And I will need your help, Huntress. Your loyalty is required now more than ever before."

"You—you planned this?" I ask.

"No—maybe—maybe in part," she stammers. "The idea was born from too much wine and too much despair, but I have thought of nothing else since then." My mother suddenly takes my face in her hands. "This is the only way. If it means you get to live, that is all that matters."

"I hope you mean it," Nova says, his voice perfectly matching the seriousness of his gaze. "Your deal includes me delivering Eve's still beating heart to the Knight. Something will have to take its place."

CHAPTER 11

Shock ripples through me like a bolt of lightning, rocks me like a clap of rumbling thunder. Mother clasps my hands between her own. She would never hurt me. I don't doubt that, but the knowledge that she had known this is what the Knight expected of her and that she would have to partake in a scheme that is destined to fail to beat him is a kind of burden I cannot fathom.

"We have very little time," my mother whispers. "Two weeks until Eve is seventeen, and the Knight will want his payment no later than midnight on that day. We are working against the hands of a ticking clock."

Nova nods.

"And we must keep Eve out of the planning," my mother says.

I whip my head around to look at her. "What? Why?"

"The less you know, the better," my mother says.

Huntress grips the hilt of her sword. "If—or should I say

when—this all falls apart, maybe you'll garner some sympathy from the Knight if you don't know the details."

Mother raises an eyebrow. "Your confidence in me has never wavered, and now you're questioning me?"

"Forgive me." Huntress puts her hand on her chest and gives a little bow. "I just think killing him is a much better plan. Eve wasn't capable, but that doesn't mean it can't be done."

"It's not that I am incapable," I say, feeling the bite in her words. "It is that the Knight isn't a stuffed straw figure standing still in a glade. He won't stand still and wait to feel your sword on his neck. He is a living, breathing monster made real, and he would have laid you out had you been there."

Huntress huffs. "I doubt that. I would have killed him." She turns to Nova. "I don't care if he's your father or not. I wish him dead, and given the chance I would strike him down without a second thought."

Nova looks at Huntress, his face still marred by some unknowable sadness. "You would try," he says. "And you would fail as all others have failed." His face gives no indication that he has taken anything Huntress said to heart.

My mother squeezes my hands again. "We can hope for something more for ourselves, but our duty is to the people of Queen's Bridge. We must appease the Knight. No matter the cost. The havoc he will cast down upon us will be unlike anything we have ever seen or feared if we fail in this."

Huntress tenses up, her eyes glassy.

I sigh and cast my gaze to the floor. Duty. That is what this has all come down to: a sacrifice so that my mother will not have to kill me and so the people of Queen's Bridge will not suffer as we disobey the Knight. Whatever hatred I'd felt for him all these years is nothing compared to the sour bitterness that now threatens to consume me.

"All right, then," my mother suddenly says to me. "Enough. Go. We will speak of this no longer."

———————

In the days that follow, my mother meets with Huntress and Nova while I travel to the Gregory farm to inform Sir Gregory of Mekhi's death. I have seen many terrible things in my life. While the images of Mekhi's broken body pressed into the snow was among the worst of them, nothing could prepare me for the look that crawls across Sir Gregory's face as I lie to him. I tell him Mekhi had become separated from me during a blizzard as we tracked the rogue wolf into the high mountains, and that the next time I came upon him he was dead, having fallen from his horse. I tell him I could not retrieve the body due to the snowy conditions but promise to bring him home the following spring. He asks where Mekhi fell, and I continue my litany of untruths. I simply cannot imagine him trekking into the mountains and digging Mekhi's body out of the frozen ground. As I relay the terrible news, Sir Gregory collapses into a heap of desperate sobs and uncontrollable tears, scattering the carved limbs of his marionettes across the ground.

———————

Two weeks later, and the plans my mother has made are being set in motion faster than I can prepare myself for whatever the outcome may be. I receive a letter written in my mother's hand, asking me to prepare for a glorious celebration, a birthday feast, and all the festivities that come with it.

I am not informed of all the details, but Nova apparently suggested that my mother not only allow the festivities but make them as grandiose as possible. It is not for my benefit or amusement. I know it is meant to give the illusion that my mother is preparing to keep up her end of the deal—what would a mother who is about to kill her only child do when faced with that impossible choice? Send me to my death in grand fashion with all the accoutrements of a proper homegoing.

The night of the celebration arrives, and I stand in front of my mirror, draped in a gown made of stardust and snow. I fashioned it myself, and it clings to my body like a second skin. The white and silver tones in the weave contrasts with the deep golden brown of my own skin. I let my hair down; the tight black coils hang around my shoulders, and set among them are finely made clips of warm honey-colored amber and blazing green emerald. As I look upon my reflection, I cannot help but feel that I am not a child of the Knight but a creation born from my mother's sincere wish to have a child. This knowledge waters the growing hatred I have for the Knight. If my disdain for him had been a ragged weed, it is now a curling poisonous vine ready to ensnare the Knight and choke the life from him.

I have to go down to the main hall and put on a brave face. That is the duty I am bound to. Trusting in my mother has never been an issue for me, but this is different. Her plans are hidden from me, which makes me feel vulnerable and exposed.

I check my reflection one last time and find Nova's wide eyes staring back at me from just over my right shoulder. I almost upend the basin as I stumble back.

"I'm sorry," Nova says quietly. He takes a step back, as if he is retreating into the shadows of the mirror. I have not seen or heard from him more than once or twice in the last two weeks. He seems smaller, more rigid. He locks eyes with me and suddenly straightens up, resting his hand over his heart. "You look—" He stops mid-sentence, and his gaze hardens.

My skin pricks up. "For a moment I thought you might compliment me."

"That would be appropriate," he says. "It is your birthday, after all."

It sounds strange. My mother has been preparing for this night, and it is exactly what I wanted, a celebration—but it comes under the worst possible circumstances, much like the wishes made to the Knight.

Nova approaches the glass from the opposite side. His face is very near the glass, and his gray eyes stare out at me. He inhales just slightly, a small gasp that is barely audible, but the sound sends a ripple of confusion crashing through me.

"You look tired," Nova says quickly, looking away.

"Ah. There it is," I say. My head clears. A beautiful face is not enough to make up for all he has done, and I'm embarrassed that I even entertained a kind thought about him. "You can't help being rude and awful, can you? It's a part of who you are."

"Awful?" he asks as his brows arch halfway up his forehead. "Is that what you think of me?"

"It doesn't matter what I think," I say, smoothing out the front of my dress, though there are no wrinkles or folds to be seen. "Why are you here?"

"The Knight has been informed that your mother and Huntress are prepared to move against you tonight. He is pleased."

"I see," I say quietly, as I try to connect the stray pieces of information together in my head. "As part of the ruse, you've told him my mother is prepared to carry out her end of their bargain. That makes sense."

Nova tilts his head. "Ruse?"

"The ruse," I say. "I know I don't have all the details, but it's obvious. This is all an illusion to make him think we're going along with the terms."

Nova's face is blank. "Yes, it is, but—did you not hear what we said before? In order to make this work you must continue on as if the terrible deed has actually been accomplished."

"I heard you just fine," I say. "We'll have this party. We'll put on whatever performance my mother and Huntress have concocted, I'll lie low for a short while. How long do you think I'll have to—"

"No." Nova's voice is low and hollow. "No, Eve. You don't understand. You won't see your mother again. Ever. You'll lie low . . . forever. That is the only way this works."

I stare into Nova's face as the world around me goes silent. My heart sinks into my stomach. I've been so focused on how we are going to make this plan work I haven't thought about the wider ramifications of it all. And yes, I'd heard what they said, but still . . .

"I won't have to hide from the Knight forever," I say. "Surely there will be a time when it will be safe for me to be with my mother again."

"The Knight has already lived an unnaturally long life," Nova says in that same dull tone. "He will outlive you and your mother and the generations that come after." Nova hangs his head. "You will never be safe from him. Not until death, and even then . . ." Nova trails off and he shakes his head.

I turn my back on the mirror, on Nova. Somewhere in my gut I know what he says is true, but I don't want it to be. I can't accept it, but it feels as if that's what I am being forced to do. I have gone from preparing to battle the Knight to trying my best to convince him that I am his pawn, and it eats at me with each passing second because none of these plans include making him pay for the damage he has done.

"I'm—I'm sorry, Princess," Nova says. "I wish things were different."

"Do you?" I ask through gritted teeth and tears.

Nova sighs. "Yes. I do."

When I look back, he is gone. I try desperately to hold myself together. I can think of nothing but the Knight. I hate him. I pull the box from under my bed and grab the maps and accounts of his treachery and toss them into the blazing fire.

They curl and catch the flames until they are nothing but cinders.

Gathering myself, I make my way to the grand hall. People are coming in from the cold, shuffling toward the hall. They greet me with wide smiles, and they speak of how glorious this night will be, a celebration to remember. What will my mother tell them when I am gone? What will my legend be? None of this feels real, and still I move toward the doors of the great hall and enter to a burst of lively music and laughing, cheery voices.

People are dancing and toasting with cups full to the brim. The Miller family crest, emblazoned on emerald flags, is draped around the room. At the far side of the room, a table has been prepared. My mother and Huntress are already seated. The table is piled high with honey-sweet confections, cured meat, and fresh bread. Vats of wine line the far wall, and a footman is serving it in copper cups to the thirsty crowd. The smell of candle wax and smoke from the roaring fire permeates the air. People dance and talk among themselves. They seem happy. There is an air of celebration, and when I enter the room everyone turns toward me and breaks into a familiar song celebrating my birth and what the year ahead will bring—good fortune, good health, prosperity.

It takes everything I have to force a smile and shake hands as I weave through the crowd. A terrible resentment pools in the pit of my stomach. I push it down. How can they know that tonight is supposed to be my last night among the living? And as I think on it, it is more true than not. My heart isn't really going to be torn from my chest and presented to the Knight like a macabre gift, but I will be forced to walk this land like a ghost from this night on. I join my mother at the table. She is dressed in robes so dark green they are nearly black. She looks as if she is clothed in despair, draped in mourning. I slide into the seat next to her, and she grasps my hand.

"Isn't this lovely?" she asks in a hollow voice without glancing over at me.

I cannot speak. A knot has wriggled its way up my throat, and if I open my mouth to say anything it will betray me and a sob will rush forth like the breaking of water from a dam. I cannot allow that. Not when there is so much riding on keeping up this terrible illusion. Not when the whole of Queen's Bridge is expecting to see me enjoying the festivities as I usher in this seventeenth year of my life. My mother stares straight ahead, unblinking. I can't stand it.

"You should dance," Huntress says.

My mother and I both look at her as if she's said something profane.

Huntress huffs. "Keep up appearances, Eve. Do not let your stubbornness get in the way of what must be done here tonight."

My mother shuts her eyes tight for a moment, then turns to me. "Perhaps it would be a good idea."

"I don't want to dance," I say.

"It doesn't matter," Huntress snaps. "Do it anyway. For your mother's sake."

I don't like her tone or the vapid look in eyes. She acts as if she has something more to lose in all of this than I do. She is also acting like she can tell me what to do. I sit in my seat and strum my fingers across the emerald green tablecloth, trying desperately to distract myself from thoughts of challenging Huntress to a duel right here and now. The flames in the candles closest to me jump up and lick at the air. A woman standing near the table glances at the flame and then at me, her eyes wide. She backs away and disappears into the crush of people.

My mother squeezes my hand. "Not now. Please, Eve."

I stare into her face, and she looks as if she carries the worry of all the world on her shoulders. She looks like she might collapse under the impossible weight of it at any moment. I give Huntress a dagger of a glance before excusing myself and meandering through the crowd of well-wishers, lost in some kind of nightmarish reality. Smiling faces twirl past, and the music grates against my temples. My chest heavy, I touch my throat to assure myself it isn't being closed in a vise as panic settles over me. My skin dampens. I feel trapped. I want to run, to fight, to scream. More swirling faces go by and the assault on my senses is too much. I step toward the door when suddenly there is a hand on my wrist. I turn, ready to decline the advances of anyone wishing to dance, and I am met with a pair of familiar gray eyes.

Nova.

He is dressed in all black and his hair pulled into a neatly twisted bun at the back of his head. He turns me around and sets his hand on my waist.

"You looked as if you would faint," Nova says. "Or bolt from the room. I can't tell which."

I don't like being so near him, but he's right. My legs are barely keeping me upright and darkness dances at the edges of my vision. Nova keeps his hand on my back, and I lean on him for support. He puts his mouth against my ear as he pulls me into the dance.

"Do I need to remind you that you need to act as if you don't know a single thing about what's to take place?" he asks.

"I don't need you to remind me of anything," I say as my head clears. "What are you even doing here? I very much doubt you've come to dance and drink."

"I don't drink," he says flatly. "I've been known to dance when it pleases me. I can tell you've never waltzed a day in your life."

Blood and heat rush to my face. That's not entirely true. I had attempted to dance with a young woman at a springtime celebration the year before. She was much better at it than I was, but she said nothing as I stepped on her shoes and tried to lead when I had no business doing such a thing. Nova doesn't hold his tongue for me, and despite my feelings toward him, I am glad he doesn't hold anything back. Nova smiles down at me but his face is pinched, his grin unnatural.

"I am here to ensure the terms or payment outlined in his deal are met."

"Just doing your wretched job," I grumble as I break from his grasp and try to find a glass of something cold to drown myself in.

"Yes," Nova says as he shadows me, mirroring my every step. "I *am* doing my job and you should do yours. Your duty—"

"Do not speak to me of duty," I snap, stepping away from him. "I know what needs to be done." The anger pooling inside me is almost too much to bear.

"I know you do," Nova says quietly. He looks down, leaving something unsaid between us.

I find an empty goblet and dip it into a large bowl of thick liquid the color of spun gold—honey wine. It's sweet on my tongue, and after several gulps I turn to find Nova has moved closer to me, his arm gently pressing into mine. He is staring down at me, and I wonder if he can see the remnants of the sweet drink on my lips. Nova breathes deep, and his gaze flits to the table where Mother and Huntress are seated. His mouth suddenly turns down and his brows push together. I follow his worried gaze across the room. Huntress has clearly had too much to drink and is draped over the arm of her chair. Her hair, in dozens of small braids, falls across her face like a curtain.

"That explains why she was so upset with me," I say. "She's easily irritated when she drinks."

"It's not an excuse," Nova says, his words tipped in anger. "She should be on alert. She's been partaking in the festivities too much for my liking. She needs a clear head."

In a blink, Nova is suddenly gone from my side. When I see him reappear behind Huntress, no one else seems to notice. He's like a ghost among the throngs of inebriated guests. Nova leans forward and whispers something into Huntress's ear, at which point Huntress abruptly stands, shakes herself, and yells something I can't quite make out amid the music and chatter of voices. The lines in her forehead are deep as she furrows her brow, and her mouth is pinched into an angry scowl. Nova remains stoic as Huntress storms off.

Suddenly, I'm caught in someone's grasp, and as I spin around, I'm met with a familiar face. Sir Gregory is holding tight to my arm.

"Princess," he says. His voice does not sound like his own.

"Sir Gregory," I say, avoiding his eyes. I want to tell him that he shouldn't have come, but that is only because I am afraid to look at his grief, which he wears like a cloak. It is draped around him, covering every part of his body. He is stooped, and his hands are covered in cuts. On his face is a permanent scowl of a man who knows he will never be as happy as he once was.

He spins me around. I try to pull away, but he holds fast to my arm.

"I didn't want to miss the opportunity to wish you a happy birthday," he says. "You're seventeen. Mekhi was eighteen. He got one more year than you, but he'll never see another."

I look Sir Gregory in the eye. I hope he can see the shame I carry. "I am sorry," I say, biting back tears. "It is my fault. I—I shouldn't have asked him to take me to hunt the wolf." I am still lying to him, but I cannot tell him the truth.

"Where is he?" Sir Gregory asks. "Where are my son's mortal remains?"

He pushes me backward, and I step on the foot of a woman dancing just behind me.

"I'm sorry," I say to her.

She smiles wide. "Don't think on it a moment longer, Princess. I was so excited to receive an invitation." She beams as she kisses my right cheek and then the left. "Happy birthday, Highness! There has never been a grander celebration!"

Sir Gregory takes a step back as people dance between us, but his gaze is locked on me.

"The mountains," I say. "In the valley at the base of Dead Man's Peak."

The woman I'd run into continues to talk, but I'm not listening. All I can see is Sir Gregory's face as he takes in the information I have given him and disappears into the crowd.

Nova is suddenly at my side again, pulling me away from the chattering woman without a single word, leading me into another dance without missing a beat.

"What did Sir Gregory say to you?" Nova asks.

I shake my head. "He blames me for Mekhi's death, as he should. It is my fault."

Nova says nothing, which I take to mean he agrees.

"We all make our own choices," Nova says. "Mekhi made his. He was very brave, but his bravery could not save him." There is something in his words that unsettles me. I feel as if he is telling me that I may soon share Mekhi's terrible fate. "Is it possible for you to put your mind elsewhere?"

"No," I say as we continue to turn in circles. I allow Nova to guide me. I feel like I am spinning inside of a nightmare—a dancing figure twirling atop a gilded music box all for the show of it.

The night drones on. Nova keeps me spinning in endless

circles. I suspect he is trying to keep me occupied. Every time I glance at my mother, my heart shatters. She's not doing a good job of putting on a brave face either, and all I want to do is go to her, put my arms around her, and tell her to hell with this plan—we will fight the Knight and if we die trying, so be it. One look at her face, her jaw set hard, her eyes narrow, tells me that she has her mind made up about how this night will go. She wants me to live, but I don't know if a life without her is worth it.

"Your mother will be fine," Nova says against my ear.

I angle my head to look into his face. Being so close to him I notice the flecks of brown in his gray eyes, the curve of his lip. He presses closer to me, one hand on my waist, the other gripping my hand firmly.

"I have never met anyone quite like her," Nova says. "Except for you, of course."

"I wish I were more like her," I say. "Maybe if I were braver, smarter, I could find a way to end all of this without having to be parted from her."

"I think you dishonor your mother by saying such things," Nova says. He pulls me to him. "You are brave and intelligent. So is she. But neither of those things is enough to defeat the Knight."

For what I think is the first time all night, I smile. "Did you compliment me?"

Nova mirrors my smile with his. "Did I? Sincerest apologies, Highness."

When the bells ring out, signaling the evening drawing to

a close, I realize I was lost in the dance with Nova. For a brief moment I allow myself to pretend that this is what my life should have been like. At the final peal, I'm dragged from that world of dreaming. Nova stands still in front of me, letting his hands rest on my waist, letting his lips brush against my hair. I break his grip and step away.

Our guests make their way to their carriages and horses. They stumble about, laughing and making plans for the following day. I envy them that they know what is to come. The torches are extinguished and the remaining food is cleared away. The musicians pack away their instruments and collect their wages. At last, it is only Nova, my mother, Huntress, and myself in the great hall. The room that had only moments before been so crowded I could barely walk now seems cavernous and too deathly still. It is as if we are afraid to breathe or move or speak. Bells chime in the hall as the clock approaches ten.

I stand in the center of the room, looking at the flags. The candles and lamps still burn, and the tears in my eyes cut the light like a kaleidoscope.

"Eve." My mother's voice is thick with pain.

I don't want to look at her, but it occurs to me that this may be my last chance to do so for a very, very long time. I turn my face to hers and in her eyes is every kiss, every warm embrace, every time we have laughed and cried together. In her gaze is the memory of my mother, Sanaa.

"We have to part," my mother says.

"Do not say goodbye to me," I say, angrily wiping away tears. "We will be together again."

My mother forces a smile. "Oh, I have no doubt of it." She is lying. I can tell by the way she avoids my eyes and focuses instead on our intertwined fingers. I trace the scar on her hand with my fingers. "I loved you before you even existed," she says. "When you were just a dream, I loved you. When you were made real, regardless of the means, I loved you even more. I will love you all the days of my life, and I am so sorry that it has come to this." Her breath hitches in her chest. "I wish I could change things, but if I had not made my deal with the Knight, I wouldn't have had these years with you. I thought that I could find another way, but we have come to the end."

I don't know what to say. I still don't want to believe that this is our only option. I feel as if I can't breathe, like I am trapped with no place to run.

My mother takes my hands in hers, slipping off her ring and putting it on my middle finger. "Keep this safe for me. Promise me."

"I promise," I say through the tears. "I swear."

My mother clears her throat and shakes her head. "Huntress has been in touch with a family who has agreed to shelter you. Even I do not know the whereabouts of their home or in what direction you will travel. It's better that way."

"Once we have staged the killing, I will report back to the Knight," Nova says. "It is my sincerest wish that this succeeds."

Huntress huffs. "The last thing we need right now are more wishes. Look where they've gotten us."

My mother hangs her head and turns her back to me.

"Go," she says over her shoulder. "Do not look back, for if you do, I might change my mind and doom us all."

I follow my mother's orders but as I turn to leave the great hall, I do look back. She has her back to me still, but Nova stands facing me, his hands hanging at his sides. The look on his face is hard to read, but if I didn't know better, I'd guess it is grief.

I don't lose complete control of myself until I get to the stables where Huntress gently rests her hand on my back as I let the anguish pour out of me.

"Come, Eve," she says, her words thick from the mead. "Wipe your tears, Princess. It will be all right."

I don't see how. I've never had any reason to think of what my life would be like without my mother. I can't stem the tears. The breaking of my own heart is almost unbearable.

"We must leave now," Huntress says, her words slurring together, her steps halting.

"Can you even mount your horse?" I ask.

She lifts her head and looks at me, her eyes half closed and bleary. "Worry about yourself."

Huntress has been at my side for as long as I can remember. Or more aptly, I have been at hers. She's led me through my training, taught me to hunt, to fight, to kill if need be. She is not a woman of many words, and her tone is sometimes sharp, but she has never been cruel. She's never been as she is in this moment. I don't fault her. She loves me, too, and her way of dealing with what is about to occur may be to put on this cold exterior. So, I humor her and turn my attention to the journey ahead, trying my best to keep thoughts of my mother far from me.

I quickly change in the frigid night air, allowing the dress I'd conjured to fall away into nothingness. I pull on clothing suited for a long journey and tuck my riding cloak close around my neck. My bag has already been loaded onto the horse. Huntress clumsily pulls herself atop her stallion and leads me out of the stables and away from Castle Veil in the direction of the South Steps, a vast mountain range that snakes out of Queen's Bridge and along the eastern border of Hamelin, continuing into the territory that butts up to the Forbidden Lands.

I do not look back as we ride into the night. The ache in my chest is unlike anything I've ever felt. I fear that if I look down, I will see a gaping hole where my heart should be. I twist my mother's ring around on my finger and spur my horse onward, trying to outrun the mounting grief. There will be no turning back. The fates of all the people of Queen's Bridge, including my mother, are at stake.

CHAPTER 12

I trail Huntress for hours, until the saddle digs into my leg and my back is racked with pain. Exhaustion is making it difficult to stay upright, when finally Huntress gives the signal to stop. I want nothing more than to dismount and lie in the snow until the ice numbs the pain. We tether our horses at the edge of a small clearing surrounded on all sides by dense black forest. The snow is untouched aside from a few animal tracks.

"Deer," I say gently, touching the indentations in the snow. "Looks like two or three."

Huntress stands with her hands jammed down on her hips. "Your tracking skills are better now?"

"I guess your incessant nagging finally worked."

Something passes over Huntress's face—perhaps a flickering shadow that makes her eyes look empty.

"We'll make camp here for the night," she says, quickly looking away.

I set to work clearing away some of the snow and gathering a few fallen branches for kindling. Huntress goes to her horse and digs around in one of the saddle bags. Overhead, a murder of crows circles. There must be twenty of them. I try to remember the last time I'd seen so many. They are solitary by nature, preferring to keep a companion or two but rarely more than that. Their calls in my head are melodic, high pitched, and confused. They round the air in a dizzying circle. It is almost chaotic.

"Have you got that fire going?" Huntress asks.

"I need a flint," I say. "This wood is too wet. It'll never catch. I didn't bring one. Do you have—" I stop short. Huntress has turned to face me, and in her hands she holds a small wooden box.

"I suppose that might work," I say. "It's very pretty. If the wood is dry, it'll catch. Are you sure you want to burn it?"

Huntress shakes her head. "It isn't for the fire."

"Oh?" I ask as my skin turns to gooseflesh under the warmth of my cloak. I have misunderstood.

"The Knight requires proof of your death," Huntress says. "A heart is needed."

I stare at the box. How she had managed to get her hands on a heart—a human heart—is beyond me. "How did you do it?" I'm not sure I want to know the real answer, but I can't stop myself from asking the question. "Please tell me it was from someone who had already died." I laugh the way one does when the conversation has become uncomfortable.

Huntress flips the box's lid open to reveal the empty space inside. I let the breath hiss out from between my teeth.

"You scared me for a moment," I say. "I thought for a moment you had added grave robber to your list of talents. What will you use? A deer's heart?" I listen for the deer. Their soft mewing call is far from me.

I smile at Huntress, and she does not return the gesture.

"I have connections from here to Mersailles," Huntress says. "In my life I've come to know all sorts of people. I could have very easily procured the heart of a young woman, but . . ." She trails off, her eyes glassy. "He would know it doesn't belong to you. He is not a fool. And a deer's heart would be an even greater insult."

I instinctively take a step toward my horse, but Huntress mirrors my movement like a shadow, blocking my path.

"How far is the residence of the people I'm to stay with?" My voice sounds far away. Breath pumps out of me in billowing clouds as I begin to unravel what is happening in these woods so far from the loving embrace of my mother.

Huntress sighs and tosses the box into the snow. "Do you know how long I have loved your mother?"

I stare into her face, and I finally place this new expression—it is pity.

"I know you love her," I say. "We all do."

"I am *in* love with her," Huntress corrects.

I am horrified at the anger behind her words. She steps

toward me, her mouth drawn down, her eyes watery and unfocused. Drink is still pumping through her.

"You're drunk," I say. "You should sit down. Rest."

"When Queen Sanaa was changed, your mother was distraught and who was there to comfort her?" Huntress doesn't heed my suggestion and instead, takes another uneven step toward me. "You were there, but you were a child. You still are. *I* was there for her. She cried on my shoulder more nights than I can count." She rushes in and grabs me by the wrist. "Your mother could have had a full, meaningful life after Queen Sanaa, but she couldn't . . . because of you."

I try to break her grip, but it is ironclad.

"What are you talking about?" I demand. "Why are speaking to me like any of this is my fault?"

"Your mother has been too distracted by you to see what's right in front of her." Her breath smells of wine. Sweat is beaded on her forehead despite the cold. "She spent all her waking moments lost in fantasies of outsmarting the Knight. All for you. All for an impossible dream of having you at her side all her life."

"She's my mother," I say. "That is what a mother is supposed to want. To have her child with her to love, to cherish." Anger clouds my vision. This is why she has been so angry with me. She wants my mother for herself and sees me as an obstacle. The Knight ruins everything he touches, and here, he has done it again. "You are not my mother," I say, pressing my face close to hers as she grips my wrist. "You don't have what it takes to be that."

Huntress blinks twice as snowflakes, full and fluffy as down, begin to fall and stick to her eyelashes. She tilts her head up and looks at the sky. "It is folly, Eve. All this planning. Don't you see? Don't you understand that we are bound by duty to—"

I shove her hard in the chest and she lets go of my arm, stumbling back but quickly regaining her footing. "Don't speak to me of duty! I have done my part! I have always defended the people of Queen's Bridge and my mother."

"And you'll continue to do so right here and now, because I won't let this ridiculous plan put your mother in danger," Huntress says, and now there is nothing but rage in her words. "We won't have to trick the Knight because your heart *will* be in that box when I return. That is your duty, your purpose."

"My duty? You want me dead?" I ask, and I sound like a child. We've all done our best to honor our responsibilities and look where it has gotten us. The Knight's reign of terror can never be finished while we are bound by duty. "What do you think this will do to my mother?"

"Do you think I'd be so careless with her heart?" Huntress asks as if she isn't planning on murdering me. "Your mother will think we have succeeded in our deception. She will never know that you died out here in these woods, and I will be there to walk with her in grief and perhaps give her some of the happiness that she so desperately deserves."

Huntress pulls her dagger from its sheath on her hip and I, out of sheer instinct, draw my own dagger and raise it in front of me, my hands trembling.

"You would betray me?" I ask, unable to fully fathom that she is willing to do this terrible task. "You say you love my mother and still, you would do this to me?"

Huntress grits her teeth and swallows hard. "I have loved you, believe me I have. But your continued existence means your mother will never be safe, and I will not allow that."

"This can work!" I shout at her as the melted snow begins to seep through my cloak, sending a chill through me. "Huntress . . . please," I say, trying to appeal to something that remains of the woman who had been my mentor for so long. "This can work if you stick to the plan."

"You and I both know that is a lie," she says. "And if you cared about your mother, you would willingly put your neck under my blade."

"This is your duty, is that right?" I ask, my voice nearly breaking. "And still you can't see that this is how we continue to fall prey to the Knight. This cannot continue."

Huntress straightens up, and for a moment I think I've reached the rational part of her. But all hope is lost as she plants her back foot in the snow and lowers her head.

"You're right," she says. "It cannot."

She springs forward with more speed than I thought her capable of in her drunken state. I step to the side, but she catches my arm at the crook and swings me down into the snow. I'm on my feet before she can swing again. She rushes toward me and I raise my foot, bringing it down on her thigh mid-step. There's a sharp crack, and she screams into the night air. She grabs at her leg but does not fall. She grits her teeth and lunges at me. I step back but slip on a patch of snow and fall hard on my back. The air punches out of me, and I hardly have time to suck in another breath before Huntress falls on me, pinning me to the ground with the full weight of her body. She raises her dagger and brings it straight down, aiming for my chest. I twist to my right but not quickly enough. Her blade slices into my shoulder like a hot knife through butter. Pain courses through me like a bolt of lightning. I scream, and she withdraws the blade with a sickening squelch. My vision goes white and my stomach lurches. She raises the blade again as I hold up my hand in front of me. I see Huntress's face through a hazy fog of pain and confusion. Her eyes are wild, her mouth open, her lips dry and cracked.

"Huntress. Please."

This time the blade pierces my palm pinning it to my chest as the dagger scrapes against my ribs. Huntress leans on the blade with all her weight. I think of conjuring a weapon, but I stop. Maybe—maybe after all this, Huntress is right. If I am dead, there is no need for my mother to pretend. If I am to die, let it be for this, my mother's happiness.

I gasp as blood fills my mouth. I cough and red droplets fly out, spattering Huntress's face, landing in the white snow like rose petals. A swirling black mass descends on us. The calls are inside and outside my head. The crows, double the number I'd noticed before, fly at Huntress's back. They peck at the bare skin of her forehead, opening little wounds like small bloody mouths. They beat their wings furiously against her. Then suddenly, Huntress is careening backward. She hits a tree and lies still for a moment before turning over on her back, groaning.

I stare up at the black sky dotted with tiny pinpoints of light. It is beautiful. I hear the melodic whistling of other birds, the strange but familiar call of the fox. They stay hidden in the woods, but I feel in their secret calls the urge to come into the grove and say their final farewells. Had the crows done that to Huntress? I hadn't thought them capable of such violence, but I admire them for it. Then someone is standing over me. A searing pain awakens my senses, and I cry out as the person removes the dagger from my chest and then from my hand.

"Eve," they say.

I know that voice. It wasn't the birds that have saved me from Huntress despite their great efforts.

"Nova."

Huntress stumbles to her feet and glares at Nova, who stands between us. I can scarcely lift my head off the ground, but I grasp my dagger nonetheless.

"Kill her!" Huntress screams. "You know your father will not be fooled! He will come for us all! You think you will be spared? You won't!"

"Did you think I could not see your treachery?" Nova says, as if he is asking her about the weather. "You wear it as plainly as the clothes on your back."

"And you would know it, wouldn't you?" Huntress says. "Your own lies tangle you up even now!" Huntress pulls a knife from the folds of her clothing, a small glinting blade. "You think I won't use this on you?"

Nova clenches his jaw and balls his fists. Huntress and Nova rush toward each other. She swings the blade near his throat but he catches her wrist and wrestles the weapon from her. As soon as it's in his hand, he runs Huntress straight through. Nova yanks the hilt up, spilling Huntress's insides out onto the freshly fallen snow. Huntress collapses, and everything around me fades to black.

CHAPTER 13

The motion of the horse under me is like the gentle swaying of a ship. The saddle digs into my hip, reminding me that I am not on some restful journey. Nova cradles me against his chest. I feel him breathing, his warm breath in my face.

Fade in.

Fade out.

My vision is a mess of jumbled images—Nova's face, the night sky, a house in the distance with a column of gray smoke billowing from its chimney, a thatched roof over my head, warmth, and then pain. So much pain.

"The wound has to be packed or she'll bleed to death," a man's voice says.

"Do it," Nova answers.

"I don't know if she will survive," the man says. "The pain alone may be too much."

"She's stronger than she looks," Nova says.

Pain.

A high-pitched ringing in my ears.

Sweat breaking across my brow.

Then nothing.

I stare up at an unfamiliar ceiling. It feels like waking, but my eyes are already open. Maybe they'd never been closed, judging by how dry and scratchy they are. Each blink feels like tiny shards of glass grating into the skin of my eyelids. I try to speak but my throat is dry as sand. Then suddenly the pain in my chest, just above my heart on the left side, forces a groan from me.

"Try not to move too much," says a man's voice.

Seated at the foot of the small bed is a burly man in a checkered shirt and brown trousers. Clipped neatly just above his shirt collar, a beard of coarse salt-and-pepper hair covers his chin. His big brown eyes are framed by two bushy eyebrows. He quickly stands and his head is nearly the height of the ceiling. He puts a cup of piping hot liquid in my hands. I try to lift it, but the wound in my palm aches.

"May I help?" the man asks. He waits for my response.

I want to say no, but the liquid smells like heaven and I'm more parched than I've been in my entire life. I nod and he lifts the cup, pressing it to my lips. I sip the liquid and, while everything else in my body is still screaming in pain, my throat feels a little better.

"Always does the trick," he says as he sets the cup on the side table and readjusts the blanket around my feet, which are hanging off the end of a bed that's too short for my frame. "Sorry about that," the man says. "My youngest boy is the only one who won't mind giving up his bed. He's always looking for an excuse to sleep in mine." He scratches at his beard. "I'd have let you take mine, but I think if I tried to sleep on this thing it'd break into a million pieces."

"Where am I?" I ask. "Where's Nova? And who are you?" Panic begins to creep under my skin. I don't know this man, and the last things I remember clearly are Huntress trying to kill me and Nova saving me. My head is spinning. I reach for my dagger and find it missing.

"That's a lot of questions, but I promise I have a good answer on all fronts." The man smiles at me, showing that one of his front teeth is missing and the others are crowded together at odd angles. "You're in my home in South Queen's Bridge. We're on the southernmost border near Hamelin, right at the base of the South Steps. Nova said he'd be returning shortly. I am Claude Kingfisher."

"Kingfisher?" The name sounds familiar, and it takes me a moment to pull it from my mind. "There's a story about a man. A Kingfisher. The man with seven sons."

Claude pulls up a sturdy wooden chair and lowers his tall, broad frame into it. He leans back and stretches his arms high over his head, rubs his shoulder like it's giving him trouble, then tents his fingers in front of him.

"You must be wondering if that story was about me," says Claude, his tone flat.

180

I look around the room. Arranged in two neat rows are a total of seven nearly identical beds. Three of them are stripped of linens and bare but the rest look lived in—their patchwork quilts folded, shoes tucked neatly underneath. There are wooden toys in woven baskets and books on the low shelves.

"The story is true," Claude says. Something dark passes over his face as he confirms my suspicions. "Some of it, at least."

I try to pull myself up to sitting, but the pain knocks me back. I wince as the wound in my upper chest pulses. Claude reaches toward me, then pauses.

"May I help you?" he asks.

I nod, and he loops his giant hands under my arms and eases me to a sitting position. He stuffs a few pillows behind my back and tucks the blanket in around my legs.

"Better?" he asks.

"Yes. Thank you," I say. "The Kingfisher story is one I've only heard rumors of. No one ever seemed to have all the details."

Claude sighs. "And I suppose you'll want some of those details now?"

"I don't even know if it matters anymore," I say.

"If it's not too pressing, I say we save this conversation for another time." His brows push together. "I have quite a lot of things to attend to."

"Of course," I say.

He quickly checks the bandages on my hand and chest. "Your wounds are clean," he says. "And they will heal in time, but you need rest."

I lean back as a drowsy haze descends on me. I have time

but how much is still a question. I watched Nova kill Huntress, and I fear our plans have gone to rot. I wonder if Nova has been in touch with my mother, if Huntress's body has been recovered, and most importantly I wonder if the Knight now knows what we tried to do. Despite all the unanswered questions, the one that sits at the front of my mind is when or if I can ever see my mother again. The haze shifts to sleep, and I lose myself in the darkness for a while.

———————————

I wake to a small round face staring at me from the foot of the bed. The child, who cannot be more than eight or nine, peers at me with big brown eyes that are identical to Claude's.

"You're awake," he says in a soft, small voice. "Father told me to tell him when you woke up. I've been watching you. Did you know you snore like a beast?"

I'm not fond of small children. There are plenty of them running around the castle district, but they always seem dirty, loud, and annoying.

"I'm Chance. I'm ten. I'm happy to make your—your—"

"Acquaintance," Claude says as he enters the room carrying a tray with a bowl of soup and a steaming mug balancing on top. "Forgive him. We're still working on greetings."

I look at the boy again, and he grins. He has several teeth missing just like his father but his are probably due to the usual course of growing up.

"It's fine," I say. I look toward the window where a gauzy

orange glow is peeking through the heavy curtain. "It's evening? I slept all day?"

"You did!" says Chance. "Every time I came to check on you, you were sleeping, snoring, your mouth hanging open. There was even some drool on—"

"Chance," Claude says sternly. "Enough."

Chance gives his father a quick nod and grins at me.

I sit up, and while the pain is blinding for a split second I push through it and lean against the headboard to catch my breath. One of the frumpy pillows littering the bed falls to the floor and Chance quickly scoops it up, plumps it, and sets it back on the bed. From down the hall a chorus of voices chatters.

"Sounds like an army has come to dinner," I say.

Claude sets the tray on my lap and watches as I ladle a spoonful of the soup into my mouth. It is delicious, and the warmth of it makes me a feel a little better.

"Nothing to worry about," Claude says. "My sons, all growing, all eating. Might as well be an actual army."

I look down at my bowl.

Claude sits in the same wooden chair as before, his ankle crossed over his knee. "I wanted to let you know that you are safe here. I will not have it any other way."

His hospitality feels genuine and not just something he is obligated to do.

"Thank you," I say.

"And I thought I might give you some of the details to that story just so that you know what is real and what is the product of rumor and outright lies. I don't much appreciate people

183

talking behind my back, but I suppose it's inevitable, our circumstances being what they are."

I lean my head back on the pillow. "I've never spoken to anyone who knew the entire thing. People only suspect that you have something to do with the Knight."

Claude bristles at the mention of his name. "Yes, well, the story is fairly new. My youngest son is nine. I expect that people haven't sniffed out all the details yet, but they surely will, in time." He sighs and runs his hand through his beard, which seems to be a nervous action that he repeats over and over again.

"I'm simply called the Kingfisher in the tale," Claude says. "And forgive me, but if I am going to relate it to you, I have to tell it like a story."

"Why?" I ask. It seems like a strange thing to do, but I wait for his answer.

"It's my life," Claude says. "And the tale is so awful that sometimes it feels too close. Do you understand?"

I think I do. I can already see the sadness creeping across his kind face.

"It goes like this—the Kingfisher and his wife longed for a child and when they could not conceive, they made a deal with the Knight." Claude continues the tale as if he is reading it from a book, keeping his distance from the reality of it. "Kingfisher made a deal and asked the Knight to bless him and his wife with as many children as possible—and they got precisely what they asked for." Claude's expression darkens, and he nervously rubs his hand over the threadbare cloth of his trousers. "Nothing more, nothing less. The Kingfishers were blessed with a son. But not long after his birth they were blessed with another son. But there was no joy in this because Kingfisher had not lain with his wife." Claude's gaze drifts to the floor. "He did not doubt her, for she had been under his watchful eye as she recovered from bringing their first son into the world. And so it went. Seven sons in seven years. The magic worked by the Knight was relentless and terrible and exactly what they had asked for but with the terrible caveat that the Lady Kingfisher did indeed have as many children as she could before her body could no longer function under the strain. She died as she brought her seventh son into the world, and the Kingfisher boys and their father lived forever with the pain of her absence."

I watch Claude as he watches me. He breathes deep, filling his massive chest and letting it hiss out between his teeth. The faraway look in his eyes ebbs, and his clear gaze meets mine.

"My wife, Leah, is gone," Claude says, shifting out of his storytelling posture. "And with her three of the infants who did not see their first birthdays. Four boys remain, and they are my reason for living."

The story of the Kingfisher was a horrible tale. I knew that even before Claude shared the complete story with me. I cannot help but pity him. The man before me seems so kind, so attentive, I cannot imagine that he has been through the events of the story and is still, somehow, able to maintain his humanity.

"You made a deal with the Knight," I say.

"Yes," he says. "We did. My wife and I. We thought it was

a simple enough wish—a large family. That's what we both wanted more than anything."

"The Knight's deals are never simple," I say. Thoughts of my mothers making the same kind of wish for very similar reasons tumble through my head.

"I know that now." He runs his hand over the top of his head, and his eyes glaze over. "I think we knew it then, too. What is it that makes a person enter into a deal with him, knowing it can never be simple or easy?"

"I wish I knew the answer to that," I say. I think of my mother, of Sir Gregory, of all the people in Queen's Bridge who my mother had tried to help after their bargains with the Knight had gone terribly wrong. It is almost too much to think about.

"I need to get out of this bed," I say. "I feel like I'm wasting away sitting here."

Claude swoops in and moves the tray off my lap before extending his hand to me. "Go very slow. I don't want those stitches coming undone. They were a bear to get in on account of the jagged angles."

I touch the bandage covering the wound in my chest. Picturing Claude stitching up the injury with his impossibly large hands makes my stomach turn over.

"It's not pretty," Claude says, eyeing the bandage. "But I did my best."

"I don't need it to be pretty," I say. "Thank you for everything you've done. I'll be gone as soon as I'm able." I know this is where I'm meant to stay, but I'm already thinking of how to leave. I don't even think I'll need to escape. Something tells me Claude may let me walk right out the front door.

Claude presses his lips together and shakes his head. "Let's worry about walking down the hallway first. If you can manage that . . . well . . ."

I look into his eyes and search for some kind of deception in them. I search for the look I'd seen in Huntress's eyes as she betrayed me. There is nothing like that. Only kindness draped around a deep, hollow sadness.

I hold fast to his arm as I stand. My legs are heavy and sore. The first step almost ends me. My leg buckles at the knee, but Claude catches me and I right myself. We navigate the narrow hall together. Every breath I take puts a stabbing pain in my chest. I try to distract myself by looking at the strange decorations lining the walls in the hall. There are deer and elk heads mounted to wooden plaques. Crisscrossed snowshoes hang from a rusted nail, and a few old bear traps sit on a high shelf. A bouquet of dried flowers hangs upside down from a metal hook. There are a few paintings of a beautiful brown-skinned woman with long black hair. I see Chance's face in hers.

"Leah," Claude says, as he follows my gaze.

"She's beautiful," I say.

He gives me a tight smile. "That she was."

I am winded by the time we enter the dining room and immediately fall into the nearest chair as four young boys stare at me in silence from their seats at the table. All of them have Claude's eyes and Leah's mouth and cheekbones. They are near identical copies of each other, with the older ones just beginning to grow scant facial hair.

"Father," says a tall gangly boy with a halo of tight black coils. "Are you sure she should be up? She looks awful."

I narrow my gaze at him.

He shrugs. "Sorry. I just meant that you have a black eye and a busted lip. You look like you need sleep and soup and not much else."

"You're not wrong," Claude says. "But she wants to be up and about."

"And that's her choice," says the little boy who'd called himself Chance as he crosses his arms hard over his chest. "Stop trying to tell her what to do, Hunter."

"I'm not," Hunter says. He turns to his father. "Chance is trying to distract you from the fact that he ate all the biscuits before anybody else even had a chance to get one."

"Greedy," says another boy.

"Am not! Father, tell Junior to stop picking on me!" Chance stomps his foot on the floor and sticks out his bottom lip.

"All right, now settle down," Claude says. The boys quiet immediately. "Eve is our guest. She's here from—someplace quite far from here and she'll be staying as long as she needs. I'd like you to help her if she needs help and leave her be when she doesn't." He turns to me. "These are the Kingfisher boys. Claude Junior is the eldest. He's fifteen. Then comes Hunter, who is fourteen. Chance you've already met, and my youngest, Grumpy."

I have to stifle a laugh, mostly because it's painful but also because I have a hard time believing the youngest boy's given name is Grumpy.

"It's a nickname," says the youngest little boy. He shrugs. "I'm grumpy sometimes."

"All the time," grumbles Junior.

Claude clears his throat. "Introductions have been made. Can we eat now? I'm famished."

The boys clap their hands and, after some excited murmuring, begin spooning dollops of mashed potatoes and corn onto their plates. I'm glad when Claude sets a bowl of soup in front of me. I don't think my stomach can handle a full meal quite yet.

"Chance, fetch a bottle of cider from the cellar," Claude says.

Chance jumps up and goes to a small hatch in the kitchen floor. He disappears into what I can only assume is a root cellar and returns with a corked bottle. He hands it to his father and Claude pours out a bit of cider for each of them. The Kingfisher family raise their cups and I copy the gesture as best I can. My arm feels stiff and sore, but I hold it steady.

"For mother," Junior says. "And for Ace, The Kid, and Fisher. We love you still and always will."

They all take a sip of their cider and set their cups down on the table. My heart has already been shattered by the events of the previous days, but this scene nearly destroys the pieces that are left.

From under the table comes a low rumble, and I freeze. The sound is audible, but as it grows louder the call sounds in my head where only I can hear it. It is the quiet call of a wolf, but it is mixed with something else, some kind of hound.

"What is that?" I ask, gesturing to the space under the table.

"Maggie," Chance says.

I lift the faded tablecloth to reveal a wolf. My heart crashes against my ribs. No. On second glance, it's not a wolf, but it might as well be one. A dog the size of a small bear is curled on the floor at Chance's feet. She raises her head and regards me lazily, and then she nudges Chance's leg with her massive head. He runs his stockinged feet over her back, and she lapses back into sleep.

"Her mother was a wolf," Claude says. "She's a big softie when it comes to the boys, but she returns to those feral instincts of hers when she senses trouble. Most loyal dog you'll ever know."

She's as big as the dire wolf Huntress and I had seen in the woods. Even thinking of Huntress leaves a bitter, angry feeling in my gut. I lower the cloth and lean back in my chair as the boys talk of hunting, which is apparently how the boy called Hunter got his nickname. They speak of fishing and a shortage of trout in the pond nearby. They laugh and joke and eat until their bellies are full and their eyes are heavy with sleep.

They clear the table, with the two older boys washing the dishes in a basin of soapy water and the younger two wiping down the table and sweeping the floor. Claude takes the food scraps outside where the boys inform me he keeps a few hogs penned up. When he rejoins me at the table, each of the boys gives him a hug, and he presses his forehead into theirs one at a time, telling them he loves them and then sending them off to bed.

"Good night, Eve," says the little boy called Grumpy. I smile at him. For someone so little he does indeed have a deeply furrowed brow that makes him look like a grumpy old man.

I stretch my hand toward the window near the front of the cozy little house and, from the frost on the sill, make the outline of a heart. Grumpy's eyes grow wide and his mouth opens into a little O. He turns to his father.

"Pa. You didn't say she was magic."

Claude looks troubled. "I didn't know."

Grumpy skips off to bed, and Claude pours me a cup of tea.

I wrap my injured hand around the warm mug, which eases the ache a little. "Can I ask you something?" I say.

Claude nods as he sips his own tea.

"Nova brought me here, but how do you know him?"

He sets his cup down and sighs. "He is the Knight's liaison."

I lean back. "So he helped you broker your deal with the Knight?"

He nods but does not look up. "Indeed he did."

"And you don't hate him for what he did? For his part in it?"

He looks up then. "I'm assuming you made his acquaintance the same way I did."

"I have never made a deal with the Knight. I'm not that foolish."

Claude winces and I immediately wish I had kept my mouth shut. "I'm sorry," I say. "I didn't mean to—"

He waves it off and takes another swig of his drink. "I'm

glad you've never been desperate enough to feel like that was ever an option for you. Some of us are not so lucky."

"My mother made a deal with him and I am at the very center of it," I say. "I didn't even know until recently."

"If a queen feels the need to seek him out, what hope is there for the rest of us?" Claude rests his hands on the table. "I'm sorry. I'm usually not so glum, but you've said it yourself. Innocent people are always hurt in the process of fulfilling his terms, and it feels like we'll never be free from him. But to answer your question, no. I do not hate Nova for his part in any of it. I sense that there is something that binds him to the Knight. Something dreadful and inescapable."

So, Nova had not disclosed his relationship with the Knight to Claude. I wonder why he had shared something he obviously wished to keep secret with me and my mother.

"He seems just as much a pawn in the Knight's game as we are," Claude says. "I have tried to forgive him because holding on to the hatred I once felt was too heavy a burden. It is not what my Leah would have wanted for me. At times, I still feel it, but it will do me no good."

I didn't know Claude's wife at all, but I wonder if that's what she really would have wanted or if it is just what he tells himself to feel better.

There is suddenly a rapping at the door, and I stop breathing. Claude goes to the door and as he reaches for the handle he also reaches into his waistband and draws out a hunting knife with a glinting serrated edge. I stretch my hand toward the flames in the hearth and an arc of yellow flame streams out and shapes itself into a dagger made of fire and ash. Claude blinks, and a smile flits across his lips. He pulls the door open and Nova quickly steps inside. He eyes the knife of flame in my hand and the one of steel in Claude's.

"Please don't kill me," Nova says.

I let the weapon I'd forged disappear into a cloud of smoke, but Claude holds tight to his knife for a moment longer before closing the door. Nova takes a seat at the table next to me and Claude retakes his chair. He does not look Nova in the eye. Nova pulls his hood away from his head. His face seems a little more gaunt than usual, and his eyes have lost some of their luster.

"How are your wounds?" Nova asks, eyeing the bandage on my hand.

"Painful, but healing, thanks to Claude."

Nova glances at him. "Thank you for agreeing to this."

"I have to try and redeem myself somehow," Claude says.

I glance at Claude. I had seen and heard nothing requiring redemption since I'd been in Claude's home.

Nova shakes his head. "You've done that a hundred times over. You are a good man, Claude."

Claude tilts his head. "I'm not. And you know it."

A silence full of pain and sadness swallows them up. Nova places his hand on the table next to mine—not touching but close enough for me to feel the warmth emanating from him. I move my hand away.

Nova turns to me. "I needed to tell you that I returned to the Knight, and he is convinced the terms of your mother's deal have been fulfilled."

I whip my head around. I had convinced myself that we had failed and that the Knight was preparing to seek his revenge. "How is that possible?" I can barely contain my relief.

"Your mother's sorrow is real and it is palpable," Nova says.

I clench my teeth so hard my jaw aches. I can't stand the thought of not seeing her again. I don't know how I'm supposed to accept it.

"That's all the convincing that was needed?" Claude asks, doubt coloring his words. "The Knight was so easily convinced?"

"No," Nova says. "But there was enough blood in the snow to convince him you'd met a grisly end." He hesitates then, and I know there is something he is holding back.

"And Huntress?" Speaking her name sends a bolt of anger straight through me. The betrayal still stings, but I need to know what has become of her.

"She did her part to convince the Knight you are dead," Nova says.

I lean forward, my chest aching. "She did?" She had been so unconvinced that she had tried to make our ruse a reality, but she somehow convinced the Knight I am dead.

Nova's eyes glass over as he looks down at the floor. "Her heart was in the wooden box I gifted to the Knight. So yes, she played her part quite well."

"You—you put her heart in the box?" I struggle to find the words to respond.

"I did," says Nova. "And I was happy to do it. She would have killed you. I have no doubt of it."

Better Huntress's heart in the box than mine, but by Nova's hand? Before I have a chance to think it through, I reach out and close my hand over Nova's.

"You saved my life. I owe you a debt."

Nova glances at me, and for a moment, there is nothing else—just he and I and some strange spark that reignites between us, something I'd seen a flicker of when we'd danced the night of my birthday celebration. I quickly draw back my hand.

Nova looks into his lap. "I am not my father. You owe me no such thing."

Silence fills the space between us before Claude clears his throat.

"Nothing quite like bonding over a murder and a dismemberment, I suppose," Claude says.

"Huntress tried to kill me," I say.

"Oh, I'm not implying it wasn't justified," Claude says. "But if we are monsters, at least let us be honest about it."

"I am not a monster," I say.

"I wasn't talking about you," Claude says, staring directly at Nova.

Nova turns his head just slightly to look at Claude, though his expression doesn't change. Something silent passes between them.

"I'm sorry," Claude says. "That is not what I meant. I've let my anger get the better of me."

"I don't hold it against you," Nova says.

"She would," Claude says, and I know he must be speaking of his wife.

Claude excuses himself from the table. He had said he didn't hate Nova for his part in his family's sorrow, but there are things just as heavy as hate—resentment, regret. I sigh, and again pain rockets through my chest and back.

"I'm sorry I didn't get to you sooner," Nova says as his gaze moves over my bandaged wounds.

"Why did you come at all?" I ask. "If Huntress had succeeded, the terms of the deal my mother made with your father would be fulfilled by now. There would have been no need for a ruse."

Nova's eyes glint in the firelight. "You think I want you dead?"

"I'm having a very hard time figuring out what you want," I say. "You were goading my mother into keeping up her part in the Knight's bargain, which meant killing me on my seventeenth birthday. But then you saved me from Huntress, when letting me die would have been much easier."

"Easier for who?" he asks, a tone of surprise ringing in his voice. He readjusts himself in the chair. "Your mother will miss you until the day she dies. Her wife is gone from her and now her daughter. Gone but not really. Both of them so close and yet so far out of reach. I think that is a fate worse than if either you or Queen Sanaa had actually died, but I still could not allow you to be . . ." He trails off, lost in his own head.

I cannot stop the torrent of tears from spilling over.

"All of this is awful," Nova says. "You will be devastated by this dreadful turn of events. And I—I am affected as well."

I glance at him through my tears. "You?"

196

He nods. "For my part in all of it. Forgive me or don't. It makes no difference, because I must live with what I have done. It never leaves me. There is no forgiveness to be had. Not for me."

"You should forgive yourself," I say.

Nova huffs. "I haven't earned that. I don't know that I ever can." He lifts his head, his gaze meeting mine. "Maybe, one day, I can earn your forgiveness. That may be the only thing that truly matters to me."

I stay quiet, because I understand now that there is something between us. I cannot deny that I find him devastatingly beautiful and unforgivably tragic. I know I shouldn't want to forgive him, but I do and I wonder what it might take for that to happen.

"Saving you was the right thing to do," Nova says. "I have not always done what is right. In fact, more often, I chose to do the wrong thing. It is in my nature."

"So which is it? Choice or nature? It can't be both."

Nova pushes his chair back and stands. "It doesn't matter."

"It matters to me," I say. "I'm alive because of you. Mekhi would be alive, too, if we'd listened to you—if *I* had listened." I bite back tears as my thoughts wander to images of Mekhi's broken body lying cold under the snow and half-frozen earth. "Maybe I *am* a monster."

Nova shifts his gaze to the fire in the hearth. "I have seen you through your mother's eyes. I can't imagine being loved the way she loves you."

"All mothers love their children," I say.

Nova looks stricken. "That, Princess, is so far from the truth I can't begin to explain it to you." He reaches into the folds of his cloak and pulls out a shining piece of jagged black glass. He sets it on the table. "A piece of the mirror from your mother's chamber. I must leave for a while. My father beckons, and if I don't go, he'll be suspicious."

A tug in the pit of my stomach makes me sit straight up. "You're leaving?"

"You'll be fine. Claude is a very capable caretaker. Not that you need it now that your wounds are healing."

I find myself searching for some excuse to make him stay. "You know Claude well, then?" I ask. "He said you facilitated the deal he made with the Knight."

Nova nods. "Of all the deals my father has struck, what he did to Lady Kingfisher was truly one of the worst things I have ever been witness to." He sucks in a breath and holds it, turning away from me. "I tried very hard to save her from her fate, but it was not to be. Claude says he's forgiven me for my part in it, but what happened was unforgivable. He should hold it against me until his dying breath."

"You want his forgiveness?" I ask. "That means something to you?"

Nova is quiet for a moment before answering. "He believes that I am worthy of that. He doesn't know me the way he thinks he does."

"Do you think you are worthy of forgiveness?" I ask.

Nova's shoulders slump, and he suddenly looks tired, worn down. "No. No, I don't think I am." He pulls his cloak in close around his neck.

I want to ask him a question, but I am afraid to know the true answer. I'm afraid it will make me hate him the way I had when I first came to realize who he is and what role he had played in my mother's suffering. I ask anyway. "Why do you do it? Why do you continue to help the Knight?"

Nova presses his mouth into a hard line. "I don't have another choice. I am bound to him. And if I am being honest, for a very long time, I did his bidding willingly. But then I—" He stops short.

"What?" I press him. "What happened?"

"I saw the deal that was made to bring you into being, the payment it required, the way he used me to manipulate your mother's feelings. I didn't want to do it, but the Knight—my father—he has ways of getting exactly what he wants and what he has wanted more than anything is to force the Miller Queen—your mother—to participate in his treachery so he could hurt her in a way that was crueler than most." Nova pauses.

"It bothered you that much?" I ask.

He nods. "Yes, but that wasn't the only thing." A weary, broken smile pulls at the corners of his mouth. "You saw the man he was torturing with your own eyes. On whom do you think he honed those skills?"

A sick feeling settles in the pit of my stomach. "Nova, I—"

"I don't want your pity," he says quickly. "You asked me why I do it, why I help him, and my answer is that I didn't have a choice and I was too loyal to him to care about what he did before I saw your mother's deal with him. It broke something in me. Something I cannot put back together." Nova sighs and shakes his head. "I have to go. If you need me—" He stops and those words hang in the air between us. "Use the mirror shard."

"Will you come back?" I keep my eyes fixed on the dying fire, taking in everything Nova has shared.

He comes to the table and puts his hand on top of mine. "Yes. But I cannot say when."

I glance up at him. He doesn't smile. He simply looks at me as if he is seeing me clearly. I want him to stay, but he turns and leaves the cabin, closing the door behind him.

CHAPTER 14

Nova appears to me in the mirror every third night for weeks. Where there had once been anger at seeing his image appear in the gleaming black stone, there is now a tempered sense of anticipation. A simmering tension still exists between us but now buries itself deep in my gut, deliciously twisting. I have not forgiven him, and he has not asked me to, but it is not necessary in these moments.

When he appears in the shard, I watch his mouth as he speaks to me of my mother, whom he has kept an eye on from afar. I want to know what he has seen, and it comforts me to know that he watches her, but I hate that he distracts me this way. I don't think he is trying to tempt me so. He cannot help himself—or maybe it is me who cannot be helped. His lips part to tell me my mother is in good health but almost never in good spirits, though she hides it well enough. His brow pushes up as he speaks of his own father, though he is always guarded.

"And you," he always asks. "What is the state of your heart?"

I feel as if he is asking me about how much I miss my mother but only on the surface. There is something else there. Every time he asks, I have to stop myself from saying that my heart trips into a furious rhythm when I see him in the shard, that my heart yearns to see him, face-to-face. But I have a terrible habit of leaving those things out. Our conversations always end the same way.

"Will you meet me at this same hour three days from now?" he asks. "It is not required, and I will not hold it against you if you choose not to."

"I will meet you," I say every single time.

"Then I will be waiting here . . . for you."

And when he disappears from the shard, and it is always he that goes first, I feel a sense of loss, of longing. I dare not speak it aloud. It is too much in the midst of this delicate and perilous situation. I am no fool. I understand that some, if not most, of Nova's actions are unforgivable, but he does not seek absolution from me, only understanding, and I give that to him. I think of all I have been trained to do—to take a life when the time calls for it—to kill the Knight and anyone who might have stood in my way. I think about my part in Mekhi's death. Nova and I are not so different, but to hear him tell it, he is a villain. He has accepted that of himself. What he did not expect was that I would accept it as well.

Claude tends to my wounds, and three weeks into my stay I have healed enough to help with daily chores. Each week, when Claude goes to work in the emerald mines on the South Steps, he's gone for days at a time, often taking Junior and Hunter with him while the two youngest boys pick up the slack at the cabin. Chance is only ten, and yet he is more capable than some adults I've met. He keeps his younger brother in line, though there is barely a year between them. I don't stand in their way. I have no interest in being a surrogate caregiver to them, and Claude made it clear that this is not expected of me. However, when they need to cut firewood to keep the cabin warm, I am more than happy to supervise so that they don't end up less any limbs.

One evening, nearly six weeks after Huntress had almost put my heart in a wooden box for the Knight, I wait on the front steps in the chilly nighttime air as Claude, Junior, and Hunter come over the nearby ridge, returning from a four-day stint in the mines. I hear them before I see them. They sing a rhythmic tune, something old and haunting. Claude says it's a melody passed to him from his great-grandfather, a man who worked the same mines Claude and his sons toil in. Their song is carried in on the wind, and when I have them in my sight, I send a blanket of starry night sky to envelope them and keep them warm as they make their way home.

"Eve!" Junior yells as he bounds up to me, wrapping his arms around my waist. "We have missed you!"

I laugh and hug him back. "I didn't miss you at all," I tease. The truth is that I miss him and Hunter and even

Claude very much when they are gone. They have become dear to me.

Claude lumbers onto the porch, and it's only then that I spy the deer slung across his back. He gives me a quick smile.

"Hope you didn't have too much trouble with that," I say, pointing to the field-dressed animal.

Claude laughs heartily and pats me on the shoulder with his free hand. "We'll eat good for the next few days because of him." He slings the deer down and stands in front of me, his face softening for a moment. He's about to say something to me when Chance bursts from the door and leaps into Claude's arms, squealing and laughing. Maggie follows him and twists herself around Claude's legs. He scratches between her ears.

Inside, after Claude and his oldest sons wash up, we sit at the table together as Chance stokes the hearth to a roaring blaze. Hunter divvies up parts of the freshly butchered deer. The smell of salted, seared meat and boiled turnips with rosemary wafts through the air and makes my mouth water. Chance and Grumpy relentlessly tease each other, each jab more pointed and piercing than the last, though they never stray so far as to hurt any actual feelings. They chatter and laugh and welcome their father and brothers home. I sit near Claude as he looks over his family. As much love as he has for them, there is sadness in his gaze, always sadness. He pats my hand when he realizes I'm watching him and eyes the healing wound, which I now leave unbandaged.

"It looks good," he says. "It's healing up nicely. I hope the boys didn't give you a hard a time while I was gone."

"Oh," Chance says, grinning. "We gave her the worst time."

Claude looks at him and tilts his head.

"There's something different about you," Claude says as he searches Chance's face.

"He's nearly bald now," I say.

Claude's eyes widen. I don't hold it against him that he didn't notice right away. There are four heads of hair in various lengths, each with a nearly identical face, and Claude isn't a man who cares much about such things.

"He slept in the barn the other night," I say. "Came back with lice so I had to cut his hair. I boiled his sheets and clothes. Nobody else seems to be affected."

Chance runs his hand over the top of his head and grins. "I like it this way."

"Your head is shiny as a seeing stone," Claude says. "I bet I could see the future in that thing."

The boys laugh and I smile, but it reminds me that my time with Nova is approaching. He doesn't usually appear in the glass shard until after the sun has set and not once in the intervening six weeks has he appeared fully in front of me. It makes me wonder about the nature of the looking glass itself. It seems that the only one Nova can travel through is the one in my mother's chamber. I had seen Nova in other surfaces, but he had never stepped out of any of them. I am convinced that this is at the whim of the Knight. It is just another way to control all the moving pieces.

The boys finish their meal and begin to make their ways to their room. When they've all gone, I push my chair back.

"Stay for a moment," Claude says. His tone is serious. I've learned that he is very careful about what he does and does not say in front of the children. I retake my seat.

"I hope you aren't too upset about Chance's hair," I say.

He waves his hand in front of him. "Not at all. In fact . . . ," he trails off, his eyes glassy. I begin to worry. "They all look so much alike and yet they all have their own ways of being."

"I've noticed," I say.

"I see them growing into who they will become and it makes me think of who their brothers might have been—the ones Leah and I lost."

The silence is delicate as the thin layer of ice that lays across the land in the late fall.

"Fisher, Ace, and The Kid." Claude says their names like prayers whispered to the gods. "I often wonder who they would be now. I think I know what they would look like, but what would they like? What would they fear?"

I place my hand over Claude's, though it doesn't cover it by half. He shakes himself and straightens up.

"I'm sorry," he says. "That's not what I'd intended to share with you."

"Now that I know their names I can speak them into the dark like I have for others who have been lost." I think of Mekhi. How many times have I said his name?

Claude nods and swallows hard. "I have something important to speak to you about, but I wanted to wait until the boys had gone."

My heart ticks up a little.

"We have a courier stationed at the mine," he says. "He runs messages from our location to nearby places. Usually orders of emerald for merchants, but often they bring with them news as well. Even from as far away as Castle Veil."

"News?" I ask. I suddenly understand what he's saying, and I stand up. "There's news from the castle?"

Claude nods and his gaze drifts to the hallway. "Yes, news. And not good, I'm afraid."

My heart is suddenly racing, and I begin to tremble. "Tell me now."

Claude takes a deep breath. "The Queen has taken ill."

"Ill?" I repeat the word as if I've never heard it before. "I don't understand."

"This illness, whatever it is, has kept our Queen locked in her bedchamber," he says. "Speaking audibly to herself for weeks. There is a real fear she has gone mad after your supposed loss and that if she cannot recover, Queen's Bridge will be left defenseless against the Knight."

I push the chair back and race to my room, a small broom closet Claude had emptied for me and that the boys had decorated with wreaths of dried sunflowers. There is enough room for a straw-stuffed pallet and my meager belongings to fit. I strip off my clothes and layer on my thickest winter undergarments. It is the dead of winter now and the ride will be long and rough.

"Eve," Claude says as he approaches. "Eve, listen to me very closely. If you go back now, all of this—everything you have done will have been for absolutely nothing."

"I have to go," I say. I'm already pulling on my boots over my two pairs of woolen socks.

"And if you're seen?" Claude asks. "If someone gets word to the Knight that you are still alive? What then?"

"I don't know," I say. "I don't care."

"Well, we care," Claude says, glancing at the closed door to the boys' room. "You've become a very dear part of this family, and *we* care, Eve." He sighs. "And I would be lying if I said my concern is only for you. How difficult will it be for someone to track you back here if you are spotted? I cannot put my family at risk, and I don't think you want that either."

I pause to look at him. That sadness he always wears suddenly seems more obvious, and a pang of guilt ripples through me. "I will wear a cloak of the darkest night. No one will see anything but a shadow. I promise." I look to the boys' room. "I would not risk their safety for anything in the world and on the impossible chance that I am seen, I will not return. I have to see her. Something is wrong. She knows that I am still alive and yet she grieves. Why?" A million possibilities tumble through my head. Did she not believe what she said when she promised we would be together again? "And if it is not grief that moves her, what is it? Why hide herself away? And who is she speaking to?" It all feels wrong, and the urgency to get to her builds in me, threatening to bring about some reckless, regrettable action on my part.

"Eve," a voice says suddenly, and I nearly jump out of my skin.

Claude glances toward my sleeping mat. I rush to my

bedside and take the shard of the seeing stone from under it. Nova's face is reflected in its glassy surface.

"If you're thinking of leaving, I would ask you to reconsider," Nova says, his voice echoing from the glass.

"You weren't going to tell me something was wrong?" I ask, annoyed. "I already have my mind made up. Don't try to talk me out of it." I sound like a petulant child. I know that. And Claude is looking at me like he looks at the boys when they get a little too mouthy for his liking. "I know the risks and I'm willing to assume them all."

"And the danger you're putting Claude and his family in?" Nova asks. "Will you assume that risk, too?"

I glance at Claude, who pulls at the back of his neck.

"If you're caught, if you're followed, they will be in danger," Nova says.

"I know what you're trying to do," I say. "But I have already thought about that part."

"I pity the person who thinks descending on my homestead would be a good idea," Claude says, his tone low and serious. "I have plenty of room for graves on my land."

I don't doubt Claude's will, but I still don't want to risk it. "I'll take a longer route back to the castle just to make certain I'm not followed. The animals will warn me if someone is nearby. I have tools at my disposal that will help me."

Claude nods but not because the answer satisfies him. He turns and walks back down the hall.

"If I can't convince you to stay with Claude, can I at least ask you to wait?" Nova asks.

I stare at his glinting eyes in the mirror. "Wait for what?"

"For me to arrive so that I may accompany you," he says.

"I don't think it's necessary," I say, though there is a part of me that would very much like to be in the same room with him for even just a moment. I haven't seen him face-to-face since that cold night just after my arrival at Claude's home.

"Give me a few hours," he says. The glass goes dark before I can protest.

I finish dressing, sealing myself up against the cold. Claude brings a sturdy horse from the stable and tethers her to a post outside. Her voice in my head is strong and clear. She is ready for the journey and so am I.

Claude packs me a few days' worth of food in a small satchel and then retires to his room without another word. I cannot help but feel as if I am letting him down somehow, but I have to get to my mother. I sit at the table in the dying light of the fire, waiting impatiently for Nova to arrive. I could go without him, I should. But I wait.

My attention is suddenly drawn to the hallway where Junior is standing in his nightclothes, sleep clouding his eyes. He looks over my attire, and his mouth turns down.

"You're leaving?" he asks.

"Yes," I say. "But it's temporary. I'll be back soon."

Junior shuffles over and sits down in the chair next to me. "Where are you going?"

I shake my head. "I think it's best if I don't say."

Junior's brow furrows, and he bites at his bottom lip. He looks so much like his father it is uncanny.

"My father thinks of you like a daughter," he says. "Me and my brothers think of you like a sister."

A knot claws its way up my throat.

"So if you leave and something happens, we'll all be very upset." Junior readjusts himself on the seat. "My parents never had a daughter. They wanted one, I think, just to change things up a little."

"That makes sense," I say, forcing a smile though my heart is breaking wide open.

"My mother isn't here anymore," Junior says, and for just a moment his eyes glass over, the firelight glinting off them. "But I think she would have liked you as much as we all do." He sighs and shrugs his shoulders.

The knot in my throat threatens to choke me. I try to swallow it. I consider staying. For the boys and for Claude but also for myself. I care for them as much as they care for me.

"I lost a mother as well," I say. "And to the Knight, no less."

Junior and I exchange glances and a dreadful knowing. Only those of us who have seen the worst of what the Knight is capable of can truly understand. I suddenly worry that I have overstepped. I search my memory, trying to recall if Claude had ever told me he'd shared the circumstances of his wife's death with the boys.

"I'm sorry," I say. "I've said too much."

"Nothing I didn't already know," Junior says. "I know about the deal my parents made with him. I know everything, even though I wish I didn't."

I close my hand over his and lean close to him. "The

Knight took one mother from me. I can't let him take another. I have to make sure she's okay."

"You have two moms?" Junior asks.

"Yes," I say. "Or at least, I did."

"I love my father, but two moms?" He seems lost in thoughts for a moment before returning his gaze to me. "It's hard to think about that much love."

He's right, and it burns me up inside.

"You said the Knight took one of them from you?" he asks.

I nod. "He did."

Junior squeezes my hand. "You have to make sure he doesn't take anything else from you." He stands, stretches, and smiles warmly at me. "Will you bring me something back?"

"Like what?" I ask.

He shrugs. "Surprise me?"

"Is this your way of making sure I come back?" I ask.

Junior's mouth pulls up at the corners. "Yes." With that, he returns to his room and closes the door.

Not a moment later, there is a knock at the front door and I answer it. Nova sweeps in, draped in black, his hair pulled away from his face. His eyes are like stars against a midnight sky. I stand in front of him, speechless. I have thought about this moment for weeks, and in all that time I hadn't come up with anything meaningful to say.

"You—you're here," I say. I hear myself say the words and wish I could take them back immediately. Heat rises in my face and stirs something deep inside me.

"I am," Nova says. "Because you don't know how to just sit still. You are impossible."

"I think we have that in common," I say. "You knew my mother was ill and you didn't tell me?"

Nova steps closer to me. The chilly outside air still clings to him. He smells of the wind. "I was going to tell you. I wanted to be the one to tell you but word—or should I say gossip—travels fast."

"Gossip? So, she isn't sick?"

Nova shakes his head. "No. She is under siege."

"What does that mean?" I demand.

Nova gazes down at me, and I find myself once again, in the midst of a serious conversation, looking at his mouth, the curl of his lip. "The Knight is confident his deal with your mother has been fulfilled, but he will not let her rest. He sends images into the mirror. Images of your death. He taunts her. He is trying to break her."

My stomach turns over. "Why? He got what he wanted. Why continue this cruelty?"

"Because he must win," Nova says. "At all costs. He would have the whole of Queen's Bridge cowering before him. Tell me, when was the last time you heard about a wish going to plan? He will have his fun one way or the other. He has finished the game he began at your mother's wish and now he wants nothing more than to make her enter into another deal with him so that he may have another chance to hurt her."

"Another deal?" I ask.

Nova nods. "I think he is hoping your mother will ask him

to bring you back from the dead or ease her heartache over your loss. He can't understand why your mother is so steadfast in her resolve and that could be a problem for us all." Nova lowers his voice to barely a whisper and leans so close to me I can feel his breath on my face. "He doesn't know you still live and that it is the sole reason your mother doesn't buckle under the pressure. She holds to that secret knowledge, but it only makes him push harder. That is her affliction. Not sickness or injury—it is the strain of torturous, relentless torment."

A white-hot anger courses through me. "And you watch it happen?"

Nova's expression shifts in the dancing light of the fire. "I told you, I don't have a choice."

That small part of me that hates him, that remembers what he has done, swells.

"I spend every waking moment trying to keep her from tipping off the edge of a chasm," Nova says. "I try to remind her of what is real while keeping our secret safe from the Knight. I do not know how long this will last. He has all the time anyone could ever ask for."

I pull my cloak in close around me as the wind whips a pattering of snow and ice against the window. I'm not looking forward to going out into the weather, but I have my mind made up.

"I'm ready to leave," I say.

Nova stands still, his gaze moving over me from head to toe.

"And I'm not changing my mind," I say. "You asked me to wait for you. I have."

Nova puts his hands on my shoulders and under my layers of wool and linen my skin feels as if it has been set aflame. I know what it's like to hold a sword made of fire, and the way the heat skips across my skin is nothing compared to this. His hands trail down my arms until our hands are nearly touching. He bends his head, and his mouth trails along my cheek. I think I hear him whisper my name, but the blood roaring in my own ears blots out the sound. He lifts his chin and a mask of uncertainty pulls itself across his face.

"Forgive me," he says, stepping back.

"There is nothing to forgive," I say.

I move past him, allowing my shoulder to brush gently against him, and step out into the blustery night air. Nova follows.

CHAPTER 15

The journey to the castle is a full day's ride but it will take us longer than that. We are traversing a far less traveled route to be certain I'm not followed or seen by anyone on the more well-worn paths through the wilderness. Before we leave the safety of Claude's land, I pull a cloak of the darkest corner of the night sky and drape it around my shoulders. A passerby might have seen a shadow among other endless shadows, nothing out of the ordinary, but we came upon no one in our first hours.

I ride through the night, with Nova keeping pace, but we do not speak. I am too afraid that someone will hear. Still, I can feel Nova's eyes on me. I want to turn and look at him but I do not, and when the sun rises we have rounded the northernmost edge of the South Steps and are heading east to the castle. Before midday, we stop to water our horses and feed ourselves.

I jump down, stretching out my legs and my back. The cloak of darkness disintegrates into wisps of black smoke. There's a searing hot pain in my left chest, and I instinctively touch the place where Huntress's dagger had ripped open my skin and scraped the bone beneath. When I pull my hand away, my fingers are wet and red. Blood. I quickly pull off my cloak and open the neck of my shirt to expose the bandage. Nova is suddenly there, staring at the blood-soaked fabric.

"How is it still weeping?" Nova asks. "It's been weeks."

"It *is* healing but the wound was jagged," I say. "Claude had trouble stitching it closed. It's fine. It's nothing." I wipe my bloody hand off on my pants.

"You're bleeding and it's nothing?" Nova looks confused.

I shrug away from him. I don't have time to be injured. I need to keep moving. Nova's hands are suddenly on me, holding me in place.

"What are you doing?" I ask, annoyed.

"Just sit down for a moment," Nova says. "We'll bandage the wound."

"I don't have time. I want to get to the castle and—" My head suddenly feels dizzy and spots of light dance around the edges of my vision. I stagger and Nova steadies me, his hands on my waist.

"Sit," he says forcefully.

I do but only because I don't have another choice. My legs go out from under me, and I collapse into a seated position. Nova darts around and soon he's got a fire going and is pulling at the neck of my shirt.

"Just take it off," he says, quietly frustrated. "I know it's freezing, but I need to see the wound in order to dress it properly."

"It's not really the cold I'm worried about," I say.

"You're worried about modesty?" he asks. "There's no one here except me."

I look into his face. "Exactly."

"Please," Nova says, dismissing my concerns. "Bleed to death or have your bare chest out. Which is it?"

I glance around. We're still a half day's ride from the castle, and I want to keep going but the lightheaded feeling rears up every time I even think about standing.

I attempt to conjure a curtain of snow to shield me but I can't muster the strength. Nova goes to his horse and retrieves a small piece of folded cloth from his saddlebag and holds it up in front of me.

"Go on, then," he says, muttering something about me being impossible as I shrug out of my overcoat and pull my shirt off over my head.

"Are you decent?" he asks.

"No," I say. "But that's not going to change."

Nova drops the cloth and leans in so close to me I can smell the wind in his hair. He tucks the cloth around my chest so that the only exposed skin is at my shoulders. He examines my wound, which has come apart at the top edge, a spot that had been tricky to mend because of how close to my collar bone it is.

"Claude stitched this?" Nova asks.

I nod.

"He should be arrested." He sits back and stares at my wound, dabbing at it with the corner of my discarded shirt. "I need to restitch it."

"No," I say as I attempt to get up. "Leave it. We need to keep going."

Nova pushes me back down, and the wound belches a crimson river. "We could cauterize the wound, if you prefer," he says. "That might be quicker but the pain will be worse. Much, much worse. And the smell—"

"Stop," I say. A wave of dizziness washes over me, and I swallow hard. I cannot continue this way.

"Lie back and put your mind on other things," Nova says, as if that is something I can easily do.

Nova produces a small leather-bound kit and with its contents prepares a length of thread slick with beeswax and a sharp needle. He pinches the edges of my wound together at the gap and begins to drag the thread through. The pain is like fire in my flesh. I feel as if I am being consumed by it. My vision goes white, then dark. I gasp for air as I grip Nova's cloak.

"Talk to me," I say. "Tell me something that will take my mind off of this pain."

"What do you want me to say?" Nova asks, his voice calm, his hands steady. "I should think you already have enough thoughts to keep your mind occupied."

I gasp as he pricks the skin again, but in the haze of pain I think I see the corner of his mouth lift. "Look at my face. You enjoy that, don't you?"

I hope that the blood loss that is keeping my mind hazy

also means there isn't enough to spare to flush my face with embarrassment.

"You think I don't see you doing it," he says. "I do."

I shut my eyes, hoping that the darkness will swallow me up.

"I watch you, too," he says softly. "I make no apologies for it. I want you to know."

I let my eyes flutter open. I haven't felt the sting of the needle after several sutures. Who would have known the key to enduring a wound repair was sheer mortification? Nova dabs at my chest with my shirt again, then loops the needle through my skin. As he pulls the string taut, he presses his free hand against my bare chest.

"You can't let the wrongs he has done to you and your family go," he says, changing the subject. "That's why you're going to check on your mother, isn't it?"

"I'm going because I need to make sure she's okay."

"I cannot say I blame you," Nova says as he pulls the thread tight. "But I can't fathom why you won't leave well enough alone. You've essentially bested him; now you're risking going back."

I huff. "Besting him means I never see my mother again and that the people of Queen's Bridge are still subject to his torment. We haven't bested him at all."

"I want him ended as much as you do," Nova says softly.

"Even though he is your father?" I ask. "There must be some part of you that—"

"That what?" Nova asks. His eyes are steely and suddenly

serious. "You cannot fathom the horrors he has subjected me to. The things I've seen . . ." He trails off. "Do you wonder how it is that I have learned to close a wound like this?"

I still cannot understand how the Knight could have done such terrible things to his own child. I hesitate for a split second before reaching up and putting my hand on the side of his face. I half expect him to pull away, but he instead turns his mouth to the inside of my palm. He closes his eyes and sighs. His breath is warm and chases some of the chill from my hand. It is then that I allow myself to think of what his lips might feel like pressed against mine.

"I'm sorry, Eve," he says. "For my part in all of this. I cannot tell you how my father's bitter aggrievement with your family haunts me."

I let my hand fall away from his face. I am unsure of what to say, but I know that what I feel for him is a dangerous spark that threatens to ignite everything in me. If I let it, it will burn through me until I can see nothing else. Nova threads the needle through my skin one final time and I am so consumed with my own racing thoughts that I barely feel it. He knots the end and lets his hands rest on my bare shoulders for a moment.

"Rest," he says. "I will keep watch for a few hours. We should ride into the city under cover of darkness."

I pull my shirt back on and tuck my cloak in around me. I close my eyes, resting my head on my bag and, to my surprise, fall into a dreamless sleep for a few short hours.

Nova wakes me as the sun is setting, and though I still feel shaky we extinguish our fire, pack our belongings, and ride for Castle Veil as the sky turns from purple to black.

When we arrive at the edge of the castle district there is an air of melancholy about the place. Castle Veil looms in the dark. My mother is just beyond the gates, and I am moments from seeing her and feeling her arms around me. I want to cast aside my cloak of darkness and leap from my horse, but I stop myself. I cannot be seen. No one can know I am here if I am to keep Claude and the boys safe.

There is almost no one in the street. Smoke billows from only one or two chimneys. The shops are closed for the evening. Even the inns and taverns are closed up tight, their windows shuttered, their doors barred. Nova rides alongside me and leans close.

"People feel some terrible change in the air," he says in a whisper. "They cannot name it, but it is him."

I feel it, too. The Knight has always been present here but now it feels as if he is in every shadow, every puff of chimney smoke, every gray cloud, lurking like a malevolent specter.

I ride straight to the stable and put my horse inside. Nova does the same and as I step out on the path, I keep a newly forged cloak of inky blackness wrapped around Nova and me. He leans on me, pressing his hand against my back.

He stays on my heel as we approach the single Queen's guard patrolling the rear of the castle. We slip past him as he turns onto the footpath and make our way up the spiral of back stairs. When we reach the hall that extends to my mother's door, I am halted. The statue that sat in the small alcove, the one I'd hidden behind so many times as a small child, lies fractured on the stone floor. The torches in the hall have left soot marks that are normally cleaned off on a weekly basis, but now the black stains extend to the ceiling above each sconce. There is a guard standing watch in front of my mother's door. He leans against the frame, his eyes closed, his mouth half open as if he has fallen asleep standing up.

I exchange glances with Nova, and he gently pushes me aside so that my back is to the wall. His chest presses against mine. I can feel him breathing, the thudding of his heart. He slips from beneath the cloak of darkness and strides up to the man, who awakens and immediately straightens up.

"The Queen has asked that you join the other guards on grounds patrol," Nova says.

The guard hesitates.

Nova feigns disbelief. "Are you disobeying your Queen?"

"No," the man says. "Of course not."

The guard marches off, and when he is out of sight I slip from my hiding spot and stand in front of my mother's bedroom door. I start to push it open when Nova gently puts a hand on my arm and presses his finger to his lips in a plea for silence. I stop and listen at the door. My mother is speaking in a chaotic rhythm, repeating the same cadence over and over, but I cannot make out the individual words.

"What is she saying?" I whisper, pressing my ear to the door.

"This is how it has been," Nova says. "It is why people say she's gone mad."

I can't bear it. I gently push on the door and it opens.

Inside, the heavy scent of smoke from the hearth wafts into my face. My mother's room is in a state of disarray—her bed is unmade, her washbasin is shattered on the floor, the shutters are closed, and my mother is standing in front of the seeing stone. Nova rushes in and throws a heavy blanket over it and takes my mother by the shoulders. The hair at the back of her head is matted, and her nightgown is dirty and tattered, hanging off her like a wet rag. My heart thuds in my chest as she turns to face me, and I am horrified when her eyes meet mine.

My mother has always been a woman whose natural beauty shone through whatever emotion weighed most heavily on her, but I barely recognize her as she stands in front of me. The hollows under her eyes are deep and purple, her lips are dry and cracked, her hair is grayer around the edges than I remembered. She is gaunt, reminding me more of a corpse than a living, breathing woman. It has only been weeks since I last saw her, but by the look of her it could have been years.

A knot crawls up my throat. "Mother?" It is all I can get out before emotion overwhelms me. I rush up to her and put my arms around her. She is small and frail under my hands.

"Eve?" she asks as if she doesn't believe her own eyes. She squeezes me tight, then moves her hands to the sides of my face. "My beautiful baby," she sighs against my hair. "My baby."

Nova closes the door to my mother's bedchamber and stands quiet.

After a few moments my mother pulls away from me and wrings her hands together in front of her. "Why are you here?

You shouldn't be here." She shifts her gaze to Nova. "You let her come back?"

"I thought we established that I cannot persuade Eve to do, or not do, a single thing," Nova says. "She is simply too stubborn to listen to solid advice."

"I had to come," I say. "The rumors—"

"Rumors?" my mother asks. Her gaze darts from side to side as if she is desperately trying to pull something from her memory. "That I've gone mad?"

I nod. "Even Nova seemed concerned and if he is worried, well, how could I not be?"

My mother lowers herself into a chair by the blazing hearth. She looks at the cloaked mirror. "Every day he shows me things—images of your death. He torments me, and when I stand in front of the mirror I feel like I cannot move."

I glance at Nova, who lowers his head. I go to my mother and kneel at her side.

"We can destroy the mirror," I say.

"You think I haven't tried?" Mother asks. "It is much like the Knight. It can't be destroyed by any means that I am aware of."

"Is this what it has been like since I left?" I ask.

My mother nods and shakes her head. "I will know no peace." She puts her hand on my shoulder. "But I will endure it if it means you are safe."

"But *I* cannot endure it," I say. "My safety isn't worth this."

"Yes, it is," my mother says.

I rest my head in her lap and she tucks a few errant strands of my hair behind my ear. "There must be another way."

"We've been through this," Nova says, approaching my mother and me by the fire. "We devised a way for this to work, and it went to plan for all intents and purposes. You are putting it all in jeopardy by being here."

I lift my head. "You would have me leave my mother to live like this?" I gesture to the room. "To be driven to madness every waking hour just because your father wants to continue his sick and twisted games?" The words are daggers that hit their mark. Nova recoils.

"He cannot help himself," my mother says quietly.

"Nova has made choices," I say. "We all have and not all of them have been good or just."

"That is not what I mean," my mother says, gripping my hand so tight it hurts. "I have come to understand something about the Knight's nature that may lead us in the direction of stopping him for good."

Nova huffs. "That you are still plotting to end him when you have seen with your own eyes the power he wields is unfathomable to me."

"Because you are his child," my mother snaps. "And somewhere, deep inside, you care for him as all children care for even their most monstrous of caregivers."

Nova opens his mouth to speak but closes it tight, clicking his teeth together. "That's not what this is about."

"It clouds your vision," my mother says. "You want to be loved by him, but you will not be because he is incapable of that. I am truly sorry for that."

Nova's eyes are wide, and he looks away.

"What I see when I look at him is not hindered by any love lost," my mother continues. "When I look at what he has done, I see it through eyes that are not beholden to him and what I have observed is that he is unable to stop himself from entering into new deals with the people of Queen's Bridge."

"We know this already," I say.

"No," my mother says firmly. "It is not simply a choice." She stands and straightens out her nightgown. "He is moved to these actions. He grants wishes as if it is a compulsion for him. Twisting their meaning and molding them into unspeakable forms. I don't think he could stop even if he wanted to and there are certain wishes, certain deals, that seem to consume him more than others." She glances at the covered mirror. "This deal that he and I entered into is one of them. Our business should be concluded. He should be on to the next reckless wish seeker." She grips her hands together. "Yet he is desperate to try and convince *me* to enter into another agreement with him. It is almost as if the fact that we both fulfilled the terms and payment of our agreement offends him in some way. He thinks he is smarter than me and is desperate to prove it. Simply fulfilling the agreement isn't what he wants this time." My mother looks at me with tears in her eyes. "He wanted you murdered on my orders. He wanted to see me grieving. He wanted to see you suffering and dying." My mother swallows hard and looks at me. "I cling to the hope that one day you and I will be reunited for good. That spark is what he hates. His goal is to stomp that out."

"I think you are right," Nova sighs. "But if you are, that

makes him even more dangerous. If he gets any sense that we have betrayed him . . ." He trails off.

My mother holds out her hand to me, and I take it. Her hand feels small in mine. "What this tells me is that he is vulnerable when he feels he hasn't won. His attempts to drive me into another deal with him have been relentless, and I fear they will only grow more frenzied."

"Why?" I ask. "He gains nothing from this torment. What is the end game for him?"

My mother's eyes widen, and she leans away from me just slightly. "The game is what drives him. The suffering is his payment." She squeezes my hands tighter. "And what do you think his ledger looks like after I have spent years encouraging the people of Queen's Bridge to turn away from him? I have taken care of them, and they have found less and less of a need to go to him with their wishes. If he revels in our sorrows, our pain, then he has less of that now than he ever had before, and he wants to punish me for it."

"Why isn't he obsessed with Sir Gregory's deal? Or anyone else's, for that matter?" I ask.

My mother's gaze seems distant. "Until Sanaa and I made our respective deals, it had been generations since anyone in our line made wishes to the Knight. I don't know for sure that we ever had." There is shame in her voice. "If wishes were made by our Miller Queens, I do not know of them. Maybe that bothers him in some way. Perhaps he sees us as a prize to be claimed."

"He will profit," Nova says quietly. "No matter the odds, no matter the circumstance."

"He cannot profit if he is dead," I say.

My mother holds my hand tightly. "And you have seen firsthand that killing him is no small feat."

Nova suddenly inhales sharply and exchanges a look of abject horror with my mother.

"Hide yourself!" my mother gasps. She shoves me toward the doors that open onto her balcony.

"What are you doing?" I ask, confused.

And then I hear it—footsteps, like the crashing of thunder, rumble in the hall. I duck through the doors that lead to the balcony and press myself against the outer wall. I stretch my hand toward the sky and pull a cloak of blackness in around me. Nova stands near the door but does not join me outside.

"Go," he says in a voice barely above a whisper, without so much as turning his head to look at me. "Now. Get back to Claude's."

"No, I—" I begin to protest, but my mother's chamber door opens slowly. The Knight's midnight-black armor is visible in the hallway like a great gaping void.

I stop breathing.

He puts one enormous, gloved hand on the doorframe and ducks his head low so that he can enter the chamber. The panels of his armor glide together and apart at the seams. Noiselessly, he enters the room and stands to his full height. Maybe it was my panicked state or the fear that was rushing through me, but as I remember seeing him in his own castle during my miserable attempt to assassinate him, I did not understand how imposing he actually is. He had been a terrible sight to see, but now, as he stands, his head far above the crossbeam of my mother's chamber door, he seems impossibly monstrous.

"My Queen," says the Knight, his voice like the resonant growl of a bear and a wolf mixed with the roll of thunder.

My mother huffs out a sarcastic laugh. "If I were your Queen, you would do as I ask and disappear from my lands for all time. You would leave me and my people in peace."

The Knight steps forward and the room trembles under his feet. "Perhaps that may be the terms of our next deal. If you can uphold your end of the bargain, I will leave this land forever."

"I would die before I enter into another one of your crooked deals."

I cannot see the Knight's face. Even the slit over his eyes is black. But I feel in my gut that he is smiling.

"You may very well be right about that," he says. He turns his head toward the balcony door and my heart almost stops.

Nova takes a step toward the Knight and bows, putting one knee on the floor. "Father," he says.

The Knight touches the back of Nova's bowed head but says nothing to him. He turns back to my mother, approaching her slowly but so menacingly that I begin to panic. My heart beats wildly in my chest. I contemplate throwing my cloak aside, reentering the room, and confronting the monster who has wrought such devastation on my family, on the people of Queen's Bridge. Could I best him in this moment? I try not to allow my anger to guide my thoughts. In my mind I see myself conjuring a sword of fire and removing his head from his neck in one fell swoop. But I tried this. I had gone to his enchanted abode prepared to end him and it had cost Sir Gregory the life of his beloved son.

The Knight slips his hand under my mother's chin. His palm engulfs her head, his fingers fully covering the sides of her face. "My Queen," he growls. "You think you have won, but I know your secrets."

My mother gasps as the Knight lifts her straight up into the air. I remove my cloak and it disintegrates, returning to the black night from which it came. I step toward the slightly ajar balcony door as I eye the fire blazing in the hearth. I stretch out my hand and the flames dance higher, hotter, brighter. The light casts the room in a fiery orange haze.

Suddenly there is a low call. It is the distinct melodic whistle of a bird.

A nightingale.

Queen Sanaa flies close to me in a hail of fluttering wings and sharp talons. She pecks at the exposed skin on my face, tearing the flesh in her attempt to push me back.

"Mother." My whisper masks a sob that threatens to break from me.

Her message is clear. Leave. Retreat. And quickly.

I glance in at my mother as the Knight holds her suspended in the air.

Queen Sanaa beats her wings against me. Berating me with her calls. I take another step back, lowering my hand. As the fire dies down and the room darkens, the Knight turns his head, his helm catching the light from the glowing embers. I see his eyes for the first time. They are black, soulless, and he sees me.

I feel like I am falling into nothingness as he stares at me from behind his blackened armor. I wonder if he will kill me now, or take me to be tortured, but he does neither.

He turns to my mother and twists her around so that she is facing the seeing stone. He holds the back of her neck firmly as her feet dangle just above the ground. He removes the heavy covering Nova had placed over the mirror, and my mother's terrified eyes are reflected in the shiny surface.

"Say the words," the Knight says.

My mother's eyes cloud over until the orbs are white as snow. Her mouth hangs open, and her body hangs limp in his grasp.

"Looking glass, looking glass, on the wall," she says. Her voice is dry and raspy. Between each word she sobs so violently that it makes her entire body shudder. "Who in this land is the fairest of all?" She gasps, like she'd been holding her breath. Her eyes suddenly clear, and she kicks at the Knight but he doesn't flinch or move. "I don't care!" she screams as she claws at him. "I don't care! Stop it!"

"Oh, Queen, thou art fair, as lovely as all I see," the Knight replies mockingly. "But Eve is alive and well, and none is so fair as she."

My mother's eyes turn white again. "None is so fair as she," she repeats in that dry, unfamiliar voice.

Nova suddenly appears in front of me. His face is a mask of pain and terror.

"Go!" he shouts, his voice like a thunderclap. "Flee!"

I hesitate. Nova reaches out and strikes me hard in the chest. I'm forced off the balcony, tumbling backward and landing hard in the snow. The air punches out of me. I cough, roll onto my side, and gasp for breath as I stumble to my feet.

I run. My legs pumping under me, the snow crunching beneath my boots. I run and trip on something as I round the castle, heading for the stables. I pitch forward and slam chest first into the cold ground. The air is forced violently from me and I struggle to breathe. My wound burns, and I fear it has opened up again. Coughing and sputtering, I pull myself up to my feet only to find another object lying in the snow just ahead of me. As my eyes adjust to the dark, the horrible realization of what I'm tripping over falls on me like a stone.

They are bodies. Dozens of them.

The people of Queen's Bridge alongside several royal guards, many of them with their weapons—swords, daggers, clubs—still clutched in their curled fingers lay scattered across the ground. They've fallen in a line in a way that suggests they were preparing to defend Castle Veil and were cut down. It could be the work of no one but the Knight.

I scramble to the stables and mount my horse. My body screams as I pull myself into the saddle. The wound in my chest burns, as does the wound in my palm. I grab the reins and steer my horse away from the castle.

As I approach the boundary of the castle district, a giant,

hulking shape lurks in shadow. The Knight's castle has perched itself in an empty field, its strange metal legs folded under it like a nesting bird. I hear its call inside my head, and I wonder again if it is alive. I ride toward Claude's as fast as I can, draping myself in darkness, pushing my horse to its limits.

The wind in my face keeps me awake and alert as I ride through the night. I stop only long enough to allow my horse to water and feed, and then I push her into the dark until I arrive at the Kingfisher house. I listen closely to her call—she is stressed and frightened, but not tired.

Maggie is on the porch as I arrive. She is waiting with her ears pinned back, and she alerts Claude of my presence with three deep but welcoming barks.

I slide off my horse and drag myself to the door as Claude and Junior open it. They look upon me in horror before Junior slips my arm over his shoulder and helps me inside. Claude surveys the woods surrounding us and waits in silence on the front porch for several moments before turning to me through the open door.

"Oh, Eve," he says. "What has happened?"

CHAPTER 16

"Are you certain he saw you?" Claude asks.

His dark brown eyes are nearly black. He is so focused on my face that I find it difficult to hold eye contact with him. Junior sets a hot mug of some fragrant liquid on the table in front of me.

"Yes," I say as I down the liquid and feel it pool in my stomach, warming me from the inside. "I think so."

"You think or you know?" Claude asks. "I need to know. You say he saw you, but he didn't come after you? He didn't even attempt to stop you?"

I shake my head. "No. He turned toward me. I saw his eyes and—"

Junior inhales sharply. "You looked him directly in the eye?" He shakes his head and takes a step back from me. "Are you cursed, then?"

Claude huffs. "Ridiculous superstitions. Go tend to your brothers and leave Eve and me to discuss this alone."

"I should be here," Junior says.

Claude leans his forearm on the tabletop and his brows arch up. "Oh? And why is that?"

"Because if something happens to you," Junior says. "I need to know everything you know so I can keep us safe."

Claude tries and fails to conceal his horror. He must have had these thoughts himself—that he might not always be here to protect his children, but it seems he hasn't considered that Junior has had the same thoughts and worries as well.

I turn to face Junior and find his expression drawn tight as if he is trying not to cry. "I would die before I allowed the Knight or anyone else to hurt you."

Claude and Junior exchange glances and something silent passes between them. Junior puts his hand, which seems so small, on my shoulder and squeezes. Then he takes his leave. I notice he is limping, testing the weight on his right foot and then thinking better of it.

I turn to Claude. "What happened to him?"

Claude runs his hand through his beard. "Chased down a boar while you were gone. Got his foot caught in the roots of a willow tree down by the stream. It should heal up fine if he stays off it, but he refuses to be still."

"He's stubborn," I say.

"Ah well, that would be a trait he got from his mother." Claude looks up and his lips move like he's saying a silent prayer. He turns his attention back to me. "You're certain you weren't followed as you made your way here?"

"Yes," I say. "I took the long route there and back, and I was cloaked almost the entire time."

He heaves a sigh of relief, but his face is still troubled. "And what of Nova?"

I take the glass shard from my pocket and set it on the table. "I have tried to speak to him, but he isn't there. The shard is empty." A terrible sinking feeling settles in the pit of my stomach. I don't know what it means that he hasn't contacted me, but it feels like an ominous harbinger of what is coming. I twist my mother's ring around on my middle finger.

"He cares for you deeply," Claude says. "I saw it in his face."

I stare at the steam coiling out of the mug on the table.

"I didn't think him capable of such feelings," Claude says. "But now that I know he is, I fear it may put us in more danger. He will want to make sure you are safe, which means he will be thinking of a way to get to you."

"You don't know that," I say.

"Yes, I do," Claude says. "I'd do the same for the woman I love." He gazes at Leah's portrait.

"Love," I say in a whisper. "No. This—this is not that."

Claude's face is a mask of concern.

"I can leave," I offer, steering our conversation away from things I can't think about right now. "That way if Nova or anyone else comes looking, I'll be far from here."

Claude pulls at his beard. "If the Knight wants to seek me out, you make it seem as if there is some rhyme or reason to him, that he would see you're gone and simply pass over this house like a storm cloud. You believe he would leave any of us unscathed? No. Sending you out into the world alone won't do at all." He sighs and cups his hand over mine. "I won't turn my back on you if you don't turn your back on us."

Tears sting my eyes, and I angrily brush them away.

"You're upset?" Claude asks. "If you want to leave—"

"I don't," I say quickly. "I don't. But is this how we're meant to live? Looking over our shoulders for all time?"

"As long as the Knight wanders these lands, yes," Claude says. "In fact, I think it is the best we can hope for." Claude shakes his head as he takes the seeing stone shard and wraps it in a thick cloth. "You should bury this. I would say destroy it, but I don't think you can. It's a magical object and things like that cannot be disposed of so easily. Bury it, Eve. At least for now. Until we know Nova's fate, I don't think it is wise to look into the shard."

He's right, but the shard is my only way to see Nova and I feel torn about locking it away. "He told me to run," I say to Claude. "He made me leave."

Claude narrows his gaze. "He said this to you? In the presence of the Knight?"

I nod. Claude and I sit in silence. The weight of what that means pressing down on us. Nova betrayed the Knight by showing loyalty to me, and I can only imagine what the consequences of that decision will be for him, for me, for all of us.

I bury the shard, wrapped in the cloth, in the bottom of a potted plant by the window and promise myself that I will move the entire thing to a more secluded location in the coming days. I will retrieve it when the time is right. When I know Claude and the boys are safe. I tell myself I will see Nova again, even if somewhere deep inside I feel it is a lie.

Claude leaves the following morning, with Hunter at his side. Junior stays with me to look after the other boys and, because his ankle is still giving him trouble, I keep the little ones occupied with games in the front yard. Claude had fashioned them several different-sized leather balls that they kick between them. They have small wooden horses and a makeshift wagon. They fight with wooden swords and pretend to be knights and robbers. They laugh until they can't stand up. I marvel at their ability to be so carefree when my world feels like it is crashing down around me. As I watch the boys play, I think only of my mother, of Nova, and of the terrible uncertainty that lies ahead.

Chance and Grumpy climb into the small cart, and I push them around the yard in the fading afternoon sun.

"Fix your face, Grump," Junior says.

I glance at Grumpy, whose expression is set in a permanent scowl. "Are you—are you even having fun?" I ask.

"Of course I am!" he says, his voice light.

"Then fix your face!" Junior scolds.

"Fix *your* face!" Grumpy shouts back. "If you even can."

"Are you calling me ugly?" Junior asks, surprise coloring his tone. "We look exactly alike, Grump. If I'm ugly, so are you."

There is a pause, and then they all laugh until they're

falling all over themselves. Grump gives a wicked little grin. I smile at them but turn and take up a spot by the fence, watching the tree line, listening to the calls of the animals. There are no warnings of danger in the air or in my head. Junior hobbles over and stands beside me.

"I would ask you what's wrong, but I'm pretty sure I already know," he says, wincing as he tries to put his weight on his injured leg.

I slip my arm around his waist to support him. "You need to be resting that ankle."

"I'm good," he says. "It barely even hurts."

"You're such a terrible liar," I say. "Stick to the truth. It's better that way."

"I wanted to show you something," Junior says. "It's just a little ways off." He gestures to a footpath that leads away from the cabin into the woods.

"Now?" I ask. "I don't want to leave your brothers unattended."

Junior turns to Grump. "You're in charge for a little while. I'm taking Eve to see the grove."

Grump and Chance stop what they are doing and both of them give a silent, solemn nod.

"What is it?" I ask.

"The grove is where our mother and brothers are buried," Junior says.

My chest grows tight. I look to Chance, who smiles softly.

"You heard him," Grump says. "I'm in charge. Chance . . . shut up."

Chance rolls his eyes. "I wasn't even talking."

Junior laughs lightly. "Grump is so annoying sometimes. Come on."

He limps toward the footpath, and I follow him.

We cut through a tangle of leafless trees, sticking to a narrow footpath. After several minutes we emerge in a small clearing, at the center of which is a waist-high headstone made of glinting gray marble and flanked by three shorter grave markers. As we approach, Junior stops and kneels. He pushes aside the snow to reveal a layer of straw that looks as if it has been strewn all over the gravesite. Pieces of the yellowish-brown material jut out of the snow across the entire open space.

"We cover the whole glade in straw before the snow comes," Junior says, reading my expression. "It keeps the ground warm so the lilies will come back in the spring. They were her favorite. And sometimes, a few of them survive even through the snow." He digs around under the layer of straw until he finds what he is looking for—a small white lily, perfectly formed, beautiful.

I accompany him to the marble headstone, and he sets the flower on top. Carved in the stone is the name Leah Kingfisher.

"She was the best person I ever knew," Junior says. "I haven't been out here in a while so I thought . . ." He trails off.

Junior is so busy being responsible for everyone else I realize that I haven't done enough to make sure he has someone to lean on. I put my arm around him.

"I will come visit her with you anytime you like," I say.

I glance at the snow and reach toward it. I will a column of ice to shape itself into a wreath of frozen flowers and lay it gently on top of Leah Kingfisher's grave. I conjure three identical ones and lay them atop the accompanying graves.

"They were all sweet," Junior says. "The boys, I mean. Me and Hunter are the only ones who knew them. Chance and Grump were born after they died." He sighs. "I think of what it would be like if the seven of us were all still here. If my mother was here, too."

I have no words. The grief is almost too much to hold.

Junior smiles gently as I glance up. A murder of crows wings their way across the darkening sky. Their calls echo in my head—a melodic ringing but at a higher pitch than I'd expect. They're frightened. It's different than it had been before. This time they seem almost sad.

"Let's head back," I say.

We take the footpath back to the cabin, and I direct the other boys to gather their things and go inside. The boys grumble and protest.

"I'll show you a trick," I offer as a bribe.

"With fire?" Chance asks, gleefully.

I nod. The boys rush inside, hang up their outside clothing, wash their hands in the kitchen basin, and settle in on the big rug near the hearth. Maggie stays on the front porch as she eagerly awaits Claude and Hunter's return. Inside, I pull swords of different shapes and sizes from the blazing fire. The boys squeal with delight as they request swords with blades as long as my arm. I conjure the weapons from the fire and when

242

the boys grow tired of the spectacle, I let the fire smolder to embers.

"Is it all swords and stabby things?" Chance asks, as sleep threatens to close his eyes right there on the floor.

"Not always," I say.

"Show us?" Grumpy asks, his voice slow and sleepy.

I go to the door and open it a crack. Maggie's ears perk up but she stays balled up, breathing slowly. I look up at the stars in the night sky and reach my hand toward them. A blanket of blue-black sky dotted with starlight descends in a rolling wave. I usher it into the house and lay it gently over the boys. They gasp and run their hands over the blanket of night.

"It feels like clouds," Chance says.

"How do you know what clouds feel like?" Junior asks.

"I just do!" Chance says, grinning.

"Is this magic?" Grumpy asks. His expression is a mask of bewilderment with only one corner of his mouth turned down.

"Yes," I say.

"How do you do it?" he asks.

I press my mouth into a flat line. I cannot bring myself to tell him the truth. That I have these abilities because of the way I came into being—a crooked deal agreed on by my mothers who only wanted a child of their own and the Knight who twisted their words and cursed us all in the process. Maybe, as Junior had suggested, I am cursed.

Maggie's call sounds in my head before she barks. She alerts with three deeply resonant tones and, when I peer out the open door, Claude and Hunter are making their way by torchlight over the crest of the nearby hill.

Hunter carries a wicker basket. When they left, they'd made sure it was filled with food and drink to last them the day. Claude has his pickaxe slung over his shoulder. I expect them to come into the house, wash up, and settle in for something to eat, but Hunter drops the basket on the porch and comes straight up to me. Hunter's eyes are wet with tears. I cup his face in my hands.

"What's wrong?" I ask him.

He stares up at me. "I—Eve, I—"

"Go inside," Claude says. "Take everyone to the room and close the door."

I look past Claude, prepared to conjure a weapon, but he rests his hand on my shoulder.

"What is it?" I ask. "Why is Hunter upset?"

Claude nudges me toward the front door, but I stand firm. Claude sighs.

"I need you to come inside and sit down," he says.

I don't want to sit down. I don't want to move.

Claude looks down at me. "Eve. I think you should—"

"Don't tell me what you think I should do," I say. "Tell me the truth. What is happening?"

Claude takes a deep, wavering breath. There is a twinge at the base of my neck. A fox is nearby. I hear nighttime birds—an owl's melancholy call, a jay's solemn song.

"News has come through the mine," Claude says. "From Castle Veil."

I swallow hard. "And it upset Hunter?"

Claude nods. "He is upset because he knows the news will be hardest on you."

I turn away from Claude, and my hands become slick with sweat as my heart gallops in my chest. "I don't want to hear it," I say. "Don't tell me."

"I must," Claude says in a voice that is barely a whisper and, to my horror, choked with despair. "Eve . . ."

I lift my chin and look into the night sky dotted with its shining stars. The chilly air laps at the bare skin on my neck.

"Eve," Claude says. "Your mother is dead."

CHAPTER 17

Wailing.

It is the sound of a wave—a roaring that builds in my gut and pushes its way to my chest, up my throat, and past my lips. I scream into the night sky as if it can carry my grief across this land so that all may feel its terrible weight.

I don't know when I stop screaming, but when I do it is only because my throat is raw and my chest feels like it might split open. I collapse into the soft pallet of straw in my broom closet of a room. I refuse to come out for days.

Claude leaves a pitcher of water and bread wrapped in a cloth outside my door and, when I don't retrieve it, he lets Maggie dispose of it. Every day there is fresh water and bread, though I cannot bring myself to consume anything but a sip of water every once in a while. Even the act of breathing feels like something I don't want to do anymore.

Claude does not allow the boys to come close, though I hear their steps in the hall in the small hours of the morning, their little voices calling my name and pushing folded pieces of paper under the door. Chance writes that he misses me and that he has fashioned himself a new fishing rod and intends to show it to me when I emerge. There are drawings from Hunter, who also leaves me a raven's feather wrapped in a small piece of cloth. Even Grumpy has left me a note. It simply has his name, his true name, Savion, scrawled in his messy but legible handwriting. I tuck them away. They feel like sacred texts to me—words that remind me there is still life beyond my door, beyond the pain that racks my mind and body, even if I am not ready to see it.

It is the dead of night on the fourth day after the news of my mother's death. I am wide awake as I most often am— unable to rest, though my body is begging to sleep. But I can't, because when I do—I dream. And the images that tumble through my head are almost as terrible as having to live in the waking world with the knowledge that my mother is gone. When I am not consumed by nightmarish sleep, I see the Knight in my waking hours, and I hear the strange words he'd forced my mother to speak into the looking glass.

Looking glass, looking glass, on the wall.
Who in this land is the fairest of all?

My mother had never been vain. She had never cared about such things. And the Knight's answer had made even less sense than my mother's question. He told her that though she was fair, *I* was fairer than she. I don't understand what it meant, and now that she is gone I never will.

In the hall, there comes a rustling. Footsteps. I pull myself up to sitting and listen. The steps aren't light enough to be Chance or Grump. Not sure enough to be Hunter. And they most definitely do not belong to Claude or Maggie. I want to lie back down and curl myself beneath the blankets, but I have the sudden, sinking feeling that if I do, there is a very real possibility that I will not emerge. The steps move closer to the door and I realize that whoever it is is favoring one foot.

"Junior," I say quietly. "I can't—I can't talk now."

"I know," he says at the door. "You don't have to."

He pushes something under the door, and his steps retreat down the hall toward the front room. I retrieve the paper and hold it in my hand, afraid to open it, though I cannot say why. Junior is much like his father—a caring person with the weight of the world on his shoulders. I think the note is one of two things: a direct order to get up and get myself together, or a simple sentence or two letting me know he's put some bread and water out for me. Care and concern all wrapped in one.

I sigh and unfold the small piece of paper.

I miss my mother, too.

Grief washes over me, dull and aching, pulling at all the pieces of me that feel barely strung together. It compels me to stand. After days of being unable to, my legs are weak and my heart knocks against my ribs.

I push the door open and stand in the dark hallway. A warm glow emanates from the front room. I walk on unsteady legs toward it, passing Claude's room where he is snoring, Maggie curled up at the foot of his too-small bed. I pause at the door to the boys' room. Junior's bed is empty as the other boys lay scattered as if they'd fallen from the sky and landed peacefully in their beds—arms and legs jutting out from under their blankets. Chance is perilously close to falling to the floor. I gently nudge him back to his pillow and cover him with a thick wool blanket. His eyes flutter open, and when his sleepy gaze rests on me, he smiles.

"You're up," he says groggily.

I nod. "Go back to sleep."

He slips his warm hand into mine. "I have to show you my new fishing rod."

"In the morning," I say.

He nods and lapses back into a sound slumber.

I make my way down the hall and find Junior seated at the table. I pull out a chair next to him and sit down. We don't say anything for a long time. Then suddenly there are lumbering steps in the hall and Claude appears in his nightclothes, Maggie trailing behind him.

He glances at Junior and then at me and his expression grows dark with concern.

"You need to eat," Claude says.

"I know," I say, nodding. "I will."

"Good," Claude says as he comes to the table and takes up a seat on the opposite side of Junior.

"When my mom died, I stayed in my room for a week," Junior says.

Claude drops his head and looks into his lap. Junior's eyes glass over as he stares into the glowing hearth like he is unlocking a door in his mind behind which his most painful memories lie.

"I was so sad I thought I was going to die, too," he says. "I felt like I couldn't breathe or move. Thinking of her hurt so much." He takes a deep, wavering breath. "But when I didn't think of her, I felt guilty. Why should I have to only remember the awful way it felt when she died? Why was that memory more important than all the other ones?"

Junior is the oldest of the boys and so I always view him as being a responsible stand-in for his father, but in this moment, I see him for what he really is—a young boy who has lost a parent, who feels the need to be much more grown-up than he should have to be. He is vulnerable and he is grieving, still. I put my hand over his and feel him trembling.

"My brothers and my father and Maggie—they're the only reason I'm okay now," he says. "My family. My mother's memory is a part of that."

"I don't have that anymore," I say, as tears stream down my face. "Everyone I have ever loved is gone."

Junior withdraws his hand from mine and stares at me in a way that is both pleading and angry.

"Everyone?" he asks, pushing his chair back and standing up. "What are we to you, then?" Tears stand in his eyes. They threaten to spill over, and my already broken heart feels like it may piece itself back together just so it can shatter all over again.

I stand and face him. "I—I am broken without her. And Queen Sanaa, she is lost to me, too. I cannot go back to take comfort in Lady Anne. Huntress is dead, and as it is she never loved me anyway. Even Nova is gone from me." The absence of his face in the looking-glass shard before I buried it unsettles me, and I have to refocus. "I am not the same as I was and I don't think I ever will be again. I don't know if I can be."

"That is the nature of grief," Claude says, dabbing at his eyes, though his voice remains steady. "It changes you. It burns you up from the inside and then you emerge from the ashes, like the phoenix."

"I don't know if I can do that," I say. It is the honest truth. How can I ever come back from this? It doesn't seem possible.

Junior lowers his gaze to the floor. "Will you try?" he asks. His voice seems so small and broken. He lifts his head and stares at me. "Please?"

"I don't know if I deserve to try," I say, as images of Mekhi's broken body tumble through my head.

My recklessness cost him his life. My arrogance in thinking I could defeat the Knight ensured that Mekhi's blood was on my hands. Do I deserve to rise from the ashes of this terrible sadness? Claude and these boys, these beautiful, messy, silly boys, cared for me again and again over the past weeks. They showed me kindness when perhaps I deserved none.

Claude stands and puts his arm around Junior. "We have all made mistakes, Eve. You question whether you are deserving of another chance to live, and what you fail to realize is that you have already been granted that. By the gods or nature or fate or sheer luck." He holds his hand out to me, and I take it. "Your mother's wish was for you to be safe. Honor her by keeping yourself safe here with us."

I breathe deep and sadness pools into the space in my chest. It fills me up. "I feel like I am drowning."

Junior puts his arms around my waist, and I rest my cheek on the top of his head.

"Don't drown," he says. "Don't sink. Don't do any of that." He pulls back and looks up at me. "Swim, Eve. For me. For us."

In that moment I picture myself in a storming sea, the water thrashing around me, the sky cloudy and full of thunder. I see myself among the wreckage of the life I had lived, the pieces of it broken and floating around me. I could let it drag me all the way to the bottom. I could allow the water to ferry me to an early grave, but instead I picture Claude and the boys standing on a nearby shore, shouting at me to swim. I kick toward them, pulling myself through the stormy sea, reaching for them until they finally pull me ashore.

───────────────

Four more days pass as I take shelter in the warmth of the Kingfisher home. The boys wear black to represent our shared mourning. They press their little hands to my shoulder as they pass me. I find solace in crafting makeshift bows and arrows to practice shooting targets made of sticks and scraps of fabric in the yard with them.

The news out of Castle Veil is bleak and seeps out like a poison infecting the surrounding lands. It is awful. Claude only shares with me the barest of details to spare me more heartache. The official messengers of Castle Veil spread the news of my mother's death to the borders of Queen's Bridge and beyond. The terrible news spreads to Rotterdam and Hamelin and even across the Forbidden Lands to Mersailles. They say Queen Regina succumbed to a mysterious illness, something that had plagued her for weeks before it finally took her life.

When Claude returns home one evening, he sits with me at the table after dismissing the boys to wash up before bed.

"I have something to share with you," Claude says.

I shift uncomfortably in my chair. "I've had more terrible news than anyone should be allowed."

Claude nods. "I would agree." He sighs and slings his tattered bag onto the table. "It's not bad news as much as it is strange."

I relax a little. "Strange? Does it have anything to do with my mother?"

He nods. "The news of her passing has spread far and wide, but there are other rumors in the mines. I heard something today that has unsettled me, and I need to share it with you. Maybe you can help me make sense of it."

I lean toward him. "Tell me."

He sits back in his chair and runs his hands through his beard. "I work with a man called Oliver whose brother worked in Castle Veil. Apparently, the messaging coming out of the castle is at odds with what people who were there in the days leading up to your mother's passing actually saw."

My heart speeds up again.

Claude lowers his voice and leans closer to me. "Oliver's brother, Ranauld, was a farrier in the royal stables and had gone into the castle on invitation from his fiancé. The woman told Ranauld that she had been in the hall outside your mother's chambers and heard her speaking some strange rhyme over and over again."

I lean forward, pressing my hands into my legs to keep them from trembling. "What rhyme?" I ask. "Did she say what it was?"

Claude nods. "I hesitate to even speak it aloud. It doesn't sound like a rhyme at all. It's sounds like magic, a spell . . ."

"A curse," I say in a whisper.

Claude hesitates to repeat the words, but I do not.

"Looking glass, looking glass, on the wall. Who in this land is the fairest of all?"

The color drains away from Claude's normally luminescent brown skin. "How did you know?"

"I heard her speak those words the last time I saw her," I say. "The Knight—he somehow made her say it. She didn't want to. She fought against it." The memory of my mother's terrified eyes turning white as the freshly fallen snow pushes its way to the front of my mind.

"What does it mean?" Claude asks. "Why would she ask such things?"

"She wouldn't," I say. "It was the Knight's doing, and now that she's gone we will never know."

"Your mother has gone on to whatever lies beyond this life but the Knight saw you with his own eyes," Claude says. "I find it hard to imagine him simply allowing the betrayal to stand, even in light of the Queen's death."

He's right, and the more I think on it the more I can't understand why he let me live. He could have ended me right there in my mother's bedchamber, but he didn't.

Claude suddenly stands up. "We've lived in this place for a long time, but home is anywhere we're all together. Maybe we pack up and move on from here. We can go wherever we like."

I shake my head and prepare to protest, but Claude cuts me off.

"I'm not saying it's set in stone, but I am considering it. Give me some time to think on it, then we'll bring it up to the boys." He sighs and pats me on the shoulder. "One more thing," he says. He goes to his bag and produces a small wooden box, handing it to me. On the top in his terrible handwriting are my name and the names of the boys.

"Open it," Claude says.

I open the box and find within it a small glass enclosure. I lift it out to get a better look. It's a small rectangular box, the sides of which are made from crystal so clear I can see the small satin pillow resting inside it. The hinges are made from ornately decorated brass and so is the small clasp on the front that keeps the transparent lid closed.

"A jewelry box," Claude says. "Chance said you don't wear jewelry, but Junior pointed out that you do have the emerald ring. Hunter also pointed out that you never take it off. So you can see we were a bit split on what to give you."

"It's beautiful," I say, holding back tears.

"Crafted it ourselves between shifts," Claude says. "We didn't tell Grump because he would have come to tell you immediately and ruined the surprise."

"Seems like something he would do," I say.

"The boy is allergic to fun and surprises," Claude sighs. "You do like it, though? I was worried you wouldn't."

I stand and put my arms around him. "I love it. Thank you."

"What will you keep in it?" Claude asks.

I stare at the beautiful glass box. "Something precious to me," I say.

Claude smiles, patting me on the shoulder.

I set the box back on the table and sit down. Claude sits across from me, his back to the hearth. I'm moved by the gift and by Claude's concern, but there is something lurking behind all those feelings, threatening to bleed into every part of me.

I had seen the Knight with my own eyes there in my mother's chamber. I saw him lift her off the ground like it was nothing. In his eyes—those empty black eyes—she *was* nothing. He had a hand in her death, of that I am certain, but I am afraid to think about it for too long. The anger that is festering inside me, mingled with the grief, is threatening to make me reckless. The same drive to track him down and end him once and for all is growing inside me again. I press my hands into the surface of the table, trying my hardest to stem the tide of hatred. The Knight should be the one laid in the ground, not my mother. I stare into the smoldering hearth, and I can feel the heat in the palm of my hand.

"Eve," Claude says. "Whatever you are thinking of doing, please reconsider."

"Am I so obvious?" I ask.

"Yes," Claude says without hesitation. "I can see the anger coiling inside you like a snake, ready to strike. But you are not ready. I don't know that you will ever be."

I glance down the hall, listening for the boys. All is quiet.

"I collected stories about the Knight," I say in a hushed tone. "I was trained to stop him, and so learning all I could about him became my obsession. I sought out people who had made wishes and recorded their stories of how the Knight granted those wishes in the cruelest ways."

Claude leans on the table, listening intently.

"I gathered the stories from all kinds of people all throughout Queen's Bridge," I say. "Yours was among them—in pieces at least."

Claude huffs. "The details were too awful to repeat, I suppose."

"They were," I say, gently touching Claude's hand and giving pause for this terrible truth. "In all my travels," I continue. "With everything I have learned, I still know so little about the Knight himself. You've been out here all these years, working the mines, hearing stories and rumors. Tell me, have you ever heard anything that is more than just a recounting of his loathsome deeds?"

Claude rubs Maggie between her ears, and a rumble of content resonates in her chest. "This land is full of scary stories."

I pause. It is not the answer I expect.

I lean toward him. "You know of other kinds of stories? About who the Knight is or where he came from?"

Claude runs his hand through his beard. "What does it matter? Will knowing him change what he has done? Will it bring Leah back? Will it save you from the heartache you've endured?"

My chest grows tight with grief. "No," I say. "It will not. But it may keep someone else from having to endure it."

"Is that your plan, Eve?"

"I have no plan until I know more about him," I say. "There must be something else about him that we don't know, something that can help us defeat him."

Claude's shoulders roll forward. "There was a woman who lived in Little Stilts when I was a child."

"Little Stilts?" I ask. "That's not in Queen's Bridge."

"No," Claude says. "It's just over the southwestern border, in Hamelin. It's not a well-known place. I don't think it can even call itself a proper village. It's more of a hamlet."

"So, you haven't always lived in Queen's Bridge?" I ask.

"I have," says Claude. "But my father worked in the mines on the South Steps. I'd accompany him from time to time as my own sons accompany me. One evening, my father was asked to make a delivery, and I went along. His horse died just over the border, and we hiked in the snow to Little Stilts to see about procuring a new one, but by the time we arrived there, a blizzard blew in and we were stranded there for six days."

"What did you do?" I ask. "Was there an inn?"

"An inn?" Claude huffs out a laugh. "It is a hamlet, my

dearest Eve. There wasn't an inn. There wasn't a market, a temple, a castle, nothing. I think there may have been fifty people haunting that place."

My eyebrows push up.

"Figuratively, of course," Claude says. "They were all much older than my father. Hell, maybe even older than his father. Anyone who was able had long since abandoned the place. At the first door we knocked on seeking shelter there was a man who looked like he'd been freshly buried and had only risen from his grave to cast us a disparaging look and slam that door in our faces." Claude shifts around in his seat. "We tried another house. A little one-room abode with a green door. A woman answered and ushered us inside. She told us her name was Nerium and that she lived alone. She asked if we were going to hurt her and my father was so offended by the notion he initially asked if I could shelter inside, insisting he would sleep out on the porch."

"He would have died from the cold," I say.

Claude nods. "Indeed, he would have. Nerium had a change of heart, and we stayed with her for six days. My father and I cleared the snow from her roof so it wouldn't collapse, and we were able to uncover her root cellar where she had a winter's worth of root vegetables and cured meat. She insisted we make sure the residents of Little Stilts had enough food to ration through the storm, so my father and I went door to door. We all ate well, and Nerium told us stories in the evenings."

My skin pricks up. "Stories?"

Firelight glints in Claude's eyes. "I am hesitant to tell

you this, because I fear I know what you will do with this information."

"Tell me anyway," I say.

Claude sighs and nods. "Little Stilts is older than Queen's Bridge by a hundred years. Most of Nerium's stories were about the great famine in Hamelin and the roving wolves of Rotterdam, but one black evening she spoke of the Knight. She knew of his treacherous dealings and spit on the floor when she spoke his name, cursing him. She said he was destined to wander these lands because of a blight on his name. She called it his 'great mistake.'"

"What does that mean?" I ask.

"I was eight," Claude says. "I didn't think to ask, but it stood out to me because no one ever spoke of the Knight's mistakes."

"They still don't," I say, as a thought invades my mind.

"I am certain Nerium is dead," Claude says as he stares at me. "I can see your wheels turning. I'd think that, by now, every person there is dead and buried."

I've already made up my mind about what I mean to do, and I am thinking about what provisions I'll need.

"The Knight doesn't make mistakes," I say. "Never once has anyone even suggested it."

"How can that fact help us?" Claude asks.

"If he made a mistake," I say. "That means he is not all knowing, all powerful. It means there is a weakness. I need to know what it is."

"It is less than a half day's ride from here," Claude says. "If you are not back in two days, I will come for you."

I round the table and put my arms around him. He hugs me tight, then disappears down the hall with Maggie at his heels. The smallest glimmer of hope dances to life inside me. It is here in this very moment that I envision a new possibility—defeating the Knight means I don't need to stay hidden. I can reclaim Queen's Bridge and keep it in the hands of a Miller Queen as it has always been. If I can find this weakness in the Knight, I can keep the people of Queen's Bridge safe and avenge my mother in the process. I can still be her right hand, her fury.

CHAPTER 18

I use the snow as cover on my journey to Little Stilts, wrapping myself in it as the wind whips up around me. Claude had marked a map tracing the route, and as I cross over the southwestern border of Queen's Bridge and into Hamelin I cannot help but feel that maybe Claude had made a mistake. As I move toward the mark on the map, I only encounter a single pair of riders on horseback. I hear their horses' calls before I see them and conceal myself in a blanket of snow and shadow as they pass by. When they pass and their voices are out of earshot, I move on.

I've seen Little Stilts on maps, its location indicated by a singular black dot. Claude had said it was more of a hamlet than a village, but as I come upon it, I don't think either description is accurate. There is a single road covered in snow and ice. Only one set of wagon tracks distinguishes it from the surrounding land. In the immediate vicinity there is one house, which looks to be on the verge of collapse. The roof is caved in and there is no front door.

Snow is heaped up in mounds farther down the road. I imagine the remnants of the houses Claude had visited in his boyhood crumbled beneath. I glance at the sky, letting my cloak of snow and ice fall away from me. If I leave now, I can be back to Claude's by dark.

A hawk soars overhead, and I concentrate, listening to his call. He is hungry, scouting for his prey, and then suddenly he is cautious and changes course to avoid something coming up the road behind me. It is a wagon being towed by a single horse and driver.

The horse makes noises like it's dying. A strangled whinny, and the driver croaks something unintelligible at it. I listen again. The horse is the oldest living animal I've ever come across, and I am stunned it's able to pull the cart and its small driver. I consider hiding myself, but the driver has already spotted me and brings the horse to a sudden halt.

I hold still, ready to conjure a weapon if need be, but my gut tells me it won't be necessary.

"You're lost," says the driver.

"No," I say.

The person laughs and gives the reins a little flip. The horse lumbers forward, and the driver pulls up alongside me. I have to bite the inside of my cheek to keep from smiling. I thought the horse was old, and I was right, but the woman guiding it is older. For a moment I wonder if I have accidentally stepped into a land where the dead walk among the living. The woman is a corpse. Her bare hands grip the reins, and her fingers are like bones wrapped in thin paper. Her face is gaunt, the entire outline of her skull visible beneath skin the texture of worn leather but with none of the softness. Her lips roll inward, like there are no teeth behind them to give her mouth a solid shape.

"Of course you're lost," she croaks. "No one who comes here does so of their own free will. Why would they?"

"I'm looking for someone," I say. It's not what I actually mean. I'm not looking for the people from Claude's story who are long dead. I'm looking for the stories they left behind. "I heard of a woman named Nerium. I'm hoping she may have kin in the area?"

The woman narrows her eyes. "No. No kin."

My heart sinks. "Is there anyone left here who might have known her?"

The woman opens her mouth and lets out the most desperate, wheezing laugh I've ever heard. I lean away from her, startled.

"This place is full of ghosts," the woman says, still chuckling. "Maybe some of them knew her. It's hard to say."

I look her over trying to discern if she herself is one of the dead.

"Come with me," she says suddenly, giving her horse a prodding with a little flick of the reins.

She steers her cart down the snow-laden pathway, and I follow at some distance. I'm hesitant, but I shake my head as I remind myself that this woman looks as if she might already be well on her way to meet her maker. I could easily kill her if she tries anything, but I immediately chastise myself for even thinking it. I didn't come all the way here to murder an ancient woman in the center of an abandoned hamlet.

The woman turns onto a pathway that leads up to a house set back among a scattering of trees. As I follow her, I study the house—a small single-story abode with a porch that looks as if it may collapse under the weight of the snow. Several of its windows are boarded up, and its front door is flecked in peeling emerald-green paint. I don't know if I believe in fate, but this may be enough to make me reconsider. Is it possible this is the same house Claude and his father happened upon all those years ago?

The woman lowers herself down from the cart, and I worry the movement will end her. She huffs and sputters and almost loses her balance. I step in to assist her, but she jerks away from me and continues to the front door in silence. Her horse whinnies, sputtering nearly as badly as its owner. I rest my hand on its bony back and feel its voice inside my head. As rough as it looks, the poor thing is still quite lucid, its low hum filling my head.

"Give her a bucket of that feed," the old woman says as she fumbles to open her door. She extends a knobby finger toward a small basket with a woven lid. I open it and scoop out a mix of dried beans, oats, and fresh hay, and transfer it to a small bucket. The horse's call nearly turns to singing as I slide it near her.

"Come on, then," the old woman says as she disappears inside the house.

I set my hand on my dagger and follow her inside. The house is just one room. There is a front door and a smaller rear entrance. A table and two chairs sit in front of the hearth where a black pot hangs from a hook over the dying embers. A neatly made bed stands in the far corner. Her small kitchen is scattered with clay bowls but otherwise tidy.

"You live alone?" I ask.

"Is there any other way to live?" she asks. She sets down a worn leather satchel and lowers herself into one of the chairs at the table. "Sit and tell me why you've come."

I take up the seat across from her. She stares at me, unblinking.

"I know a man who said he came here when he was young," I say. "He met a woman who lived in a house with a green door. He said her name was Nerium and that she knew something about the Knight."

The woman's eyes light up at mention of his name. I keep my hand on the hilt of my dagger. No one should be so eager to hear his name.

"So, you have come to chase ghosts," the woman says.

"The Knight is not a specter," I say, leaning my elbow on the table.

The woman shakes her head. "No. But he is *something*, isn't he? Something unnatural?"

"I would agree," I say. "I don't mean to be rude, but if you didn't know Nerium and you say she has no kin, I think I may be wasting my time and yours."

"Not everyone wants a bunch of needy rats clinging to

them all the days of their lives," she says. "Do you know what it would have cost me to bring children into this world? Do you know how much they consume? How much they cry?" She looks disgusted at the thought.

"I wasn't specifically talking about you," I say.

The woman draws her lips inward, then sighs. "If you're talking about Nerium, then you are talking about me."

"You?" I ask, looking her over once again and trying to assess the passage of time in Claude's story. "You're not implying that you are Nerium, are you?"

"It's the name my mother gave me," she says. "She named me after a poisonous plant. Pretty but deadly to those around it—in case you were wondering what she thought of me."

I sit quietly for a moment. There is a question I want to ask, but I cannot bring myself to do it in a way that seems tactful. I decide to leave any pretense behind.

"How old are you? The man who came here as a boy is graying now." It occurs to me that I don't know exactly how old Claude is, but I'd say he'd seen fifty winters. "He said Nerium was elderly even when he was a boy."

The woman visibly cringes. "Longevity runs in my family. Did you come here to ogle at my date of birth or to ask me something?"

I can't say I believe her at all. Maybe she knew Nerium when she was a girl. There seems to be no one left in this place who would care if she took up another woman's name, perhaps her home and possessions, too. I decide it doesn't matter if she can give me the answers I need.

"Nerium," I say hesitantly. "What can you tell me about the Knight?"

"No," Nerium says, stiffly.

"No?" I ask, confused.

Nerium shakes her head. "No. I can tell you the same things we all know about him. He's ruthless, evil incarnate, that the wishes he grants are full of deception and double meanings."

"I know all that already," I say.

"Exactly," Nerium says. "So, what is it you really want to ask me?"

"No one can stand against him," I say. "Not unless we learn something new about him. Something that can help us strike at the heart of who or what he really is."

"Ahhhh," Nerium says, her voice wet and gurgling. "Another collector of stories." She readjusts herself in her seat and stares across the table at me. The embers in the fire suddenly leap into flames and wash the room in an orange glow. "What did you say your name was?" she asks.

"I didn't," I say. I extend my hand toward the flame and the fire arcs out, gathering in my hand and forming itself into a short dagger of red-hot flames. I hope my meaning is clear.

Nerium rests back in her chair, and the fire settles. I allow the weapon to dissolve.

"The Knight is unstoppable," Nerium says. "But that is only what he wants us to believe. He has been bested but only once."

I lean forward, my heart ticking up. Claude's words echo in my head. "His great mistake."

Nerium nods. "The details of this defeat are scant. I believe someone in my line was there as the events transpired, though I cannot say who. The broken pieces of the tale have trickled down to me."

"Tell me," I say.

Nerium clasps her hands together in front of her. "The Knight's great mistake involved a young girl. She made a wish to him and he granted it, but somehow . . ." Nerium trails off for a moment, and I stay silent as she pulls the story from her mind. "This young girl bested him. She found a way to circumvent his deal, and he became so enraged that he vowed to curse her but she never again wished to him. She never allowed herself or her children to wish to him. It's said he went even more mad than he already was. He almost destroyed himself in his fit of anger. Beaten at his own terrible game by a young girl? I think he could not live with himself after that." Nerium sighs and clears her throat. "But he still lives, so I think he has made his entire life about righting that wrong done to him."

"He has never been bested," I say. "Never."

"You're wrong," Nerium says. "And you should be glad that you are. You wear whatever grief he has caused you like a prisoner wears a shackle. Now you know he's been outdone once in his miserable existence, perhaps you can make lightning strike twice." Her gaze moves from my hand to the fire and back again.

This is what I came here for, and still it is another incomplete story. I press my hand into the table. "That cannot be all there is."

"I'm sure it is not, but that is all I have to say on the matter," Nerium says.

"Do you know of anyone who might have more to tell?" I ask.

Nerium tilts her head to the side, and as she inhales, the air rattles inside her chest. "I'm sure there are others who collect stories. You're not the first to ask about the Knight's great mistake, but something tells me you may be the last."

"Do you always talk in riddles?" I ask, as I push back my chair and stand.

Nerium says nothing but smiles a nearly toothless grin.

I leave Nerium at the table and mount my horse outside. As I ride away from the house with the green door, I look back only once to see Nerium standing on the front step, her arms folded across her chest, a wicked smile on her mouth.

CHAPTER 19

I ride straight to Claude's and collapse on the mat in my room. I sleep into the next morning and awaken on the ninth day after my mother's death. The boys still slumber, and while Claude snores in his room, I dress and go to the potted plant that hides the shard of the mirror in its soil.

I never moved it to a faraway place in the surrounding forest as I'd intended. I pretend that it is because I have been preoccupied with other things, but I know that is just the lie I tell myself to justify keeping the pot with its buried treasure close to me. I need to know if Nova is trying to call out to me. I've considered digging it up a hundred times, knowing it's not the right thing to do, knowing the risks. But as my fingers press into the dirt and find the shard of magic mirror wrapped in cloth, I feel a sense of relief. Perhaps Nova will be there. If I could just talk to him, hear his voice, maybe it would calm this terrible sense of restlessness that has settled over me in the days since my mother died. I need to ask him if he knows about the Knight's great mistake, if there is anything he can add.

Grief clings to me and, despite Claude's warnings, I allow it to fuel a burning sense of hatred inside me. All I can see is the Knight. All I can feel is the white-hot anger bubbling inside me—and it scares me because I know where it leads. Nerium is right. Even though I cannot put together the entire meaning of what she shared with me, I now know that someone had the tools to defeat the Knight at his own game, which means that I may yet see him dead by my hand.

I pull the shard of seeing stone out of the dirt and unwrap it. The glinting black glass is quiet, empty.

"Nova," I whisper. "Where are you? I need you."

I stare into the glass and see only my reflection. After staring into it for far too long, I tuck away my rage and go into the kitchen to clear my head.

Claude and the boys usually leave the kitchen spotless before they go to bed but there is a dirty bowl on the long wooden counter that runs along the back kitchen wall. The early morning light slants through a large window that overlooks the rear garden, which is covered in patchy snow. I set the shard down and rinse the dish off in the washbasin, setting it out to dry on a checkered cloth. I put my hands on the countertop. Cleaning dirty dishes seems like such a mundane thing to do as my mother lies cold somewhere in the belly of Castle Veil and as the destruction of the Knight seems more out of reach than it ever had before. My chest aches as grief rushes in like the tide. I grip the counter's edge to steady myself.

Tap. Tap. Tap.

I glance up and find myself staring into the face of a woman. Startled, I stumble back. At first, I mistake her for Nerium, but after a moment I realize that this woman is taller and broader at the shoulders. She raps her hand against the stained-glass window, and even at a bit of a distance I can see her knuckles are knobbed, her fingers partly curled.

"Don't be frightened, dear," the woman croaks from outside the window. "I—I seem to have lost my way."

I can still hear Claude snoring down the hall. The door to the boys' bedroom is ajar. They're all still sleeping soundly. I go to the rear door and push the bolt back. I open it just a crack. The woman shuffles closer. She's draped in a floor-length black cloak that is tattered at the hem as if she'd dragged it across every jagged rock in her path. The hood covers her head and partially obscures her face. She's clutching a woven basket.

"You're lost?" I ask.

She nods. "I was taking my—my apples to—to market and I—" She stumbles over her own feet, and I rush forward to catch her by the elbow.

"Oh, thank you, my—my dear," she says. Her voice cracks and snaps as she speaks. She breathes hard, her chest heaving.

The arm I cradle in my hand is not much more than skin and bones.

"I'm so—sorry," the woman says. "I've frightened you. I—I didn't mean to."

I'm not frightened, but I am curious. I watch the tree line and I listen to the creatures that dwell there. The birds and foxes and rodents all seem calm.

The woman trembles in my grasp. "Come inside," I say, guiding her toward the door. "Have a rest and then we'll help you get where you need to go."

She leans her head against my shoulder, and I feel a sense of warmth radiating from her. I bring her in and sit her down at the table. I poke at the nearly extinguished fire and throw another log atop the glowing embers. After a few moments, it catches and begins to warm the room.

I sit down next to her, my chair facing hers as she sets her basket on the table and pulls off her hood. A massive braid of tightly coiled gray hair falls down her back. Her face is a maze of lines. They are so numerous I wonder how many years she has walked in this world. The delicate skin of her eyelids droops down, nearly obscuring both her eyes, which could be brown but a milky cloud has begun to cover the centers, creeping in around the edges like milk dripped into a strong dark tea. She sets her hand on the table, and the paper-thin skin on the back makes her veins look like tiny ropes beneath. Her nails are long and yellowed, and she gently taps them against the table.

She sighs. "I am—I am so very tired."

"Were you traveling on foot?" I ask.

She gazes into the fire. "Yes."

"Alone?" I ask.

The woman looks me over, her clouded eyes moving over my face. "You are—very pretty."

Her cadence is strange. It's almost like she's unsure of what she's saying. "Thank you," I say. "Try to rest. You're welcome to stay if—"

Down the hall there's the creaking of boards, and Grump emerges in the hallway. Still in his nightclothes, he is wiping the sleep from his eyes.

"Morning," I say.

He marches straight up to me.

"I snuck out of my room and ate a bowl of leftover soup and then went back to bed."

I try my best not to smile. "Why are you telling me? I've already cleaned the bowl. No one will know."

He shrugs. "I know I'm not supposed to be out here in the middle of the night and—" He seems to suddenly register the woman and his mouth opens into a little O. "Who are you?"

The woman turns her head toward him but says nothing.

Grump looks to me. "Who is this old lady?"

"Savion," I say, using his real name to let him know I'm serious. "That's rude."

He looks confused. "She *is* old."

He's not wrong, but that's not the point. "She's lost. She was taking her apples to—"

"Apples?" Grump's bushy eyebrows push up. He eyes the basket and then, without asking, he squeezes between me and the woman and fishes around in her basket.

"I'm so sorry," I say to the woman as I pull on Grump's oversized nightshirt, but it's too late.

He produces an apple and holds it close to his face.

It is the greenest apple I've ever seen. The waxy skin is perfectly smooth, not a blemish or bruise. The stem is nearly black and protrudes perfectly from the crown of the fruit.

"Where did you get this thing?" Grump asks. "It's still snowy outside. This looks like you just picked it."

Grump is right. Fall has long since passed and the season for apples is over. And the nearest orchards aren't anywhere near Queen's Bridge.

"Where did you say you were coming from again?" I ask, as a feeling of unease spreads through my chest.

"I—I am going to sell my apples," the woman stammers. "I got lost along the way and—and you should try them. They're really very—sweet."

Grump grins and brings the apple to his lips.

The old woman is breathing like she's just run a race. A thin film of sweat breaks across her brow. "Sanaa—loves—apple seeds," she says between gasping breaths. She reaches out, her hand trembling, and snatches the apple out of Grump's hand.

My heart kicks up. "What did you just say?"

"Nothing—nothing, dear," the woman says, her gaze wildly darting around the room.

I put my hand on Grump's shoulder and move him away from us. "No," I say. "You said Sanaa. How do you know that name?"

The woman's gaze settles on me. "She—loves—apple seeds—" Before she can utter another word, she launches herself out of her chair and knocks me backward.

I land hard on my back, the woman on top of me, the unnaturally green apple in her hand. She grips it hard and tries to press it against my mouth. She's stronger than I imagine she could be. She could barely stand, but now she's pinning me to the floor with the weight of her body.

"Eat the apple!" she screams. "Eat it!"

Bits of the apple skin flake off beneath her jagged nails, and a green liquid oozes from the punctures beneath. I hold tight to her wrist, keeping her from pressing the apple into my mouth, but some of the green liquid drips down and lands on my cheek. It burns like a hot poker being pressed into my skin. An agonized cry erupts from my throat. I push hard against her chest and a necklace she had strung around her neck comes loose, dangling just above my face. An emerald cut into the shape of a star. My gaze instinctively moves to her right hand. There among the withered skin is a scar running like a map to the truth of who she is. I stop breathing as I stare up into her face. A face that is much older than it should be.

"It cannot be," I say.

"Looking glass, looking glass, on the wall," she whispers, her lips wet with spittle, her eyes milky white. "Who in this land is the fairest of all?"

She pushes the apple toward me once more, but suddenly there is a calamitous rush of footsteps. Claude races into the room with the other boys trailing him. He puts his shoulder down and runs directly into the woman, knocking her off me. Her head strikes the table leg and her body goes limp. The apple rolls out of her hand and across the floor.

CHAPTER 20

Claude stands panting by the table as all four boys crowd around us. They've armed themselves with wooden spoons, sticks, and hammers. Junior has a hatchet, and Hunter has equipped himself with a broom handle. Maggie stands close to Junior. Her head is nearly as tall as he is, her teeth are bared, a low growl rattling in her chest. Saliva drips from her open mouth onto the floor.

"What is happening here?" Claude asks breathlessly.

I crouch close to the woman as she lies on her back. Her eyes are closed and her mouth is open. She's breathing but in a labored, heavy way. I put my hand to her cheek, and it's then that I know why I had opened the door to her with hardly any hesitation, why I had immediately wanted to be near her. I turn to Claude.

"You won't believe me," I begin, my voice trembling. "I don't know how, but this is my mother."

Claude looks to the woman and then to me.

"What's this?" Hunter asks as he reaches for the strangely green apple.

"Don't touch it!" I say.

Hunter steps back.

"I think it's poison," I say. My face still burns where the green liquid from inside the apple had touched my skin.

Claude grabs a cloth from the kitchen and wraps up the apple, being careful not to touch it with his bare hands. He sets it on the counter and returns to my side.

"Eve, I know you're grieving, and I understand if you're confused," Claude says. "But this cannot be your mother."

"It is," I say. "I don't know how, but it is. She said Queen Sanaa's name. She is wearing my mother's necklace, and she has the same scar on her hand. She is my mother, but she is changed."

"She looks like she's a hundred years old," says Hunter.

I nod. "Help me move her into the chair."

"We'll tie her up," Claude says.

I don't protest. Claude helps me lift her and settle her in a chair with her wrists and ankles tightly bound. I support her head as she weaves in and out of consciousness.

"Eve," Claude begins, but I shake my head.

"I already know what you're going to say, but please," I say. "Just wait. Let her wake up and we'll have her explain it."

Claude pulls his lips between his teeth like he's trying to keep a few choice words to himself. He sighs. "I am glad you made it back safely. Did you find what you were looking for in Little Stilts?"

"I found Nerium and the house with the green door," I say.

Claude's eyes go wide. "Impossible."

"I thought the same thing, but she was there."

"She cannot still be living," Claude says. "She was at death's door when I was a child."

"Maybe she and death are working hand in hand," I say. "She was alive and well, but no, I didn't get what I was looking for. She only left me with more questions."

"Looking glass, looking glass," the woman mumbles as her eyes flutter open. They're brown, with none of the milky white edges—and they are familiar to me as my own reflection.

"Mother," I say, softly touching her shoulder.

She flinches as if I struck her. She looks around the room. "Where am I?" Her voice is still gravelly and rough, but I recognize it, too. "How did I—" She turns her head and her gaze finds me. She breathes deep, and tears fill her eyes. "Eve?"

I lean toward her but Claude steps between us. I try to push past him, but he stops me.

"What are you doing?" I ask. "Move."

Claude plants himself like an oak. "I will not. This woman came into our home and tried to kill you." He glances at the bundle of cloth containing the poisoned apple. "She nearly succeeded. You call her mother, but the Queen is dead."

"No," my mother—and I have no doubt that it is her—says. "No! It is the Knight! This is his doing!"

She begins to sob, and I want to rush into her arms but Claude is right, something beyond my understanding has happened. Claude and I exchange glances, and he steps aside.

"Why did you try to poison me?" I ask, swallowing the knot in my throat. "How could you?"

My mother—in this new form, her hair gray, her skin a maze of lines and folds, her frame skeletal—looks as if she is going to fall apart.

"I could never," she says. "I would never. The Knight used some kind of magic, some spell, to enchant me. That night when you came to see me, he realized our ruse and I thought he would be enraged and simply kill us all right then and there—but he didn't."

"Why?" I ask.

"Because the terms of our deal have not been fulfilled," she says. "You were to die on my order. He wanted me to order your death so that I would know all my life that it was I who was responsible."

"The cruelty is always the point," Claude says.

She nods. "When he realized the terms of our deal were not fulfilled, he forced me to look into that mirror. He didn't let me eat or drink, he forced me to recite those terrible words. Looking glass, looking glass . . ."

Her eyes start to glaze over, the edges of her brown irises turning white. I step toward the boys, and Claude balls his hands into fists. She swallows hard, and after a moment her eyes clear. She struggles to catch her breath.

"He—he tried to seed a bitter jealousy in me," she says. "He thought he could make me hate you enough to come here and—and end you myself."

"He does not know you," I say.

"And yet," Claude says. "You're here trying to do just that and looking like you've lived an entire lifetime twice over."

"It is a punishment the Knight thought would be fitting," my mother says. "He turned me into a crone, thinking it would stoke the flames of jealousy. As if being in this form is some kind of an insult." She huffs. "He knows nothing of the love a mother has for her child or herself. When this new plan did not yield the outcome he wanted, he resorted to other methods. A spell to make me bring you the poison apple, feed it to you from my own hand, and watch you perish. That is what he wanted, and I fought it every step of the way, even though I felt my body moving against my will but never my heart." Her voice hitches in her chest.

"I think we should kill her," Grump says.

Junior clamps his hand over Grump's mouth and drags him backward. A paring knife falls from his grasp in the process.

"Savion, please," Claude says, rubbing his temple. "Forgive him. He's very protective of Eve."

My mother nods.

Claude stands in front of her, looking her directly in the eye. "It is clear you are under some enchantment. Can you control it?"

She sighs. "I—I have been trying to. I don't know. I feel its effects waning."

Claude shakes his head as he glances at the boys and at me. "That is not good enough."

"No," my mother says. "It's not. I know that. Perhaps it is best to keep me restrained until I am certain."

Claude nods and takes a few steps back.

"Why does everyone think you're dead?" Junior asks. "The whole of Queen's Bridge is in mourning."

"The Knight cast this spell on me, and the transformation kept me bedbound for hours," my mother says. "I couldn't move. I couldn't breathe or speak. I felt as if I were dying or maybe already dead, trapped inside my own mind and body. Lady Anne kept vigil, and when I lay still, she checked for the sound of my heart and found it so scant that I believe she thought I was gone. She covered me with a sheet and told the messengers to spread the news."

"And the doctor, he didn't check to see if it was true?" Claude asks. "Isn't that the way of things?"

My mother nods. "He didn't have the opportunity. Lady Anne left my chambers to fetch the doctor, and in her absence the Knight reappeared and handed me the apple. He told me where to go to find you and before I even knew what was happening, I was moving. Trudging through the snow with only a single thought in my head." My mother looks at me, her eyes full of shame and sadness. "Kill Eve."

"It's not you," I say, rushing to her side and putting my arms around her. "It's not what you're really thinking or feeling. You would never hurt me. Never."

My mother looks up at me as tears stream down her face. "Eve, my baby, my love, I would put out my own heart before I ever harmed you. And I tried—I tried to stop myself from continuing this awful journey. I fought his will every step of the way but it made little difference."

As I cradle her head against my chest, a terrible thought occurs to me. "Mother," I say, my voice and hands trembling. "The Knight—he told you to come here. He *knows* I'm here."

The room falls into a dead, solemn silence. We had all been so preoccupied with my mother's transformation and the circumstances of her arrival that we had not thought about what it means that she is here in the first place.

"He does," my mother whispers as fear invades her. "He knows, but I cannot say how, and now that he has once again failed to force me to comply with the terms of our deal, I fear what he will do."

Claude turns to me, desperation distorting his kind features. "You learned nothing in Little Stilts that may help us?"

"Nerium told me the Knight had been defeated only once," I say. "She called it his great mistake. Someone, a girl, made a wish to him and she somehow found a way to leave the terms unfulfilled."

Claude sighs. "That can't help us now, can it? How could Nerium think it would?"

"His great mistake . . . ," my mother says, trailing off, lost in her own thoughts.

I put my hand on her shoulder. "What is it? Do you know something about this?"

Mother shakes her head. "We do not wish to him. It is a

hard-and-fast rule passed down to the Miller Queendom for generations. A rule that has been broken because of me."

"Do not guilt yourself this way," I say. "We cannot go back."

"No. I know," my mother says. "But why?" She seems confused. "Why have such an ironclad rule?"

"Because his deals are treacherous," Claude says, as if it is the most obvious thing in the world.

"No," my mother says firmly. "No. It is more than that for us."

My mind reels as I think about everything my mother has ever shared with me about my family's place in Queen's Bridge and the deeds of our foremothers. The Knight's pursuit of us, terrorizing our people in the process, has always felt personal. It has always felt as if he simply cannot help but torment us. He wanted so badly to make a deal with my mother, and he continues still to force us to comply. A terrible thought occurs to me.

"It is us," I say.

My mother and Claude stare at me.

"We are connected to this great mistake somehow," I say, putting the pieces together. "He could not let it go. He will not allow us to—"

There is a sudden call inside my head—a high whistling filled with fear and angst. I rush to the window to see a gathering of crows so massive it looks like a swirling storm cloud, blotting out the sun. Claude's expression is a mask of fear. He nods to the boys, and they spring into action as if they'd had a plan all along. They close and lock the shutters and bar the doors. They change into warm clothing and gather in the front room by the hearth.

My mother, still bound by her wrists and ankles, sits quietly in her chair as I move into the kitchen, retrieving the shard of seeing stone I'd left on the counter. Down the hall I set the shard on my bed and change into something I can fight in—thick pants cut high at the waist, a long-sleeved woolen sweater woven so tight it is nearly impossible to cut, a pair of sturdy boots. Standing in the small confines of my room, I feel helpless. The fear of what I know is coming threatens to crush me. The Knight *will* come for me because somehow all of this leads back to us. I turn to leave when a guttural scream cuts through the air. I trip out into the hallway. Junior and Hunter are by my side in a blink.

"What is it?" Junior asks. He grips a small dagger so tightly his knuckles are ashen.

The scream sounds again, and I realize it is my name being called aloud, coming from the shard. Rushing back into my room, I grab hold of the glass and see Nova's wild, terrified eyes staring back at me.

"Nova!" I scream. My voice doesn't sound like my own. I knew I had been longing to see him but until this moment I hadn't realized how much. "Where are you? Can you come here? Something has happened and I need—"

"Eve!" Nova cuts in. "Eve! Listen to me!" He's suddenly gone from the seeing stone as if he's been snatched away.

I grip the shard. "No! Nova!"

There is a terrible rumble from the glass, the sound of scuffling, Nova's desperate gasps.

"Nova!" I scream. I grip the glass shard so tight it cuts into my palm. If there is pain, I do not feel it. Blood seeps down my arm and soaks the sleeve of my sweater.

Nova's eyes appear in the mirror again. "He's coming! Eve! He's coming for you! Run!"

CHAPTER 21

I have broken my promise to keep Claude and the boys safe. It was never my intention to put them in harm's way, but my presence here has done just that. I leave the shard on my bed and rush back to the front room.

"Can we get the boys someplace safe?" I ask. "If we leave now, is there somewhere they can go?"

Claude looks at his boys as they train their eyes on him, waiting for him to give them an answer.

"He's coming," I say. "The Knight."

"Now?" Claude asks, the color draining away from his face. I nod.

"Then it is already too late," he says. He looks to his boys and then to me. "He has taken so much from us already. I will not allow him to take anything more." He snaps into action, gathering the boys and shepherding them to the root cellar under the kitchen floor amid heavy protest.

"We can fight!" Junior says.

"We know how!" Hunter chimes in.

Chance puts his arms around Grump.

"No!" Claude says. "You will stay quiet and hidden until this is over."

Until this is over.

What does that mean for us? How does this end? My stomach sinks as the possibilities tumble through my head, none of them giving me even the slightest glimmer of hope. I reach to untie my mother and, when I've freed her hands, she clasps her hands over mine.

"Don't," she says. "I don't know if I am fully in control."

"I'm taking these off," I say. "We don't have time for you to be unsure." I grip her hands in mine. "You are in control."

She nods, and I finish untying her. She stands on shaky legs.

"What can I do?" she asks. She glances at the dagger on my waist. "I don't know if I can fight. I can barely stand, but I'm willing to try."

"I don't need you to fight," I say. I glance toward the hatch in the kitchen floor. "I need you to keep the boys safe. They are precious to me. Can you do that?"

My mother nods. "I would stand beside you, regardless of how I feel."

She's in no shape to do so and she knows it. She has never been the type of person to back away from a fight. She feared nothing save losing me, and if I did not insist she join the boys in the cellar she would be at my side as I have always been at hers. As she descends the short ladder and joins the boys,

Grump has somehow gotten his hands back on his little paring knife. He points it at my mother.

"If you act funny, I'll end you," he says. His voice is small, but I do not take him for a joke. He means it.

My mother backs away until she is pressed into the wall. "You'd be well within your rights to do it, but it will not come to that."

"I hope not," Chance says. His hands flit to his weapon of choice, a short length of wood with several rusty nails poking out of the end.

"Where did you get that?" Hunter asks as he laments his weapon, a large rock he's palming in his right hand.

"I made it," Chance says. "I'll make you one when we get out of here."

Hunter nods and grips his rock a little tighter.

Suddenly, there is a terrible rumbling in the earth beneath my feet. The sound reverberates in my bones as it shakes the house. Bits of gravel bounce around on the dirt floor of the root cellar. Dishes rattle in the cabinets. Grump slips his hand into Chance's. Hunter braces himself while Junior stares up at me, his eyes wide and fearful.

"Close the hatch," Claude says.

As we lower it together, I look upon my mother and the boys. A small voice in my head tells me it may be for the last time.

I roll a rug over the hatch and move to the front room with Claude, who has armed himself with a long broadsword. It is a weapon that requires brute strength of which Claude has plenty. Maggie sniffs around his ankles, grunting and huffing. The sound emanating from her is not fear, it is anticipation. She wants to sink her teeth into something bloody and warm. The ground rumbles again, and I look to Claude, whose mouth is drawn down.

"It is his castle," he says. "It's close."

"I'll go out to meet him," I say. "I'll try to draw him away."

"It won't work," Claude says, sighing. He turns to me and leans so close I can feel the rage rippling off him like the heat from the midday sun. His eyes are wet, but his voice does not betray him. He speaks to me as if he is speaking an incantation or a prayer. "We don't let him hurt the boys. Do you understand me? We die before we let him do that."

On this, we agree.

I open the front door and walk out into the bitter, biting cold as the Knight's castle pushes its way through the towering pines. It emerges like a beast from a cave. The moon lights up the land around us, glinting off the metal of the Knight's cursed abode. Black smoke billows from its chimneys as it comes to rest just outside the fence in the front garden. It crushes the trees around it like matchsticks as its legs fold under it.

I focus on my breathing—in and out, in and out. I try to remember every lesson, every mistake I'd ever made in my training. I cannot afford to make a single misstep now. Claude stands beside me, his eyes narrow. The look stretched across his face is one of a man who is about to confront for the first time the creature that caused his wife's death—it is pain and agony and bitter hatred. I am with him in his grief and resentment, his regret and his fury. I hope that together we can burn the Knight out of this world and send him to whatever exists for fiends such as him.

The hatch in the belly of the metal beast of a castle opens, stretching down to the ground. The ramp shudders, and from the hatch a disheveled figure in a tattered cloak tumbles out. They land hard on the snow that is packed so tightly it offers no cushion from the fall. They cough and blood spatters into the snow—drops of crimson on the white cold. I take a step forward as the figure stumbles to their feet, their hair loose around their face.

Nova.

His gaze flits to me. His face is bruised and blood traces down his chin. I take another step forward, but he holds up one trembling hand.

"Don't come any closer," he says. His breaths are frenzied. His eyes dart from me to Claude and then to the house. "Did you get them out?"

I shake my head. "No time."

Nova's eyes widen in the dark as terror claws its way across his broken and bloodied face. He closes his eyes and tilts his face up to the sky in a silent plea.

Footsteps echo in the dark. Metal on metal, thunderous and inhuman. I stare at the blackened opening to the Knight's castle, waiting for him to emerge, and when he does it is as if he is materializing out of a nightmare. His black armor is polished to a high shine. Even at a distance, I can see myself and Claude reflected in it. His helm glints in the moonlight, but I cannot see his eyes. He steps toward Nova.

"The people of Queen's Bridge call me a monster," the Knight says. His voice sends a bolt of terror straight through me, but I do not let it show.

"They are right," Claude says through gritted teeth.

The Knight angles his head toward Claude. "As monstrous as you? A man so desperate for a family that he would sacrifice his beloved wife—what was her name—Leah?"

Claude's intake of breath is sharp and pained. He grips the hilt of his sword. "Do not speak her name."

The Knight takes another step toward Nova. "Am I as monstrous as a son who would betray his own father?" He tilts his helm toward me. "And you, dearest Eve. A girl made of the night itself, imbued with the power to do wonders, and what was it all for? So that your selfish mothers might have a few fleeting years with you?" He laughs, and it is the most terrible sound I've ever heard. "I may be monstrous, but I am nothing compared to the rest of you."

"None of that matters now," I say, extending my hand toward the icy blanket of snow that covers the ground at my feet. "The deals you've made with my mother are finished. We will not comply with your terms. We will not offer payment."

The Knight angles his body toward Nova, and his hand, in its armored glove, clenches and his shoulders rise just slightly, like he has taken a breath and is holding it in, stifling something inside himself. I flex my fingers and a column of ice juts out of the snow. I grasp it, willing it to form a blade. It obeys, and I hold the icy sword in my hand as the Knight wraps his hand around Nova's throat and lifts him into the air.

"Let him go," I say.

Maggie is suddenly at my heel, snarling and snapping her razor-sharp teeth.

The Knight flings Nova into the air. His body collides with the underbelly of the castle. When he lands back in the snow, he is still. Too still.

A cry erupts from my throat. Claude and I move toward the Knight in tandem. I rush left as he goes right. Claude brings the blade of his sword across the Knight's chest. The Knight barely flinches as the blade ricochets off his armor. He lowers his shoulder and hits Claude directly in the chest. Claude is tossed into a snowbank and groans in pain, gasping for air.

I swing my sword with all the strength I can muster and when it makes contact with the Knight's armor a spark bright as the moon lights up the night for one brief moment. In the flash of light, I see the Knight's eyes through the slit in his helm. The irises are black as coal, the skin around them withered and dry. He is a monster now, but has he always been? Is there something human under this monstrous façade? If there is, that means he can be killed.

"I know your secret," I say through clenched teeth. It is not the full truth, but I speak the words as if nothing else matters. "I intend to follow in the footsteps of the girl who bested you."

The Knight is so still I cannot see his chest rise and fall.

"You know nothing," the Knight says. "If you did, you wouldn't be here."

I don't want to hear anything else. I rush forward again as the Knight conjures a blanket of darkness from the night sky and flings it toward me. It covers me and everything goes black. I lose sight of Claude, of Nova, of the house. I stumble in the pitch black as somewhere beyond it, the Knight laughs uproariously. Maggie growls and snaps, then yelps in pain. I think I hear Nova grunt and then scream. I feel relief and terror at the same time. He is alive but he is screaming. I slash at the blanket of blackness, and when I break through I catch sight of Maggie, who is limping but has put herself between Nova and the Knight. Nova is standing, a long sharp dagger with a silver blade clutched in his hands. His hair is plastered to his face.

"You raise a weapon against me?" the Knight asks.

"I do," Nova says. "I will not be a pawn in your twisted games any longer."

The Knight lowers his head and Maggie snaps at him. He raises his arm, preparing to strike her.

Claude rushes in, throwing his full weight against the Knight and planting the hilt of his sword in the Knight's chest. The breastplate buckles as the Knight appears to flinch. Claude grins maniacally and hocks a mouthful of bloody spittle on to the ground. The Knight brings his arm down hard on Claude's shoulder. There's a loud pop, and Claude's body lurches to the side. He screams in agony, his shoulder visibly dislocated. He drops his sword and sinks to his knees.

The Knight laughs, tilting his head back. Just then,

something splits the air in front of me, passing so close to my face I can feel the cold rush of air left in its wake. When the Knight levels his head, an arrow protrudes from the slit in his helm. From the placement, the arrow is stuck firmly in his cursed right eye.

Claude is still clutching his shoulder as his arm hangs at an unnatural angle. Nova rushes to his side, grabs his arm, and yanks it back, popping the shoulder back into place. Claude bellows as another arrow glances past me. This one bounces off the Knight's shoulder. I follow the path of the arrow back to its source—Junior standing on the front step, bow in hand, arrow notched.

The Knight reaches up and plucks the arrow from his face. Stuck to its tip are tendrils of bloody flesh. I think I hear the Knight gasp.

"Run!" Claude shouts.

Junior's face is a mask of terror as he scrambles off the porch and then my mother is there, pulling him away. The Knight picks up Claude's sword and launches it directly at Junior. It collides with the front stoop and explodes in a hail of wooden shards. Junior disappears in the cloud of debris.

A ragged cry escapes my throat as I rush the Knight, swinging my sword toward him, and in a blink he has conjured his own sword from the ice. Our blades clash against each other. We are close now. So close I can see the details of my face in his gleaming helm as he bears down on me, pressing his blade into mine. My arms tremble under the strain and I am once again struck by the feeling that this man—this monster—is smiling at me. I plant my foot in the ground and grit my teeth, pushing back against him. In my head there is a low rumble, and suddenly Maggie rushes in, gripping the Knight's forearm. Her teeth pierce the metal and the Knight swings her entire body to the right. Maggie goes flying and lands with a thud in the snow. I take the opportunity to bring my sword up under the Knight's chin, but the tip glances off his armor and I stumble to the side.

There comes a groan from the broken pile of timber that used to be the front step of the Kingfisher house. From the rubble, Junior emerges, and he is dragging my mother's limp body from under the wreckage.

The Knight lunges toward me, his sword raised, but I sidestep him and bring my own sword down across his back. He slips forward and the tip of his sword goes into the ground. As he bends to retrieve it, I slip past his arm and race toward my mother.

"She pushed me out of the way!" Junior says as I fall into the snow beside her.

"Mother!" I cry as I brush her hair away from her bloodied face. She coughs, wincing in pain.

"My ribs," she gasps. "They're broken." She clutches the right side of her chest.

Claude lets out a groan, and I turn my attention back to him. His sword missing, he instead wields a stick as large as a small tree, brandishing it at the Knight who only looks on. The Knight stalks toward Nova, ignoring Claude altogether.

I loop my arm around my mother and force her to stand.

The pain snatches her breath away. All she can do is whimper.

I grab Junior and pull him close. "Take her to the shed. Hide there until I call for you. Do not come back here. Do you understand?"

Junior nods. "I shot him right in the eye."

I cannot help but smile at him. "Go."

He rushes off, practically dragging my mother along with him. I turn and conjure a short dagger from the ice, something that can slip between the plates of the Knight's armor.

"Stop this!" Nova cries. "Let this be done!"

"It is done when I say it is done," the Knight says as he looms over him. He gestures with his hand and the snow begins to gather, swirling into a cocoon of frigid ice that surrounds Nova. He beats wildly against it, but it is no use. "The Queen has failed to uphold her end of our bargain," the Knight continues. "A deal is a deal, and I will have nothing less than her full compliance." He laughs. "What will the people think of me if I allow her to cheat me out of what is rightfully mine?"

There is so much anger in these last few words it gives me pause.

"The people?" I ask as I move toward him, my blood pumping through me, warming me against the biting cold. "You care what the people will think of you? The people of Queen's Bridge already know what you are! You are a liar! A deceiver!"

The Knight squares his shoulders and faces me as Claude collapses on the ground near Nova, clutching his chest, opening and closing his eyes like he's struggling to stay alert.

"I have granted the people of the wretched land all their hearts could desire," the Knight says as he steps toward me. "And still they try to cheat me, to swindle me."

I grip my dagger made of the frigid ice, the biting wind, and the sharp malice that fuels me as I make my forward march.

"At what cost?" I ask.

"I don't force them to make the wishes," the Knight snaps, the cool exterior of his controlled façade slipping. There is anger and desperation in his tone. "But once we have entered into a deal, there can be no backing out, no . . . modifications. Do you know how many times your mother begged me for just a few more precious years with you? Do you know that she offered me riches?" He huffs out a laugh, and a puff of white steam erupts from the slit in his helm. He grips his sword. "She is not the first to do so. How I delighted in her pain as I denied her that." I cannot tell if he is speaking of my mother . . . or of someone else. He tilts his head, and I can feel him looking at me—into me. "You still have not put the pieces together, have you, Eve?"

I raise my dagger and push off the ground. I rise up high enough to swing my weapon, slicing him across his helm. A lightning bolt–shaped crack snakes its way up the faceplate. He swipes at me with his gloved hand and I land, one knee bent, giving me just enough leverage to sidestep him, but he catches me by the back of my shirt and wrenches me around, taking hold of me by the neck. I strike at him near the joint of his shoulder where there is a fissure in the armor. The blade slips in and the Knight wails—a hollow, echoing sound. He yanks the blade out, and it disintegrates in his hand. I try to quickly will another blade to form, but the Knight squeezes my neck so hard my vision blurs. He sticks his sword in the snow and raises his now free right hand.

"You think you have nothing left to lose, no reason to ask me to grant your wishes, but you haven't thought it through," the Knight says.

"I will never wish anything of you!" I shout.

The Knight spins me around and shoves me forward, holding me by the back of my neck. He leans down so that his voice echoes in my ear. "Are you sure?"

He wants to make another deal. My mother's words echo in my head: *I don't think he could stop even if he wanted to and there are certain deals that seem to consume him more than others.*

I try to crane my neck to look him in the face. "I won't do it."

He steadies me and suddenly there is a great cracking sound. From the corner of my eye, I catch the Knight's free hand opening and closing as he conjures a piece of jagged ice from the frozen ground. The ice coalesces into a spinning orb that hovers just above his outstretched palm. It's the size of a wagon wheel, and it spins rapidly.

"Sweet Eve," says the Knight. "Daughter of the Queen, protector of Queen's Bridge—you can't save them. They are not worth saving."

The ball of swirling ice launches from his hand. It flies through the air and finds its target. A target I didn't know was there. And now it is too late.

The icy ball strikes Junior, who has emerged from his hiding place, directly in the chest as he stands at the side of the house. The force of the impact lifts him off the ground, and he lands in the snow just in front of the tree line.

Claude screams, and I can only watch as he runs, a hitch in his step, toward where Junior lies motionless on the ground. I watch him as he approaches Junior and then collapses next to him, sinking to the ground as if he wants to be swallowed by it. He grabs the boy and pulls him to him. The snow beneath him is red with blood, and steam rises in tumbling clouds from the terrible wound in Junior's chest. The sound that comes from Claude is unlike anything I have ever heard, and that is how I know what has become of the oldest Kingfisher boy. Junior, the most responsible, the most caring, the one who had shown me a light when I was lost in my own grief, the boy who missed his mother as I missed mine, is dead.

CHAPTER 22

The Knight lets go of my neck, and my legs give out. I suck in a chest full of cold air and grit my teeth so hard something pops in my temple. Pain blooms there but it is nothing compared to the growing ache in my chest. Claude's anguished cries ring out in the open night air. Mingled among them is the call of birds, and the crunching of snow—a parade of footsteps. The other boys appear from around the side of the house. They see Claude cradling Junior's body and begin to wail like the wind.

I stand and face the Knight who begins to conjure another deadly projectile of ice, looking past me through the slit in his helm. The boys cry out, and Claude looks between them and Junior's body. His gaze darts around wildly, his mouth hanging open in an expression of abject grief and horror. The Knight laughs, and I know that this is the moment when I can make good on my promise to the other Kingfisher boys and to Claude.

"Don't!" I scream. "Please don't!"

Nova beats wildly against the wall of his ice prison. A crack ripples up the side, but the structure keeps him confined.

The Knight tilts his head down. "I don't have to, but I will. Unless . . ." He pauses, waiting.

I know what he wants. I have run out of any other options. "Unless I make a deal with you," I say.

The Knight's entire frame stiffens. It is as if the mere idea of it fills him with anticipation. He cannot help himself. I watch as the ball of ice swirls above his open palm, ready to strike down anyone in its path.

I can't allow him to hurt anyone else, but I know this will go wrong. A deal with the Knight, a wish granted by him, may end in my death or with me cursed in some unfathomable way. If my words are not precise, if my intent isn't clear, it will end in tragedy. Others have tried—my mothers, Sir Gregory, Claude and his precious wife, countless people in Queen's Bridge—but none have succeeded in the way they wanted. The Knight always finds a way to make them suffer.

The Knight flicks his wrist and the ball of ice crashes into the side of the house, shattering the window and bringing part of the roof down in pieces. Something catches in the rubble, perhaps a spark from the now demolished fireplace, and the orange glow of a smoldering fire lights up the night.

"Fire or ice?" the Knight asks. "How would you like them to die?"

"I want to make a deal!" I scream. "Grant me a wish!"

"Don't do it, Eve!" Nova shouts, his voice muffled by the ice. "Don't do it!" He slams his fists against the ice once more, and the crack in the side widens.

The Knight turns his head toward Nova, and his shoulders roll forward just slightly before he quickly straightens up and turns his attention back to me.

"Anything your heart desires, Princess," says the Knight. I can hear the satisfaction in his voice. "Tell me, what would make you happiest in all the world?"

I close my eyes for a moment. I can still hear the sounds of grief washing over the Kingfishers in waves. I can hear Claude struggling to keep them afloat. Nova is pounding his fists against the ice, the fire is now roaring, my mother lies injured somewhere, the people of Queen's Bridge are probably still collecting their dead, and in the sky above me is the unmistakable melodic hum of a bird—not just any bird but my nightingale savior—Queen Sanaa.

I open my eyes as she flutters down and lands on my shoulder. She coos against my neck. She has flown miles to be here with me in this moment when it feels as if everything is ending.

"I want these boys and their father and all the people of this land to be rid of you," I say. "I want them to never again have to look on your hideous visage. I want you gone."

The Knight paces in front of me—left to right, right to left. "A tall order, Princess. A very tall order indeed. And what shall it be—terms? Payment? What suits you?"

I have nothing to give. It is clear that the Knight does not value riches and so there is no amount of gold or emeralds or land or livestock that can assuage him. That leaves me with only one option, and it is a terrible risk. It can only end in catastrophe. "Terms."

The Knight steps forward and leans down so close to me I can see his wounded, empty eye socket and his remaining eye like a black orb glinting in the firelight. "Terms it is." He puts out his hand and I take it, a signal that we are entering into this damnable agreement. "I will leave the people of Queen's Bridge in peace," the Knight says. "I will grant no further wishes from them. I will leave and it will be as if I have never existed here." He squeezes my hand so tight I feel as if it might break. I grit my teeth and stare into his eye. "And in return, my terms are thus—I will have your life."

"I will gladly give it up," I say, glancing at Claude who looks on with vacant eyes.

"As easy as that?" the Knight asks, his tone pitching up in a way that unnerves me. "I cannot deny that seeing you dead by your mother's hand has been something I have wanted from the very beginning but . . ." He trails off, and a puff of gray steam escapes from the crack in his helm as he exhales sharply. "Somehow, that is simply not enough for me any longer." His voice is nearly singing with delight. "No. We will do this another way. I will have a life but it will not be yours. You will choose one person to die in your place. Someone who is here right now. Someone you love. The price of my compliance is one life, and you must watch the light leave their eyes. Make your choice."

He shoves my hand back toward me.

"The deal is made," he says. "Fulfill your promise to me so that I may grant your wish." He turns his back on me. "Fail," he says over his shoulder. "And you will pay a price so steep your soul may never find itself whole again." He gestures toward the boys and to Claude and then he looks in the direction of Queen's Bridge. "Look upon your sacrifice, Eve. Now."

I stare at the ground. It is an impossible choice, and the price is not one I can easily pay. And what will my punishment be when I cannot comply? My hands begin to tremble and sweat slicks my palms. It has already gone wrong.

From behind me there is the crunching of snow and I turn, instinctively. My mother is limping toward me, clutching her chest.

"Mother," I whisper, as dread chokes the words from me. "Get away from here! Go!"

She does not listen. She moves toward me and stops a few paces from where I am. She turns to the Knight.

"You must always win," she says.

The Knight huffs. "And I do, my Queen. Always."

"So let it be done," my mother says. She turns to me and smiles. "I'm here, Eve. Let it be me. Save them." She gestures to the boys and to the horizon in the distance. "Save the people of Queen's Bridge."

"I—I can't," I stammer. "I can't do it." I turn to the Knight. "Take my life! I'm offering it to you right now!"

"That is not part of our agreement," he says.

"Must it be by her own hand?" my mother asks.

The Knight stills himself, then shakes his head. "No. But she must watch."

All I can think is how cruel he is, how his brutality knows no bounds. My mother suddenly reaches into her cloak and produces the unnaturally green poison apple. The Knight steps toward her, seemingly enthralled.

My mother holds the apple to her lips. "I love you," she says as she looks me dead in the eye.

I move toward her, reaching for the apple as her teeth brush its deadly flesh, when suddenly a dark figure darts in front of her. There is a brief scuffle as my mother falls hard onto her back. The figure turns—Nova is there, apple in hand, a wicked grin twisting his bloodied lips. He bites into the apple and swallows the poisoned flesh as he keeps his gaze locked on me.

"Nova?" the question comes out because I can think of nothing else to say or to ask. I rush to his side as he collapses in a heap. I pull him on to my lap and cradle his head as the poison spreads like black tendrils under his skin. "No! No, please!"

Nova's eyes roll back, and he mutters incoherently. "He is not who—who you think. Know—know his name. I—I am—sorry—sorry, Eve." He breathes slow and shallow. "It was you. You are the reason I—the reason I didn't want to be a—a monster anymore."

"You are not a monster," I say as tears make a watercolor painting of Nova's beautiful face. *You are not a monster.*

His lips curl into a soft smile. "Yes, I am. But I—I am yours. I love . . ."

I press my forehead against his and shut my eyes as his words die in his throat. His body goes limp under my hands.

The Knight has moved closer to us and is standing like a statue . . . watching. I gently rest Nova's lifeless body on the snow-covered ground, touching his cheek gently before stumbling to my feet in a haze of grief and anger. The Knight stays close to Nova's body as I back away. My chest is so tight I can't breathe. I can't see anything other than the Knight. I want him dead.

"Did you look into his eyes as he died?" the Knight asks as he stares down at Nova's body. "The terms were clear. You were too busy crying over him to look into his eyes as the light left them. Our deal is unfulfilled."

And here it is. It occurs to me in this moment that words will never be good enough, the intentions can never be clear enough. Every deal the Knight makes is in bad faith and so there can be no resolution, no closure. I extend my hand toward the flames now consuming the rest of the Kingfisher house. An arc of orange flame connects to my palm and a blade sharp enough to pierce the night sky forms under my grasp. It is unlike any weapon I have ever conjured before. It is burning and bright and full of white-hot rage. The Knight is still looking at Nova. Does he care that his son now lies dead on the cold ground? He nudges Nova's corpse with the toe of his boot and grunts.

Everything inside me—all the hatred and grief and

anger—rushes out in a flood. I lurch forward, the fiery sword blazing, a roar in my chest that pushes past my lips. I strike him at the back of the knee first. The blow buckles him, and he sinks to the ground. I raise my sword and bring it down hard across his back. It cracks the armor and a large piece of it falls away, revealing a piece of leathery flesh beneath. The Knight turns and scrambles to his feet. Stumbling back, he conjures a sword from the broken pieces of the ice that had surrounded Nova only moments ago. It is a tapered sword—sharp, deadly. He swings it toward me and as I pitch left, the tip catches the flesh of my thigh, tearing it open. A warm rush flows down my leg. I wince, but the weapon I've built from the flames requires both hands and I cannot take the time to push the wound closed. I ignore the pain as I swing at the Knight again. I catch a plate of armor covering his left forearm, and it buckles and falls away from him. The arm beneath is small, shrunken. I look into his eyes and for the first time I see the unmistakable flash of fear.

I catch a glimpse of a figure rushing in behind the Knight. Claude is clutching a hunting knife with a blade as long as my arm. I raise my sword high, preparing to strike just as Claude rushes in and sticks the blade of his knife into the crack at the back of the Knight's armor.

The Knight rears back, howling like an animal. The sound cuts through the air and frightens every living creature in the nearby wood. Their calls go up like the blaring of trumpets. Claude does not let go. He holds tight to the hilt of the knife, pressing farther into the Knight's rotten flesh. The Knight wrenches his hand back and sends Claude flying into the snow. I move in and thrust my blade at the Knight's chest. The point punctures his breastplate, and I can feel the hot heat of the blade running him through. Screaming, Hunter rushes past me and kneels at Claude's side.

I let go of the flaming sword and it disintegrates, leaving a smoking black hole in the Knight's chest. I catch a glimpse of the snow—white as down—on the other side. He stumbles and then collapses in a heap.

I run past him, my leg bleeding profusely. I press it closed with my hand as I come upon Claude. He is still.

"Pa!" Hunter yells. He turns to me. "Eve! Help me!"

I kneel down and press my ear to Claude's chest. "Please," I whisper into the cold night like a wish. "Please." A slow, rhythmic thumping sounds in his chest. "He's alive."

Hunter bursts into tears and lays himself over Claude.

"Eve!" my mother's ragged voice calls.

She is cradling Nova, but she is pointing toward the tree line. The Knight has disappeared and left a trail of blood, black as the night, in the snow. I find my footing and follow the bloody path that tracks into the woods along the footpath, leading to Leah Kingfisher's grave.

Moonlight slants through the trees. The cold is even more biting, the shadows longer, but I keep my head down and track the Knight through the wood.

Trudging through the snow, my boot strikes something hard, something metallic. I squint in the dark. It is a piece of the Knight's armor. I kick it aside and keep moving only to find more pieces of the midnight-black suit mingled among the snow and blood—the left arm plate, the leg guards, the backplate.

I pause when I come upon Claude's knife. The Knight must have somehow been able to dislodge it as he stumbled along. I clutch it firmly. Suddenly the trees thin and the moonlight shines brighter. As I enter the small glade where Lady Kingfisher's grave lies next to her beloved sons, I have to hold my breath. The air is filled with a putrid stink so foul it makes my eyes water, and I immediately put my hand over my nose and mouth. It's the smell of decay, of impending death. In the center of the clearing kneels a figure. The last bits of the Knight's armor lay scattered around it.

"I can track something if it's bleeding," I say angrily.

But as I approach and the silvery light from the moon shines down upon this strange figure, I don't know if I'm looking at a man, a monster, or something else altogether.

He is naked and small, much smaller than the Knight had been. The skin of his back is wrinkled and sagging off the bones. The wound Claude inflicted is like a deep hollow near his right flank. The wound I inflicted left a hole that runs straight through him.

His head is mostly bald aside from a few wispy hairs at the nape. Straight down the center of his back, tracing the path of his spine, is a line of stitches. They hook into the skin on either side of a monstrous cut that runs from the top of his head to his buttocks. The stitches are crude, set so wide that the skin looks like it might come apart at any moment. I grip the knife so hard the wound in my palm begins to bleed after being dry for weeks.

"You and I at the end of it all," he says. It is the Knight's voice and not, at the same time. So much of what had made it unbearable to hear was the deep resonance as it echoed through his suit of armor. Now that is stripped away.

"Not the end of it all," I say. "Just the end of you."

He turns his head, and I gasp as he stares at me head-on. Slowly I move in front of him as my heart beats wildly in my chest. My gut is telling me to run, but I can't take my eyes off this creature.

The wound that ran the length of his back from top to bottom extends to the front of him as well. It curves over the top of his head, traces down the bridge of his nose and continues down his chest and abdomen until it disappears beneath his hands, which are cupped in his lap. This wound is also poorly sutured and allows me a glimpse of his skull and breastbone as he heaves in rasping breaths.

"What—what are you?" I ask, unable to look away.

"Does it matter?" the Knight asks. His remaining eye darts from side to side, but I keep Claude's knife trained on him.

"Yes," I say. "I want to know what kind of man—what kind of terrible creature would do the things you've done." I step forward and put the blade of Claude's knife under his chin. "You have taken much from me. Too much."

His wild gaze narrows on me. "I knew a girl very much like you once. She thought she could outthink me, too." He unfolds his right arm and I press the knife into his neck just a bit more.

He winces but plunges his hand into the snow and pulls out a piece of the broken straw that litters the ground. He holds it in his hand and it begins to glow, bathing us both in warm light. I step back, stunned. When the light fades, the piece of straw has been transformed into a finely spun piece of gold.

"That girl tricked me," says the Knight. "Sent her spies to find the one thing that would void the terms of our deal. It was my . . . great mistake."

"What was it?" I ask. "What were the terms of your dealings with her?"

The Knight's gaze in his one good eye rests on me. "My name."

I can't understand. "Why would anyone care?" I ask.

"If she knew my name, then I would not take her baby," croaks the Knight.

A new wave of horror and revulsion washes over me.

"She cheated me out of what was rightfully mine," the Knight says. "I was so angry I ripped myself in two." He traces the wound running down his chest with one blackened finger. "You haven't heard my story, but others have. I made sure anyone who ever tried to cheat me would pay. Dearly. And would you like to know something, Eve?" His one good eye blinks. "I found out that fate is not so cruel as one might think."

"I think it is very cruel," I say.

"It is delicious." He licks his lips and his bloody tongue is stitched down the center as well. "It has brought me back to you and your family."

I pause. "*Back?* What does that mean?"

"Time is a wheel," he says. "A spinning wheel. Much like your beloved family crest, wouldn't you say?"

Nothing he says makes sense to me, and I am growing wary of allowing him to continue to exist. I peer at the pieces of armor scattered about the clearing. "It kept you together."

The Knight smiles. It is the most wicked thing I've ever seen and unnerves me so deeply I have to look away.

"It did," he says. "No longer."

Nova's terrified face flashes in my mind and anger overtakes me again. "Nova . . . you killed him," I say. "He was your son."

The Knight huffs. "A creation born out of a wish." He pauses. "I can grant my own, you know."

"I don't care," I say.

"My wish to have a child was much like your mother's. But like all of you, fools that you are, I did not remember to ask that he be obedient, that he be loyal. Those things, well, I had to use force to get those out of him. You'd be surprised at how persuasive a branding iron can be."

I have heard enough. I circle around him and put the blade at his throat.

"Nova is dead, and I—I loved him." It is the truth I wish I had been brave enough to admit in the weeks and months that came before, but it is too late now.

"Pity, you'll never know how much that's worth," he says.

"What?" I ask, confused at this.

The Knight glances over his shoulder in the direction of the house. It cannot be seen from where we are, but he looks back anyway.

"A deal of my own making," mumbles the Knight. "Sleep like death, consume. Until hands and lips touch." He cranes his neck to look up at me. "Strike me down, dearest Eve, and mourn forever."

"As you wish," I say. I remove his head in one fell swoop and it tumbles into the snow, mouth open, eye wide.

For the Knight, there is no peaceful rest, only the further dismantling of his mortal remains, which I burn on a pyre. When it has stopped smoldering, I gather the ashes and spread them in the River Farris over the course of ten separate nights. There will be no resurrection for the Knight. No amount of thread could sew him back together after what I have made of him.

For Junior, the ceremony is one befitting a boy who was as beloved as he. We wash his body and dress him, and I place my mother's emerald ring on his right hand. We place him in a wooden coffin, built from the trunks of a few felled pine trees. Claude digs the small grave right next to the place where Leah Kingfisher rests and lowers Junior's casket into the hole himself. I think a part of him goes into the dirt as well. We stand at the graveside for what feels like hours, hoping that maybe it isn't true. Magic allowed me to exist, to conjure weapons from fire and ice, to pull down the sky itself, to understand the woodland creatures—surely it can bring Junior back to us. Surely it can mend the hole in our hearts. But it is not to be.

The grave is filled and smoothed over. My mother plants more lilies in the frigid soil atop the burial and tells us that they will sprout in the spring. Claude cuts the headstone from a quarry near the mines and lugs it home on his back. He carves Junior's name and epitaph into it himself.

Claude Kingfisher Jr.
Beloved son, brother, and friend.

I want the same thing for Nova, but it, too, is not to be but for a much stranger reason than grief or mourning. Nova's body lay in the confines of the cold root cellar for days as we prepared a coffin for him. We went to retrieve him, expecting to find his body in a sad state, but he looked the same as he did the day he was struck down by the poison apple.

"How can this be?" Claude asks as my mother and I stand around Nova's body.

My mother looks on, confused. "He bit the poison apple. It was deadly. He should not look . . . like this."

Claude sighs. "I don't feel comfortable putting him under the ground."

My heart lurches in my chest. He looks like he's sleeping, but Claude's words remind me of the reality.

"What other choice do we have?" I ask.

Claude thinks for a moment. "Wait here." He disappears up the ladder and returns a few moments later with the glass box he'd made for me. "What about this?"

He sets the box in my hands, and I stare at him questioningly.

"It will take time," Claude says. "But I can make a bigger

one. Nova can rest inside so that you may look upon him." He stares down at Nova. "I don't know what kind of magic it is that keeps away the rot. Perhaps it is not for us to understand."

I look at the glass box and then to Nova, nodding.

My mother returns to Castle Veil and her throne. The people welcome her home with open arms, though her ordeal has since become fodder for all manner of rumors. Some say she is a witch; others say she looked upon the Knight and was cursed. We let people speculate, because the truth is still something none of us fully understands. She looks three times her age and this effect has remained unchanged since the Knight cast his magic on her. Her physical appearance has changed but she does not lament this. She embraces it. She is free from the Knight's influence and delights in telling the people of Queen's Bridge they need never fear the Knight ever again. She also delights in burying the cursed seeing stone in a location that she has assured me she will take to her grave. Celebrations of the Queen's return continue for weeks. While I am joyful, I do not partake. In fact, I have asked that my mother not alert anyone to my whereabouts or correct them when they speculate about what has become of me.

I stay with Claude, and we work into the night for weeks crafting a coffin of glass and emerald for Nova. My beloved Nova. It is not lost on me that I mourn someone others only saw as a villain.

When we finally finish, Claude places the coffin in the

woods far beyond the graves of his wife and beloved sons. We transport Nova to the glass coffin and lay him inside on a blanket of starlight I'd willed down from the heavens. It cradles him like a cloud. I tuck little sprigs of white flowers I'd grown on the newly repaired sill of the house into the glass coffin before Claude and I close the glass lid over him.

And it is here he lies for one year and then another.

CHAPTER 23

TWO YEARS LATER

It is easier to track a story if it is bleeding. That is to say, if the heart of the tale is beating, if it is real and not just the fanciful embellishment of some frightened villager's imagination, I can find it.

While Nova lies unchanged in his glass coffin for what feels like an eternity, I have given up hoping for anything more than a chance to look upon his face whenever I venture to that secluded corner of the wood. I spend my days with the King-fisher boys, with Claude and Maggie, and I mourn all that I have lost while trying my best to appreciate what I have gained. Another family, my mother's embrace, and a reinvigorated sense of purpose. I no longer hunt for the Knight; I hunt for his stories, and I have reason to believe I am not alone in this.

Today, I am on my way to make sense of a rumor.

It began several days prior. Claude and I left Castle Veil in the late evening after a visit with my mother. Claude had the sudden urge to have a drink, and we stopped at a small inn just south of the castle. The keeper gave Claude a pitcher of mead, which he drained, causing us to have to stay away a little longer than we had planned. While he slept off his drink, I stayed in the front room of the small inn, huddled by the fire, enjoying the warmth and the quiet. Keeping my cloak hood up and the handle of my dagger visible, I made sure no one bothered me. As much as I loved the Kingfisher boys, they were constantly making noises no human being should ever make. They were in a constant state of trying new things, loud things—homemade instruments, songs, bird calls. Quiet was a seldom found luxury. I was there in the front room of the darkened inn, enjoying the quiet, when I awoke with a start. I'd fallen asleep, and I glanced outside to try to gauge how long my impromptu nap had been. An hour, maybe less. It was a tapping at the window that roused me. A crow sat perched like a living shadow on the outside sill. It pecked at the glass until I awoke. It was another moment before I realized I was not alone and that my finely feathered friend had been warning me.

People were coming in and out that evening, renting rooms from the keeper, enjoying their drinks and bowls of sweet-smelling stew, and then dragging themselves off to sleep much like Claude. But in the small space by the fireplace, there were now two women in the far corner who partook in neither drink nor food. They huddled together in the deepest shadows of the room over a small table. When I realized they were there, they sank deeper into the darkness, talking in hushed voices to each other. And then I heard it. The thing that has set me on the path that I am on right now.

One of the women leaned toward the other just as there was a lull in the roar of the fire and the clanging of dishes. I heard her words clearly.

"He spun the straw into gold," she said. "Three times in total."

The memory of the Knight turning that little errant piece of straw into gold before my eyes rushed to the front of my mind, and I stood up. The women turned to me. The one with more gray in her jet-black hair smiled.

"I knew it," she said. She got up and approached me. She placed a folded piece of parchment in my palm. "Not here," she whispered. "Meet us tomorrow." She closed my fingers over the paper, turned and gathered up the other woman, then disappeared down the hall.

I wanted to follow them to their rooms but thought better of it, and I spoke to the innkeeper instead.

"Who were those two women who were just here?" I asked. "They're guests?"

The keeper tilted her head. "Sisters, I think. They've been here a week. Seems they're waiting on someone, but I don't know who or what for." She shrugged. "I don't know, but I know I've heard them speaking all manner of strange things. Sound like stories for children, but full of things that no child ought to hear unless you're trying to ensure they never sleep again." She shuddered. "It is good to see you,

Highness. My condolences on your passing. A terrible tragedy indeed."

She and I exchanged a little nod. I love the people of Queen's Bridge more than I can say. They continued to shelter me when I needed it most.

I woke Claude, against his sincerest wishes, and forced him to make the trip home so that he could sleep off whatever was left of his drink-induced stupor in his own bed.

Now it is the morning after, and I am riding, with Chance and Grump following me on their own horse. They're arguing about who is going to ride in front on the way back, and Grump is insistent that he will be in the front, regardless of Chance's protests. They very nearly come to blows and I have to tell them that if they don't stop, I'll be forced to turn our horses around and go straight back home.

They quiet immediately because this short journey is something that intrigues them both. When I explained to Claude what I was doing and what the woman at the inn had told me, Chance had overheard and convinced me to allow him to come along. Grump said he was going to come whether I liked it or not and, knowing him, I didn't take it for a joke.

The ride is not long from the Kingfisher house. By midmorning we arrived, cresting over a small rise and seeing the little hut, smoke billowing from its chimney, in the bottom of the valley below. There are very few homes in this part of the wood. Close to the southernmost border of Queen's Bridge, it is mostly dense forests, and so the house seems out of place.

I tether my horse to a post just off the front step, and

Chance and Grump hop down from their perch atop a horse who would need a week's rest after dealing with them. They've both become exceedingly efficient with a bow, but only Chance has his slung over his shoulder. Grump has a small dagger in a sheath on his belt.

"Wait here," I say as I ascend the steps. I knock, and a moment later one of the women from the inn opens the door.

"Ah!" the woman with the graying hair at her temples says, smiling. "Clio! She's here!" She ushers me inside and then registers the boys. "And she has guests! Come in, gentlemen."

Grump narrows his eyes. "I have a knife."

I sigh. "He's very protective. He doesn't mean anything by it."

"It means I will stab you if you even look at Eve or my brother in a way I don't like," Grump says.

I quickly grab him by the arm and haul him inside. Before I shut the door, I catch a glimpse of Queen Sanaa circling high overhead. I feel her call in my head. All is fine for the time being, and she will send word to Claude should it become necessary. I also catch the remnants of Maggie's low rumble. She is just a short way off, and I pity the person who steps between her and myself or the boys.

I stand with Chance and Grump just inside the front door. The small hut is well built but cramped. It is essentially one room with a large table strewn with piles of parchment and quills. There are dozens of books and folios containing even more parchment. A small fire burns in the hearth.

"Please come in," the woman says. "I'm Maeve and this is my sister, Clio."

Clio gives us a wave from her seat at the table. Black ink discolors her fingertips, and her eyes are narrow and suspicious. I flex my fingers at my side and the fire in the hearth burns brighter.

"Clio!" Maeve snaps. "Do not start. We have work to do here." She turns back to me. "Please, won't you sit?"

She gestures to an empty chair at the table, and I sit while the boys take seats on the floor by the fire. Grump keeps his hand on the hilt of his dagger. Neither Clio nor Maeve speak, so I decide to make introductions.

"I'm Eve," I say.

"We know," Clio grumbles.

"This is Grump and Chance," I say, gesturing to the boys.

Clio whips her head around. "You poor boy. Your parents call you Grump?" She shakes her head. "A shame."

"Don't make fun of me," Grump says. "Or maybe you'll find out how grumpy I can be."

A wide grin breaks across Clio's face. "Are you always so polite and cheerful?" she asks, sarcasm dripping from every word.

"Yes," Grump says, scowling even more than usual.

I shift in my seat and lean my elbow on the table among the paper and quills. "When I saw you in the inn, I heard you say something that struck me as—"

"Odd?" Maeve asks hurriedly. "Odd or familiar?" She sits in the last empty chair at the table so that she is across from Clio and on my right. I can strike them both down in quick succession if need be. Grump won't even have to dirty his little blade.

"Familiar seems like the right word," I say.

Clio readjusts herself in her chair. "I'm not surprised."

"Why not?" I ask. "Why were you at the inn in the first place?"

"We were waiting for you," says Maeve.

Chance shifts the bow from his shoulder to his lap and Grump pulls his dagger from its sheath, gripping it tightly.

I listen for Queen Sanaa again. Her song is calm in my head, and Maggie has reached us and is sitting, from what I can tell, just on the other side of the front door. Clio and Maeve exchange glances.

"We collect stories," Maeve says. "We've been doing this work nearly our entire lives. I don't know if you've noticed, but in these lands, there are some very strange characters, wouldn't you agree?"

"You're speaking of the Knight," I say. "He is dead. So no, there aren't strange characters here any longer."

Clio laughs outright. "Oh, my dear girl. You've slain the head of a beast. Three more may rise in its place."

I straighten up and allow my left hand to hang at my side so that I can conjure a blade of fire if need be.

"What she means is that the Knight was not the only despicable monster roaming these lands," Maeve says. "Don't you recall visiting a strange woman in Little Stilts?"

Memories of my visit to the desolate little hamlet flood my mind. "How did you know I was there?"

"We passed you on your way in," Maeve says. "We seem to have just missed you in Hamelin and in Dead Man's Peak. Our paths crossed on the road to Little Stilts, but we were so caught up with what we had learned from Nerium—"

"You knew her?" I ask.

"We know her still," Clio says.

I decide not to think too hard about how Nerium is still alive after all this time.

"Nerium is a keeper of stories," Maeve says. "Parts of them, at least."

"For whatever reason," Clio says. "A terrible magic affects this place. Not just Queen's Bridge either. From Rotterdam to Mersailles to Little Stilts, there are strange tales. It is in the soil, the air. This land breeds monstrous things. Your story will join the tome of others," Clio says as she scratches some words onto a parchment. "The Queen with the enchanted looking glass."

I stare into Clio's wide eyes.

"Oh, yes," Clio says. "We have heard. Of course, the truth is much stranger than the fictions being scattered by rumor and gossip, isn't it? They say your mother sent you to the woods to die because she was jealous of your beauty."

"Lies," I say.

"Yes, but what you don't seem to understand is that as we record these events we have to tell them in a way that allows some truth to be seen, so that the people will know it, but—"

"But we must exercise caution," Maeve cuts in, finishing Clio's sentence. "We collect stories to keep record, but we cannot be too obvious. There are forces at play here that put us all in very real danger. The source of the evil that lurks in these lands is hard to understand. Its power may extend beyond anything we can comprehend."

"Evil?" Chance asks, concern clouding his expression.

Clio nods. "We record the stories and keep their true meaning hidden to all but those who would choose to look—to really and truly see." Clio points to a beautifully illustrated picture of my mother sitting in her throne room, a wooden box in her lap. "Before your reemergence after the defeat of the Knight, the story says it was your heart that lay in the box."

"It was Huntress's heart," I say. "Nova—he was the son of the Knight—he did that to keep me safe after Huntress tried to kill me."

Clio dips her pen in the ink and draws a stylized H on the front of the wooden box. It has so many flourishes it almost looks like an E, as if it's meant to represent me and not Huntress unless someone knew the real story.

"What's the point of all of this?" I ask. "Why collect them in code? Why bother and why bring me here to tell me this?"

"Because one day someone, if not us, is going to string all of these stories together and realize that the terrible magic that runs through each of them comes from a common, ancient source." Maeve sounds exhausted. "And we need to ensure that only those really seeking the truth can find it. Scary stories entertain, but the truth is far worse than anything we've written here."

"It won't be us," Clio says. "We're already getting old. The work will have to be passed to someone else at some point, but for now we do this work in the hope that some sense can be made of it."

I take a moment to let all of that settle in, when something else occurs to me. "You said something about turning straw into gold when we were at the inn," I say. "Why did you say that?"

Clio's eyes brighten. "We thought you might have seen him do it," Clio says.

"The Knight?" I ask.

Maeve nods. "That is what he was known as to you. We weren't certain but now we understand—the Knight is the guise he took on after . . ." She trails off, seemingly lost in her thoughts.

"After what?" I ask.

Clio sets down her pen and shuffles through a stack of odd parchment until she comes to a loosely bound tome. She flips through and pushes it toward me. The title at the top of the page reads *Rumpelstiltskin*.

"Listen to me very carefully," Clio says, running her fingers across the page. "This is a story about a girl who was courted by a king. Her father was a greedy man who had his crooked eye on the king's fortune. He offered his only daughter, but the king was greedy as well. He told her if she could spin straw into gold he wouldn't kill her and that perhaps he would make her his queen."

"An impossible task," I say.

"Nothing a little wish-granting can't fix," says Maeve.

"Someone heard her cries for help as she sat trapped in the king's quarters with a bale of straw at her side and spinning wheel under her hands. Someone who was born of these cursed lands and who had the power to grant wishes but often at a terrible price."

I level my gaze with Maeve. "Wishes?" I whisper. It is odd but as I think on it something else claws its way out from the depths of my memory. Scattered by the horrors of the past few months, it is hard to fully realize. *His great mistake.*

"Indeed," Maeve says, picking up where her sister left off. "A strange man appeared to the girl and took as his payment a ring. He spun the straw to gold and the king was pleased. But it stoked the king's greed, and he required the girl to do this task once more. The strange man came to the girl again and this time his payment was a necklace."

"The task was done in one night," Clio says. "But of course, it was not good enough for the king and he asked the girl to repeat the task a final time, this time ensuring that if she did as he asked, she would be his queen. The girl was elated and she called on her strange friend a final time."

My mind circles back on itself to memories I have kept locked away for the better part of two years because the pain of what happened is sometimes more than I can stand. The Knight, in his dying moments, spoke of the girl who had deceived him and how it had driven him mad with anger and set him on a path to hurt all those he could. But he seemed fixated on connecting me—my family—to this terrible tale. Nerium spoke of his great mistake and the girl who bested him. My skin turns to gooseflesh beneath my sleeves. I glance at Grump and Chance, who sit in silence by the fire.

"The Knight," I say in a hushed whisper. "He spoke of this tale to me."

"And this?" Clio asks as she pushes a drawing of my family's crest toward me. She rotates it upward, and as I look on it in its new orientation it resembles a spinning wheel wound with golden threads.

I can do nothing but stare at her.

"You are a Miller, descended from the miller's daughter, as was your mother and her mother before her," Maeve says. "Royalty born out of a broken deal with the Knight."

"No," I say, getting up and stepping away from the table. "My mother would have told me."

"She herself did not know," Clio says. "Great effort was made to rid the world of the memory of your family's founding. More from fear than anything else, but vestiges of that understanding remain—your family's stance on never making a deal with the Knight, for example. The crest, your surname."

"Finish the story," I say to the sisters. "Tell me what happened to the girl and her child."

"The girl told her strange friend what she needed," Maeve says. "But she also let slip that she desired very much to be the queen for she had fallen deeply in love with the greedy king."

Clio sucks the air between her teeth. "Foolish girl."

"Some girls are foolish," Maeve says. "They still deserve grace."

Clio rolls her eyes. "The girl's strange friend became

330

insanely jealous, for he had hoped she would love him instead. When she told him she did not love him, he refused to work the straw into gold. She begged him, offered him all the riches he could ever want. He denied her."

"But then he thought of something he wanted," Maeve says. "Something that would hurt her more than anything else he could think of . . . her firstborn child as payment."

Chance gasps, and I glance over at him as his mouth hangs open.

"She agreed, wanting desperately to marry the king," Clio continued. "A year later a baby was born, and the strange man returned demanding his payment."

"Vile," I say. Both that she would agree to it and that he would come to collect.

"Those were the terms of his deal, and he would not allow her to go back on that," Maeve says. "She told him she wanted to make another deal, any deal that would allow her to keep her baby if she could fulfill the terms."

"He could not refuse, could he?" I ask. That was the nature of the Knight. His deals, his wish making, were his purpose, and he could not avoid it as a person could not avoid breathing.

Clio nods. "He told her a riddle. And if she could untangle it in three days' time, he would allow her to keep the child. If not, he would take her by force."

I press my hand into the tabletop as the pieces fall into place.

"Brew beguiling wishes three," Maeve says, quoting the cursed riddle. "Play with me a simple game. Rack your head and whisper to me, my one and only name."

Maeve and Clio sit in silence for several seconds. It feels as if we've spoken some forbidden incantation aloud.

"Names have power," Clio says. "Knowing the true name of a spirit or daemon can allow a conjurer to call it down or banish it."

"Princess Eve," Maeve speaks my name like a spell. "Eve— the darkest night before the coming of the new morn."

The little hairs on the back of my neck stand up.

"The girl sent her closest allies near and far to try and track down the name of the strange man," says Maeve. "Finally, on the third day, one of the girl's spies saw the strange man in a heavily wooded area all alone. He danced naked around a roaring fire. He sang to himself of his deceit and the joy he took in it. During this rueful song and dance, he said his name aloud. The spy rushed back to the girl and shared with her what she had seen."

Clio shakes her head. "The strange man came to the girl that very night and demanded her baby. He said he would boil it and use the fat to make a potion that would allow him to fly."

I swallow hard as my stomach turns over.

"The girl shouted his name aloud," Clio continues. "Rumpelstiltskin! Rumpelstiltskin! Rumpelstiltskin!"

Maeve huffs. "The man was so shocked, so stunned that their deal had come to a conclusion and that he had lost what he hoped to gain, that he planted one foot in the ground and kicked his opposite leg so hard it tore him in two. Split him right down the middle."

I don't dare move. My legs will give out. All I can see in my mind are images of the Knight after he had shed his armor. He seemed so much smaller, so frail. As I recall the sutures that held the ragged edges of his skin together, I want to vomit.

Maeve leans closer to me. "You haven't laughed or smiled."

"Why would I do that?" I ask.

"Because most people believe these tales to be a tool for teaching young children some profound life lesson," Clio chimes in. "Be obedient. Don't be greedy. Be resourceful."

"And keep your promises," Maeve says. "Or something dreadful might happen."

Clio stands, leaving her quill and ink on the table. "We recorded Rumpelstiltskin—what? Twenty years ago? The story came from a woman out in the middle of some godforsaken countryside. She'd been told the story her whole life, and she was nearly on her deathbed. We had no idea when the original events of the story actually took place, but we have always wondered what became of him. His magic was too powerful to simply fade into the vastness of time."

"There were rumors and hints that he lived, still," says Maeve. "We hoped that we might find what became of him when we came to record your story, Eve. The girl they say was made from the freshly fallen snow and a drop of blood."

"From the evening sky and the stars themselves, actually," I say. I feel lost in a haze and I can barely keep track of what is real and what is not.

The sisters glance at each other.

"People like to tell stories, and we collect stories," Maeve says. "Farther out from Queen's Bridge the stories are much different from what we suspect is the truth."

"They call you Snow White," Clio says, pointing to another story in the book. "They say your mother, jealous of your beauty, poisoned you and now your dead body rests in a glass coffin."

I cannot understand how the rumors have spread so far and yet they contain kernels of truth. Sometimes I wish it *were* me in that coffin instead of Nova.

"Let them believe what they want," I say. "It makes no difference to me."

"We did not make the connection to the miller's daughter and your family until we got here, and by then you'd already ended him."

"And the world is rid of him," I say.

Maeve looks thoughtful. "But something still bothers you, doesn't it?"

They know so much already—these storytellers—it doesn't seem to matter much now, but I tell them what I know.

"The last thing he said, before I removed his head, was an incantation of some kind," I say. "It felt like a curse."

"What did he say, exactly?" Clio asks. "Can you remember it word for word?"

"I can't forget it even though I have tried," I say. "He said 'Sleep like death, consume. Until hands and lips touch. Strike me down, dearest Eve, and mourn forever.'" I grit my teeth at that last string of terrible words. "If it is a curse, then he has gotten his way for the final time."

"You mourn?" Maeve asks. Her eyes are kind, but she is pressing her lips together as if she is trying to keep a torrent of words from spilling forth.

I nod. "Every day of my life."

"It wasn't a curse," Clio says.

I dab at my eyes, swallowing the sadness. "What?"

"Not a curse," Maeve says. Her eyes are wide and her hands are clasped together in front of her. "A magical contract . . . a final deal."

Clio quickly returns to her parchment and scribbles down the words.

"Sleep like death," she mumbles, before her head snaps up and she narrows her eyes at me. "Why do people think you're dead in a glass coffin?"

"That's very specific," Maeve says.

"I'm not dead, clearly," I say. "But someone I loved is. He is kept in a glass coffin."

"Kept?" Clio asks. "Why would you want to see him rotting away?"

I flinch at the thought, and Maeve pinches Clio's arm.

Clio winces. "I don't mean to be insensitive, but it seems an odd thing."

"There is no rot," I say. "He looks the way he did when he died."

Clio runs her hands over the words. "Until hands and lips touch. Strike me down, mourn forever."

Maeve inhales sharply. "Eve executed him, she mourns her love still. Hands—"

"And lips," Clio says in a voice so small it is only a whisper.

Maeve grabs the folio of collected stories and flips through. "Eve, my dear, you have not fulfilled the terms of the traitorous Rumpelstiltskin's final deal, and what he asks is something we have seen before."

I move to her side so I can peer down at the book. "What do you mean?"

"Here!" Maeve says, giddy with excitement. "This girl, locked in a tower by an evil witch. The spinning wheel pricked her finger and she fell into a sleep like death."

My heart thuds hard in my chest as I stare at the image of young woman lying on her back, hands crossed over her chest. "What became of her?"

"She was awoken by a kiss," Clio says. "Not just any kiss. True love's kiss."

"It sounds very much like a fairy tale, but it is much more than that," Maeve says. "It is a powerful bit of magic, able to rescue one from the evil that powers most curses."

I have to grip the edge of the table to steady myself. "She woke up?"

"She did!" Maeve says. "She lives still, to this very day!"

Until hands and lips touch.

I glance at Chance and Grump, who have been sitting in rapt attention.

"Go," Clio says. "Go fulfill your end of the bargain."

Bidding them goodbye, I ride as fast as I can, with Chance and Grump following behind me at a perilous speed. Maggie trails us and Queen Sanaa circles high overhead. We get back in half the time it took us to ride out. I leave Chance and Grump at the front of the house and make the rest of the trip on foot.

Springtime has brought with it green foliage and warm breezes. The path that leads to Nova's final resting spot first leads to the grave of Leah Kingfisher and her boys. While I am eager to get to Nova, I stop and place a handful of lilies, now blooming all around the gravesite, on Leah's grave marker, which has been newly decorated with little painted rocks and toys made from sticks. I bend and kiss Junior's headstone.

"I miss you," I say against the stone. "I always will."

I move past the gravesites and deeper into the wood. The path to Nova is well worn, although mostly by me. The boys come to see him on occasion and clearly someone had seen him in his glass coffin in order for Maeve and Clio to have heard a rumor. I don't know how, but I'm past caring. I push through the newly bloomed foliage and finally emerge in the small clearing.

Nova lies as he always has beneath the glass—his hands folded neatly, his face serene, like he's sleeping. The cloth I'd forged from the night sky surrounds him.

I lean close to the glass, which I don't often do. It's hard for me to be so close to him, knowing I could not have saved him because he was determined to die for me. Tears sting my eyes. What if the sisters are just storytellers? They admitted as much, but what if they are just that? Women obsessed with the strange tales of these lands. Could there be any truth to what they said or am I hoping for something impossible?

There is movement in the woods behind me. I turn to find Claude emerging from the footpath, his woolen cap pressed against his chest.

"The boys told me you came straight back here," he says. "They were a little worried." He glances at Nova's glass coffin. "Do you want to be alone?"

Normally my answer would be yes. But not this time.

"I need your help," I say.

I've thought this through. It is the only thing I've been thinking of since I left the strange little cottage and the company of the sisters, Maeve and Clio. If the Knight's final words to me had been his final act—a deal of his own making—then it seems to offer me something none of his other deals had: hope. I don't believe that the Knight had been capable of compassion, or even love. He'd used his own son as a tool and didn't seem at all moved as he watched him die. I don't think his final deal was meant to offer me anything but a lifetime of torment. How could he know that his story—the one that told of who he was before he took on this visage of the Knight—would reach me and help me unravel the terms of his deal?

I put my hands on the lid of the glass coffin and glance at Claude. "Help me lift it."

He steps forward. "Eve, what is this about?"

"Please?" I ask him. "I found something. A clue to how this might end."

"Is it not already over?" Claude asks, looking mournfully at Nova.

I slump against the glass and put my head in my hands. I want so badly for this to be a beginning, not an end, but maybe Claude is right. He sits down in the grass next to me.

"What did you find?" he asks.

I wipe angry tears from my eyes. "The last thing the Knight said to me were the terms of a deal. I thought it was simply his intention to make me mourn forever, but I've learned something about who he was before he was the Knight."

"Before?" Claude asks.

I nod. "He was as cold and heartless as we knew him to be, but he tried to trick a young woman into giving up her baby to him and she outsmarted him. He never let it go. It is why he tormented the people of Queen's Bridge and why he was obsessed with the deal my mother made with him. We come from the woman who outsmarted him. We are her distant kin, and the Knight knew it."

Claude is silent for a long time. "He has ruined so many lives and all for what? Because he could not accept that he could be bested?" He sighs and hangs his head. "Why did you want to open the coffin?"

"I thought—" I begin but stop myself. It sounds foolish. "I thought maybe there was some other meaning in those last words he spoke to me, but now I am doubting everything."

Claude suddenly stands and puts his hands on the coffin. "Come on, then. Help me move it."

I scramble to my feet, and Claude smiles warmly at me.

"There's no worse feeling than a lingering question of whether you could have done something else, something different," Claude says. "I know that all too well. So let's not leave anything undone."

I nod and together we remove the delicate glass lid of Nova's final resting place.

The air that wafts up is sweetly scented. The blankets I'd conjured for him are gently shifting as the stars in the sky do every night. Nova's face is serene. Unchanged.

I pull down the covering so that I can see his hands. I gently interlace my fingers with his. His skin is frigid, but his hand is soft.

Claude exhales slowly. "What do you mean to do?"

I repeat the words the Knight had spoken to me. "Sleep like death, consume. Until hands and lips touch. Strike me down, dearest Eve, and mourn forever." I have mourned enough. Nova has slumbered enough. And I struck the Knight down myself. There was only this last term to fulfill and then maybe . . .

Grasping Nova's hands, I lean down until my forehead is resting against his. I breathe in the sweet smell of jasmine. I kiss him gently. Pressing my lips to his, letting the tears fall onto his face. When I pull away, he lies still, unmoving, unchanged. My heart shatters all over again.

Claude rests his hand on my back. "I'm sorry, Eve. I'm so very sorry."

"I need a moment," I say.

Claude nods and leaves me alone with Nova. I sit down in the grass, my back resting on the edge of the platform that cradles his body.

I cry until there are no tears left. Once upon a time, I thought I would slay the Knight and be the champion of the people, my mother's right hand, a hero of my own making. It is strange that this is almost exactly what happened but in ways and with consequences that I had never imagined. Fairy tales are strange and mysterious things. My journey to this point has been much like the deals the Knight made—unpredictable and horrible in ways one could scarcely comprehend. I stand and walk to the head of the footpath. There, I tilt my head back and look into the sky through the canopy of spring leaves.

There is a rustling behind me.

My heart almost stops.

"Eve," says a familiar voice.

I turn to find Nova sitting up, his skin ruddy at the cheeks, his hair loose around his face. He pulls himself up, but I cannot move. I am stuck where I stand. Nova stands on trembling legs, the haze of his long sleep shaking free from him with each step. He limps toward me and when he is close enough, I reach out, afraid this isn't real, afraid that when I try to touch him, he will disappear. He takes hold of my outstretched arms. He is real. He is breathing and warm. He is right here with me after all this time. He takes me in his arms, pressing his face into my neck. I hold him for a long time, in disbelief.

"Is this—is this real?" I ask. "You—you're alive. You're here."

"I've been asleep a long time," Nova says.

"Yes, you have," I say softly.

He cradles my face in his hands and brushes his lips against mine.

"It was a sleep like death," he says. "And I dreamed only of you."

He presses his mouth to mine, and I wrap my arms around him, breathing him in.

Of all the stories I have collected—tales of monstrous beings and unfathomable cruelties—I wonder if our story, the story of Nova and me and my mother, will be the one that lives on. After all, it is Nova and me at the end of it all. Free from the Knight and his terrible deeds, now and for all time. A happily ever after of our own making.

ACKNOWLEDGMENTS

When I was drafting *Cinderella Is Dead* in 2016, I knew it wouldn't be the only fairy tale I would attempt to reimagine. Now, eight years later, I'm watching my spin on Snow White go out into the world. It's a wonderful, albeit surreal, feeling. *Sleep Like Death* is a story within a story. If you're familiar with my work, you know there is nothing I love more than a good hidden history.

Here, we get to explore the story behind "Snow White" and how this specific tale intersects with other stories in what I like to think of as the *Cinderella Is Dead Literary Universe* (lol). The secrets hidden inside the fairy tales we think we know will always be a fun and exciting space to work in. I love telling these stories and I'm grateful that together, we get to return to this world of dark magic, mysteries, and myth.

On a more personal note, *Sleep Like Death* is a story about mothers and mother-figures. Eve's relationships to the women in her family and in her community are a focal point because I understand how important those relationships can be. This story is dedicated to the women in my life who stepped up and showed me how to navigate the world when I didn't have a mother who was willing or able to do that. Rolanda, Gwen, Pearl, and Annette all went out of their way to show me the kind of care and concern that all young girls are deserving of. I wouldn't be here today without them.

I'd like to thank Jamie Vankirk, Mary Kate Castellani, Alexa Higbee, Lily Yengle, Kei Nakatsuka, Erica Barmash, Carla Hutchinson, Emily Marples, Sophie Rosewell, and everyone on both the US and UK Bloomsbury teams. I'm so thrilled that we get to continue to tell these stories! Thank you for all your hard work. None of this happens without your dedication to the readers and to the work. Go team!

I'm forever grateful to family—Mike, Amya, Nye, Elijah, Lyla, and Spencer. I love you all so much. I couldn't do any of this without you.

For the librarians, educators, and booksellers who have made sure my work gets into the hands of the readers who need it most, I don't think there are words to adequately express how much I appreciate you. I know, especially in the world we live in right now, that your job is harder than it should be. Thank you for showing up every day and fighting the good fight. We are in this together.

To my readers . . . THANK YOU. I've said it before but let me take the opportunity to say it again, I don't get to be here telling these stories without your support. You make all of this possible. Thank you for reading!